# FUGITIVE RED

## Also by Jason Starr

**Thrillers**

*Cold Caller*
*Nothing Personal*
*Fake I.D.*
*Hard Feelings*
*Tough Luck*
*Twisted City*
*Lights Out*
*The Follower*
*Panic Attack*
*Savage Lane*

**The Pack Series**

*The Pack*
*The Craving*

**Film and TV Tie-In Novels**

*Ant-Man: Natural Enemy*
*Gotham: Dawn of Darkness*
*Gotham: City of Monsters*

**Crime Novels Co-Written with Ken Bruen**

*Bust*
*Slide*
*The Max*
*Pimp*

**Graphic Novels**

*The Chill*
*Punisher Max: Untold Tales*
*Wolverine Max: Volume 1*
*Wolverine Max: Volume 2*
*Wolverine Max: Volume 3*
*The Returning*

# FUGITIVE RED

## A NOVEL

JASON STARR

ISBN 978-1-60809-328-1

Cover Design by Christian Fuenfhausen

Published in the United States of America by Oceanview Publishing
Sarasota, Florida

www.oceanviewpub.com

10 9 8 7 6 5 4 3 2 1

PRINTED IN THE UNITED STATES OF AMERICA

*For Mom*

*"There is nothing safe about sex. There never will be."*

—NORMAN MAILER

*"Reality is merely an illusion, albeit a very persistent one."*

—ALBERT EINSTEIN

# FUGITIVE RED

# CHAPTER ONE

IN THE TWO-BEDROOM penthouse on 73rd, near 3rd, Rob McEvoy said, "I like it, man, I like it." Then, as he went ahead through the short foyer, into the kitchen area, he added, "Breakfast bar, love it. What kind of wood?"

"Teak," I said.

"Sweet."

"Installed a few months ago by the owner," I added. "Countertop's Blue Louise, that's top-of-the-line granite, and those're all new appliances—Sub-Zero, Wolf—with a fully integrated dishwasher."

Rob was walking away, toward the living room, asking, "Fireplace work?"

"Yep. And you don't see many apartments with working fireplaces in Manhattan."

"Living room's kinda small."

"Yeah," I said, "but there's a separate dining area and an open floor plan with lots of light and two exposures."

"Southern?"

"Northern and eastern."

"It's okay. I get enough sun in L.A."

He smiled with his shiny, new-looking capped teeth, which seemed even whiter in contrast with his overly tanned skin. He looked so different than he had—Jesus, twenty-four years ago—when we were both struggling musicians, living on the Lower East

Side. If we hadn't reconnected on Facebook, if I'd just ran into him on the street, I probably would've walked right by him.

"It's actually a very bright apartment, especially in the morning," I said.

"Yeah, and the living room really isn't so small. Enough room for a big, wide couch, and that's all that really matters, right?"

He winked at me, then went toward the door to the terrace and said, "Wow, let's have a look."

We stepped out onto the terrace that was staged with lounge chairs from Crate & Barrel.

"You won't find a terrace this size for this price," I said. "It's three hundred square feet. Some apartments in Manhattan aren't three hundred square feet. You can barbecue, throw parties . . ."

"This is awesome," Rob said. "Totally what I've been looking for. How much is it?"

"The owner's asking two mil, and I don't think it's negotiable. He recently dropped the price and it's an investment property and he's not desperate to sell. I mean, you can try to nudge him to one nine and change, but I don't think he'll budge. The maintenance is nineteen-sixty, which is actually extremely reasonable, so if you put twenty percent down you're looking at a nut of—"

"I'm paying cash," Rob said.

"Oh. Oh, okay." I knew Rob was doing well—he'd started Music Mania, his own music licensing business, in Hollywood—but I didn't expect him to fork over two million in cash. "That's cool," I added.

"I also want to close on it fast," he said, "within a month or two."

"Assuming we can get all the paperwork done, and there are no issues with the board, I don't see why that should be a problem."

"Sweet." Rob lay in one of the lounge chairs. "Gonna be honest with you—I've been out with a few other brokers, seen a couple of other places I like, but this is my fave. And all things being equal, I'd rather you get the commish than some stranger."

Was he saying he wanted to make an offer? Sounded like it, but I wasn't sure.

I'd been doubting everything lately. My only deal in the last three months had been a one-bedroom, non-doorman rental, and I'd had to split the commission with another broker. Living in Manhattan, on the Upper East Side, wasn't exactly cheap, and Maria and I had been struggling lately to pay rent, bills, and expenses for our eight-year-old son. We hadn't gone on a vacation in years.

But selling a two-million-dollar apartment could turn everything around.

"That sounds great," I said, thinking, *Go for the close, go for the close.* "If you have any more questions, I'd be happy to answer them, and I can also contact the seller for you, and feel them out on the price, I mean, if you're thinking about making an offer."

Gazing out at the view of rooftops, Rob said, "Man, I love this view."

"It's pretty awesome, isn't it? I mean, it's hard to get an unobstructed view in Manhattan these days. Or you think you have a great view then a building goes up and blocks it. But you don't have to worry about that here. Those are all multimillion-dollar townhouses and they're not going anywhere."

"I like that it's private," he said. "You could fuck somebody here in the middle of the day and no one would see you."

I wasn't sure if he was joking or not, but I smiled, said, "Ha, yes, that's true. That's very true . . . So, do you think your wife will like it?"

He looked at me like I'd said something offensive.

"My wife?"

"Yeah," I said. "You guys are gonna use it as a *pied-a-terre* when you're in the city, I guess, right?"

I knew he'd mentioned his wife in a couple of the emails we'd exchanged, and his Facebook status was "Married." I glanced at his ring finger, at his thick gold wedding band.

"No, *I'm* gonna use it as a *pied-a-terre* when *I'm* in the city," he said, showing off his fake smile. "My wife? She's never gonna even know about it. You know it's like what they say—what you don't know can't hurt you."

He walked by me, back into the apartment. I followed him.

He said, "Yeah, if I take this place, first thing I'll do is get a decorator in here. iHome the fuck out of it, get some hip furniture, a bar, the right lighting, a kick-ass sound system. And a great bed. That's the most important thing, right?"

I smiled along with Rob, not wanting to judge. I needed this sale.

"Well, I think you'll really enjoy yourself here," I said.

"Oh, I'll enjoy myself, I guarantee you that."

I forced another smile. Then, when he looked away, I rolled my eyes.

As we rode the elevator down to the lobby, I gave Rob more basics about the building and the neighborhood.

"If you have any questions, just let me know," I said. "I don't want to put any pressure on you, but I know other brokers are showing this apartment, and there's been some serious interest and I don't think it'll last."

Actually, I had no idea if other brokers were actively showing it or if there had been any interest at all. But from experience, I knew I had to do whatever I could to get him off the fence. If what he'd told me was true, and he was considering other apartments, I needed him to make a decision as soon as possible.

"Don't worry, I won't fuck you over," Rob said. "I'll turn this around fast, I promise."

I didn't want to let him go without making an offer, but there was a limit to how hard I could press.

"Gotchya," I said.

I was looking forward to getting back to my office and, well, away from Rob, when he said, "Hey, you want to grab some lunch?"

"Love to," I lied, "but I have some stuff to take care of at the office."

"Come on, man," he said, "lemme buy. It's not like we see each other more than once every, what, twenty years? We have a lot of catching up to do."

I knew this was a bad idea. When you're trying to close a deal, it's always a mistake to hang out with the potential client—nothing good comes from closeness.

On the other hand, I didn't want him to think I was blowing him off.

"Yeah, okay, cool," I said. "I guess I can catch a quick bite. I mean, what the hell, right?"

# CHAPTER TWO

Rob had an Uber drop us at Le Veau D'Or, an upscale French restaurant on East 60th that I'd passed many times but had never gone into. Rob was in a black sport jacket over a designer black tee shirt—the big-shot music mogul look? I felt way underdressed in jeans, sneakers, and a plain gray button-down.

"Um, maybe we should go someplace a little more casual," I said.

"Chill, my brother," Rob said. "You look great. A little low budg, yeah, but you're Jack Harper—you're a rock 'n' roll guy, you're hip. You think Bono gives a fuck how he looks when he goes out to lunch?"

I was going to say, *Yeah, I think he probably does,* but we were in the restaurant already, so I figured we might as well just get seated.

As the hostess, an attractive, leggy blond, was leading us to our table, I saw Rob's gaze zeroing in on her ass, then he looked at me and in an exaggerated way mouthed the words, *Holy fucking shit.*

I was already regretting my decision to have lunch with him. Would schmoozing with him really increase the odds of closing the sale? If he sensed how jerky I thought he was, it could actually hurt my chances. Sometimes less is more.

At our table, Rob said to the hostess, "Actress or model?"

His voice boomed—a few people were looking over—but I didn't get the impression he was accidentally loud; no, he *wanted* people to hear. The hostess, probably used to getting hit on by sleazy businessmen, seemed unfazed.

"Actress," she said.

"Fifty-fifty shot, right?" Rob was fake smiling. Then he shifted to an intense, focused expression that was just as fake. "You have beautiful eyes. I mean, I don't think I've ever seen that shade of blue, except when I was sailing in the Aegean."

I tasted vomit.

"Thank you," she said. "Enjoy your meals, guys."

As she headed back toward the front of the restaurant, Rob turned to check her out.

"I'd give her the best two minutes of her life," he said. "Who'm I kidding? Twenty seconds."

Again his voice had boomed and the older woman at the next table shot me a look. My response was a helplessly embarrassed shrug, as if saying, *It's not me, it's him.*

"And you know she'd be into it," he continued. "Nine times out of ten a girl her age meets an older guy, of course she's gonna fall for him, know why? Because her boyfriend's probably some twenty-two-year-old jackass—never compliments her, always puts her down, doesn't respect her. That's the key—*respect.* We know how to respect women, we know how to be . . . what's that word I'm looking for? The old-fashioned word, Knights and King Arthur and shit?"

I had no idea what he was talking about.

"Chivalrous," he said, "that's it, thank you. Remember when we were twenty-two? We didn't know jack about how to treat women back then, but now that we're older guys, we have what younger women want—respect, intelligence, worldliness—class, I'm talking about class."

The waitress came to our table. She was Asian, young, attractive. Rob gave her a smarmy, "Heyyy," but spared her a lame pickup line.

"Can I get you some drinks to start?"

"Vodka gimlet," Rob said.

"Water's fine," I said.

Rob looked at me like I'd caught fire. "You sure, bro?"

"Yeah, positive."

The waitress smiled and left.

"Come on, you can have one drink," Rob said. "I mean, we have to celebrate getting back in touch after twenty-two years. It's a beautiful thing."

"Actually, I'm in the program," I said.

He gave me a look like he thought I was joking. When he realized I wasn't, he asked, "Since when?"

"Been sober six years, five months."

"That's great," he said. "I mean, it's great you have that kind of discipline. God knows, I don't. So what prompted it?"

"What do you mean?"

"Going cold turkey. I mean, I remember the old days, you went out drinking every night."

"That's what prompted it."

He smiled, then said, "I hear you, bro. I mean, half of L.A. are friends of Bill W. I'm just surprised you are, too."

"Yeah, well, a lot of shit has happened in twenty-two years," I said, purposely leaving it vague, not wanting to get into a whole discussion about my alcoholism and the other mistakes I'd made. I added, "It was just time to deal with shit so I dealt with it, you know?"

"That's cool," he said. "So how's the music going?"

Speaking of topics I didn't want to discuss.

I reached for the glass of water, then realized the waitress hadn't brought it yet.

"Actually, I haven't touched a guitar in ages."

"You?" Rob said. "You're kidding me. Music was your life—that's all you ever wanted to do. When you weren't playing, you were writing songs, or talking about music, or checking out bands. I know music can be a rough career, you gotta pay bills, but how could you just give it all up?"

"Life got in the way. I had a kid, new responsibilities. How 'bout you? Still playing?"

I wanted to steer the conversation away from an uncomfortable subject—me.

"Seven days a week," he said. "Actually I'm thinking of putting together a band in L.A. Nothing serious, just to mess around, but already booked some gigs at this bar in West Hollywood. Hey, I have an idea. Next time we're in town, we should get together and jam."

"Maybe," I said, but I had no intention of playing with Rob, or ever holding a guitar again.

The waitress brought my water and Rob's gimlet and took our lunch order: seafood casserole for me, poached salmon—"sauce on the side"—for Mr. L.A.

As the waitress walked away, Rob turned to look at her ass.

"So do your kids play any sports? Soccer or anything?"

We talked about our kids for a while—I told him about how my son, Jonah, was taking karate and chess classes this year and how he loved Pokémon.

"My son's into Pokémon, too," Rob said. "Big Golisopod fan—huge. See, I'm a good dad, I keep up with this shit." Then, after taking a long sip of his gimlet, Rob asked, "So how're the mothers at the school? Any hot ones?"

Rob may have been forty-four, but his brain age was sixteen.

"I'm just curious," I said. "Aren't you worried about your wife finding out?"

"Finding out?"

"You know, about your . . . *lifestyle*. Aren't you worried about your life turning into a huge train wreck?"

He made a face like I'd suggested something ridiculous, some impossibility.

Then he said, "Come on, I told you, I'm not a moron. That's who gets caught—the dummies. I'm not gonna have some obsessed woman calling the house; I'm not gonna rub it in my wife's face. I have my life at home and I have my other life and I never let the two lives meet."

The way he was talking to me about it so openly—and loudly—I doubted he was very careful.

"Don't you feel guilty?" I asked.

"You kidding?" he said. "Cheating saved my marriage. If I didn't cheat, Julianne and I would've gotten divorced years ago. When my youngest was a year old and she went through this whole crisis and shit with her father dying, we would've split for sure. A lot of guys in my position would have taken off. But I'm a good father, a good husband, too. Thank God that I was fooling around, that I had that outlet."

I could practically hear Oprah's audience booing.

"I don't know how you do it," I said. "I think I'd go crazy if I had to live my life that way. I mean with all the lying and deceit."

"You get used to it," he said casually.

He flagged down our waiter and ordered another gimlet. I didn't think it was the most tactful thing in the world, to get drunk while having lunch with an old friend who was a recovering alcoholic. But, then again, tactfulness had never been Rob's strong point.

"Okay, lemme ask you a question," Rob said. "You happily married?"

Maria and I hadn't had sex in four and a half years.

"Yes," I said.

"You hesitated."

"I did not."

"I was watching," he said. "I could've counted to three before you answered. Okay, maybe two, but it's okay. Admitting you have a problem is a process—look who I'm talking to. You know how it is. You're still in the denial stage right now. There's no shame in that."

"Thanks," I said. "I feel so much better about myself now."

The sarcasm soared over his head.

Smiling with one side of his mouth, like a parody of a used car salesmen, he said, "Okay, Mr. Happily Married Man Who's Never Cheated. What about fantasizing? Have you ever fantasized about another woman?"

"Of course," I said. "I mean everybody has fantasies. But that doesn't mean—"

"I used to fantasize," he said. "And I'm not just talking about turning around to check out a pretty girl on a hot summer day. My fantasizing went deep. It was vivid, all the time. That's when you get to the next step—making the fantasies real. You start flirting more, you notice female attention, and you start to seek it out. You know what I never understood? I never understood why some guys have a crisis when they hit forty. When you're in your forties and fifties and you're a man, with Viagra, Levitra, that's like the golden age for getting laid."

I smiled. Rob's skewed logic was ridiculous, but amusing.

"Okay," I asked, "so where do you meet your . . . I don't know what you call them . . . girlfriends?"

"Online mostly," he said. "You know, the extramarital dating websites."

"You're kidding me. You really do that?"

"That used to be my attitude," he said, "until I tried it. What do you think I do, meet women at work so I can wind up in a Me Too, trending on Twitter? I like taking risks when I'm ziplining, not when I'm trying to get laid. Online is the safest way to cheat, and these cheating sites are the best thing for married men since Monday Night Football. One I go to most is D-Ho, short for Discreet

Hookups. Go on D-Ho, your first time it seems lame. A lot of the guys are catfishing and the women are smart enough not to bite. But eventually, you get to know the women and start emailing, IM'ing, sending virtual flowers. Corny, I know, but I'm tellin' ya, the shit works. So far I've met eleven women and got laid eight times. Not a bad percentage, right?"

"Aren't you worried about hackers stealing your credit card info?" I asked. "Making the client list public?"

"If an alligator bites off a golfer's hand, do you quit playing golf?"

I had no idea what he was talking about.

"I don't get it," I said.

"Syphilis, AIDS, herpes, pregnancy—sex has always been risky," Rob said, "but people still do it. You should see the one I'm meeting tonight. Married, two kids, sexy as hell. I hope she looks like she does in her pics."

He held up his phone, showing me a photo of a very attractive woman, probably in her mid-thirties. She was smiling, holding a drink, looked like she was at an office party.

"What can I say?" I said. "Looks like you've got it all figured out."

He squinted, as if trying to solve a complicated problem, then said, "I'm sensing jealousy, Jack. Is that what this is all about? Your music career didn't go the way you wanted it to go, you quit drinking, you have no excitement in your life now, so you wish you were playing with your old buddy Rob on the other side of the tracks. Am I right or am I right?"

He wasn't one hundred percent off-base, but I said, "No, I'm just curious. So what do you do, just meet these women to have sex?"

"No," he said, "we meet to *fuck*. I mean, like tonight, we're meeting at my hotel bar, but I doubt we'll get through the first drink. Oh, man, I should show you some of the texts she's been sending me. She's so raunchy and nasty, I love it."

"Doesn't it bother you that she's cheating on her husband? That she has kids?"

"Not my business."

"What if her husband finds out and they wind up getting divorced?"

"She's an adult, she can make her own decisions."

I laughed.

"Answer me honestly." Not even smiling. "If you could cheat on your wife, and I guaranteed you there was zero chance of her ever finding out, would you do it?"

"Come on, that's a ridiculous—"

"In other words, yes."

"I didn't say—"

"Any guy would," he said. "And you'd be surprised, most women would, too. And if you're gonna tell me you'd never cheat, it's wrong, it's amoral—you're full of shit. Because what's the alternative? You *don't* cheat? You have the same dull, routine sex with the same woman for the rest of your life? I mean, like I said, I love my wife, don't get me wrong. I wanna grow old with her and spoon-feed mashed prunes to her at the nursing home when we're ninety, but when you think about it, you have to be crazy not to cheat. I mean, like they say, you're damned if you do and damned if you don't, and I say, Why not be damned and get laid?"

Our lunches arrived. While we ate, I managed to steer our conversation away from extramarital sex onto other subjects. Mostly, we talked about people we knew from back when we lived together. I'd stayed in touch with a few whom Rob hadn't, so I caught him up on what they were doing now.

By the end of the meal we were both straining for topics to talk about, and it was a relief when the check came. I suggested splitting it, but he insisted on paying.

"Compliments of Music Mania," he said.

Leaving the restaurant, he immediately put on his mirrored Aviators, even though it was overcast and drizzling.

"So let's have a think about the apartment and let me know where your head is at," I said. "I think you'd love it there, I really do, and if you want to make an offer and close fast, I'll get right on it."

I could tell he wasn't listening.

"Sounds like a plan," he said, staring at his cell. "Fuck, it's late. Gotta hit a meeting, then it's back to my hotel to rest up for my big date tonight. I'm not expecting to get much sleep." He looked at me. "You're so jealous right now. Deny it all you want, but you can't hide it."

We hugged, slapping each other's backs, and then walked away in opposite directions.

# CHAPTER THREE

I KNEW MY one thirty was going to be a bust the second I saw Larry Stein. On the phone he'd sounded older—I'd assumed forty—but he was in his late twenties, thirty tops. Worse, he'd sounded like a serious buyer on the phone, said he was currently renting, worked on Wall Street, and was looking for a large one-bedroom convertible to two or a small two-bedroom "in the million range." In person, he was in a cheap suit and was wearing an imitation Rolex that he'd probably bought on the street for ten bucks.

I screened him in my office—or tried to anyway. I asked him more about his career and background, and that was when he mentioned, in passing, that he was the assistant manager of a luggage store on Wall Street. Apparently he'd meant "I work on Wall Street" literally. I asked him if he had another source of income, and he said he had "other assets."

I was skeptical—he seemed like a ballbuster, the type of guy who went to open houses on weekends "just for fun"—but I showed him the apartment on Ninetieth anyway. He had nonstop questions: *How are the building's finances? How's the co-op board? How're the doormen? Is heat included in the maintenance?* After we had spent about twenty minutes in the apartment—he must've gone in and out of the bathroom six times—he asked, "So what would my monthly expenses be?"

"Assuming you put twenty percent down, about thirty-six hundred a month."

"Why so much?" he asked.

Thinking, *Um, maybe because it's a million-dollar apartment,* I feigned patience and said, "Well, with a sixteen hundred dollar maintenance that's just the way the numbers crunch."

"That's way out of my range," he said.

After a deep breath I asked, "Would you like to see some less expensive apartments?"

"Don't have time today," he said, "but I'll reach out to you next week sometime."

I knew I'd never hear from him again.

Walking back downtown along 3rd Avenue, I texted Rob McEvoy: *So cool seeing you today, man! Great to catch up and if you have any more questions about the apartment just gimme a shout!*

Rob was my hottest prospect right now. Well, let's face it—my *only* prospect, and, worse, I needed the sale desperately. Commission on a two-million-dollar apartment was $120,000. In this case, I'd have to split the commission with another broker and my company got a cut as well, but after taxes my share would still make up practically all of my income for the entire year.

If I didn't close the sale . . . Well, I didn't even want to think about that.

A text from Rob arrived: *I will . . . and I will !!!!!*

Okay, I'll admit it—I was jealous of Rob. Not of his philandering—of his career. He was an asshole, yeah, but he was making money, working in the music business. Before I got married, I'd been a studio guitarist, and sometimes I toured with bands around the country and once Europe. My pay was erratic—I was often broke and living on friends' couches—but I was a damn good guitarist, and it had been the happiest time of my life.

I missed having a career that I loved.

* * *

In the courtyard of P.S.158, a massive prewar elementary school on York Avenue, I waited with the other parents for Jonah's class to arrive.

This was always the highlight of my day. Because Maria had a full-time job in public relations at a midtown financial services company and my hours were flexible, I could do all of the pick-ups and drop-offs, rather than hiring a babysitter like a lot of Manhattan parents did. It might've been an annoying situation for some guys, but time with Jonah always felt like time with my best friend. I went on all of his class trips, was his reading and math buddy every other Friday, and took him to the major school events such as tie-dying day, the walkathon, dance night, and the Halloween Boo Bash.

A seemingly endless stream of shrieking, energetic kids exited the school, but Jonah's class was late. Upper East Siders could be as cliquey as their kids, and parents congregated in their usual groups. There were cliques of working moms, yoga moms, SoulCycle moms, PTA moms, grandmothers, stay-at-home dads, and babysitters. In the morning there was the clique of "dads in suits"—uppity pricks, who seemed to all know each other from somewhere, who always seemed to be dropping references to their "firms" and "mergers" and "buyouts." If I were more business savvy, I could've used the pick-ups and drop-offs as an opportunity to schmooze—the way some people schmoozed at the A.A. meetings I attended. I could've injected myself into every conversation and handed out business cards, saying, "Hey, if you know anybody who's looking for an apartment, gimme a shout," but it wasn't my style to kiss ass.

Standing around, I ended up on the periphery of a conversation between Stacy Katz and Geri Sherman from the PTA clique. I didn't say anything, just smiled and nodded once in a while. They were talking about the curriculum and an upcoming class trip to the South Street Seaport.

I'd never really thought about Stacy and Geri in a sexual way. I mean, I'd noticed they were attractive, but I hadn't actually *thought* about it. But now I couldn't help hearing Rob in my head—*You should see the moms at my daughter's school*. If Rob were here, he'd definitely hit on Geri. She was a good-looking, petite brunette in her early forties, and she was in the midst of a divorce. From a dad, I'd heard that she'd cheated on her soon-to-be ex—i.e., just Rob's type.

I glanced around, wondering what other moms Rob would hit on. Karen Schaeffer, one of the SoulCycle moms, was happily married, but that wouldn't deter Rob; he'd consider her a challenge. Or maybe he'd go after one of the yoga moms—Kirstin Lasher or Jenny Liang or Danielle Freidman—oh, yeah definitely Danielle. She was married to a workaholic neurosurgeon and had been the subject of affair rumors since Jonah was in kindergarten. She was in her late thirties but still looked great. Typical Danielle outfit—tight jeans, high-heeled boots, and a low-cut top showing lots of pushed-up cleavage. Recently, she'd been having a lot of play dates with Greg Langley, a stay-at-home dad who, I'd heard, was in marriage counseling with his wife, so it wasn't hard to imagine that there was some *real* dating going on there as well.

Although I knew that Rob's idea that everyone cheats on their spouse at some point was ridiculous, I'd read that something like seventy percent of all married people cheat at some point. If that were true, it meant there had to be a lot of illicit relationships going on with the parents at the school—ones I hadn't heard anything about.

"Hi, Daddy."

I looked down and saw Jonah standing there in front of me. I'd been so distracted by my thoughts that I hadn't noticed his class come out.

"Hey, kiddo," I said, kissing him on top of his head. He had shaggy light-brown hair, but it would probably turn darker eventually because Maria and I had dark hair. "How was school today?"

"Okay, can we get ice cream?"

"Nope, no ice cream. You've had ice cream two days in a row."

"Come on, Dad, *please*."

"You can have a healthy snack at home," I said, "and then how about we go to the park and play some basketball? Sound cool?"

"Sounds cool," he said, and we high-fived.

* * *

Later, after basketball and ice cream—yeah, I caved—we arrived at our apartment building—a modest, yet well-maintained postwar doorman building on 83rd between 1st and York. Unfortunately we were renting—we couldn't afford to buy—because owning on the Upper East Side would have been a great investment. Now that the Second Avenue Subway had finally opened, demand in the neighborhood had been skyrocketing, thanks mainly to an influx of hipsters from overpriced Williamsburg. Trendy restaurants and bars, many with live music and even burlesque, had opened throughout the neighborhood, and recently I'd passed a couple of new vegan cafés—always a surefire sign that a neighborhood was taking off.

Our apartment could've been marketed as a "junior four," but it was actually an average-size one-bedroom. Jonah had the bedroom, and we'd put up a wall in the living room alcove/office space to create a second bedroom. It was way too small for three people, but it was all we could afford on Maria's salary and my commissions. We'd managed for a while, but it's hard enough for two people to live in a one-bedroom—put a kid in the mix and it's nearly impossible.

I was in the living room, helping Jonah with his homework, when Maria entered. She had been away for a few days on a business trip to Houston and she pulled her suitcase into the apartment behind her. She was in a conservative navy dress, her hair back in a tight ponytail.

"Mommy!" Jonah rushed over to Maria by the door.

Bending over to hug him, she said, "Hello, sweetie, how have you been? I missed you so much."

"Missed you, too," he said.

"I want to hear all about everything you've been up to. Let me just change out of my work clothes, okay?"

"Okay."

"Hey," Maria said to me.

She kissed me quickly on the lips then went into the bedroom.

Our relationship was so different than it had been thirteen years ago. When I met her at one of my gigs downtown, she was in a tight leather miniskirt and fishnets and had short, spiky hair and a nose ring. She was alone at the bar.

Usually I was shy about approaching women, but without hesitating, I went right over and said, "Hey, I'm—"

"Jack Harper," she said.

"Sorry," I said, "how did you—"

"I was at your show last week and the week before that in Brooklyn." She was glowing. "I love your music. You're insanely good."

We began dating. After a week we were calling each other soul mates. She came to my shows, always cheering for me at the front of the stage. Her enthusiasm felt over the top, but it was flattering to have my sexy girlfriend cheering me on. Within two months, I moved in with her. Six months later, we were married.

My friends warned me that we were moving too fast, but I wasn't interested in logic. Maria and I had a great year or so together, then she grew out her hair, lost the nose ring, and got a corporate job. I was happy for her and happy that at least one of us had a stable career, but we grew apart. She didn't seem as interested in music anymore, especially my music. She stopped coming to my gigs, saying she needed to "get up early" or gave other excuses.

Meanwhile, my music career had hit a rough patch. My band wasn't getting as many gigs, and studio work was drying up. Maria and I had talked about wanting a family, and I knew I'd need to find a way to bring in more income.

I'd had a drinking problem since—well, since I had my first drink in high school. When Maria got pregnant, I promised to cut down, but I didn't. When Jonah was born, I stayed home with him during the day while Maria worked, and at night I played gigs and got drunk. I never drank when I was around Jonah, but I was often hungover.

Finally, I decided to do the right thing for my family and got sober. Maria, to her credit, stuck with me throughout this dark period. My music career had continued to dwindle so I got a real estate license to help bring in more income.

Beating booze helped me to become a better father and a better man, but it didn't help my marriage. Maria and I were living like roommates—roommates who didn't get along most of the time. We got into a bad pattern of tag-team parenting—I was with Jonah during the day, and when Maria came home from work, she took over.

We didn't have a date night and didn't socialize together. I hung out with friends from A.A. a couple of nights a week, while Maria entertained clients. We'd never had a lot of "couple friends"—just Maria's college friend Steve and his wife, Kathy. But since they'd moved out of the city to Westchester, we didn't even see them very often.

Our sex life dwindled. Maria was focused on her career and began to travel more often for work. Whenever I initiated, she said she was too tired. She never initiated herself so I eventually stopped trying. I suggested marriage counseling many times, but she was opposed. She had never been in therapy, despite a difficult childhood, and she seemed threatened by the whole idea. I went into therapy myself for a while, but it takes two people to fix a marriage.

Getting a divorce began to seem like a logical solution, and it would've been the best thing for Jonah. Maria and I weren't exactly modeling a happy, loving couple. I had a feeling that divorcing Maria would be a nightmare, though. She could be charming, but she also had a vindictive side. Her cousin Michael was a cutthroat divorce attorney, and with the lower tier lawyer I'd have representing me, I'd be in huge trouble, especially if Maria pulled "the alcoholic card." She could leave me broke and try to get full custody of Jonah. I could counter that I was sober now and that I'd been a major part of Jonah's life since he was born, but would these arguments hold up in court, especially with Michael representing her?

With no viable option to escape my marriage until Jonah was in college, we muddled on.

Rob had asked me if I fantasized. Yeah, I fantasized, but not about sex with another woman.

I fantasized about getting out of my bad marriage, about breaking free.

* * *

After Jonah did his last few math problems, I went into the kitchen where Maria was unpacking our order from Seamless—Chinese takeout. We had a recurring order of chicken with snow peas, assorted mixed vegetables, General Tso's chicken, and a large wonton soup.

"So," I said, "how was Houston?"

After a long pause she said, "Productive."

"Productive sounds good," I said. "Better than nonproductive."

She seemed distracted, checking her phone.

"Isn't that IPO coming out soon?" I asked.

"IPO?" She sounded confused.

"For that biotech company," I said. "That's why you were in Houston, right?"

"That IPO was two months ago," she said. "I told you about it, remember?"

I didn't remember, but I said, "Oh, that's right."

She was tapping out a text or email on her phone. Maybe a minute went by.

I knew she wouldn't ask me about my day unless I brought up the subject myself, so I said, "Well, my day was interesting. I showed an expensive apartment to Rob McEvoy."

"Who?" She was still tapping, looking at her phone.

"Rob McEvoy," I said. "You remember. My old roommate, we played in a couple of bands together."

Maria had never met Rob, but I'd told her stories.

"Oh, *that* Rob." Now she looked at me. "Isn't that the guy you've always thought was an asshole?"

"The one and only," I said.

I explained that he was looking for an apartment in Manhattan, leaving out that the apartment would be his fuck pad.

"Well, let's hope that comes through," she said, as she plated the General Tso's.

The comment might've sounded benign to a casual observer, but I heard, *Let's hope you finally bring in some money because I'm resentful as hell that I've been bringing in most of our income lately.*

"What's that supposed to mean?" I asked.

"It means I'm rooting for you," she said.

"Are you?" I said.

Jonah was watching us.

"Come on, Jack, let's not get into this now."

Maria was right for not wanting to argue in front of Jonah, but I didn't like how she was twisting things. She'd made a passive-aggressive comment, and because I'd challenged her, she acted as if I'd said something wrong. She'd done this before. It was a subtle way of stifling me, one of our many unresolvable problems.

At dinner, the focus was on Jonah. Maria talked to him about school and his homework, and I talked to him about soccer. I wasn't very into soccer myself, but since Jonah was into it, I'd boned up about Messi and Ronaldo, and I could hold my own in a conversation with an eight-year-old.

A great thing about takeout—no after-dinner dishes. While Maria had some one-on-one time with Jonah, helping him with his homework, I went to an A.A. meeting at St. Monica's Church on 79th Street near 1st Avenue.

Whenever I could—usually a couple of times a week—I attended meetings throughout Manhattan. I went to St. Monica's most often, though, because it was local and I had a lot of friends there. Many of my friends had moved out of the city over the years, others I'd had fallings-out with, and A.A. had become my main social life. Well, that or meet-ups and "sober parties" at friends' apartments.

I often spoke at meetings, but tonight I was in the mood to just listen. Ricardo spoke for a while, and then a couple of new members shared their stories. After the meeting, I caught up with some friends, including Dave, a young, red-haired guy whom I was currently sponsoring. Dave was twenty-six, an ad exec, and he'd been sober for almost a year. After a rough period when I spoke to him maybe ten times a day, he had been doing well. He had a new job, a new girlfriend, and looked happy and healthy.

When I was about to leave, he took me aside and said, "I just want you to know how much you've meant to me, Jack. Seriously, I don't know how I would've gotten through any of this without you."

"Hey, it's why we're here," I said.

He gave me an energetic hug.

When I returned to my apartment, at around ten, Jonah was already in bed, asleep.

Maria had gone into the bathroom and was washing up, getting ready for bed. I sat on the couch with my laptop and checked my work email and my schedule for tomorrow. Then my attention drifted and I checked out some Facebook statuses. Rob had posted a picture of his daughter dressed as the cat in her school play of *Peter and the Wolf*, and had written: *So proud of my baby girl.*

I "liked" his status—his daughter really was adorable.

While I was online, Maria went into our bedroom and shut the flimsy door. She usually got into bed by ten—an hour before I did—to read, and was usually asleep by eleven. She got up early, at six thirty, to go to the gym before work.

I watched TV for a while the way I always did at night, with a headset so I wouldn't disturb Maria and Jonah. I flipped around—the local news, part of an *Arrested Development* I'd seen a few times. I was zoning out a lot—worrying about work, hoping the sale with

Rob came through. He hadn't reached out to me with an offer, but then again, he was distracted tonight with his date. I imagined them in Rob's hotel room, having wild, screaming sex.

At eleven, I turned off the TV, turned out the lights in the living room and kitchen, and joined Maria in bed. Reading on her Kindle, she didn't seem to notice me. A few minutes later, she put the Kindle on the night table, turned out the reading light, and shifted onto her side, facing away from me.

When I heard her light snoring, I turned in the opposite direction and fell asleep, too.

# CHAPTER FOUR

AFTER MORNING DROP-OFF at Jonah's school, I rushed uptown to 95th between Park and Lex for a showing. It was a new-on-the-market, gut-renovated two-bedroom co-op on the third floor of a nice brownstone building on a tree-lined street, a block away from The Lower Lab, a desirable Upper East Side elementary school. The owners of the apartment were getting divorced and were eager to sell. There was so much tension between the sellers that their attorneys were showing the apartment to agents and the apartment was undervalued by about fifty thousand dollars. I knew the owners would agree to the first decent offer from the first preapproved buyer, and I had the perfect prospect—Alex Korin, whose wife had just given birth to their second child. Alex and his wife had gone out with me to look at apartments several times, and they were preapproved for a mortgage. The problem was four brokers were already viewing the apartment when I arrived, and they also probably had clients interested in it.

I reached Alex on his cell and said, "You have to get your ass uptown right now, I've got the perfect apartment for you, man."

Alex was in his thirties, owned a couple of bars in the city. I could be casual with him.

"I just got to work and I have meetings all morning," he said.

"I'm telling you," I said, "this is exactly what you're looking for and it won't last."

All real estate agents say that the apartments they're desperate to sell "won't last," even if they'd been stagnating on the market for months. Although this time I actually meant it, as far as he was concerned, I was full of shit.

"I might be able to get there after three, but I'll have to reach out and let you know."

"It'll be gone by then, I'm telling you. Can your wife come see it?"

"No, she's taking my daughter to the doctor this morning. Looks like strep."

I tried to persuade him to figure out a way to see it, but he said it was impossible for this morning. I ended the call, dejected. I overheard Sally Engle, a seasoned, very well-known agent for a major realtor, telling the owners' attorneys that she had several interested buyers on their way over. The other agents also had buyers rushing over, and I knew the apartment would probably be sold within an hour.

It was raining. I didn't have an umbrella, but I walked to my office anyway, not really caring or even noticing that I was getting soaked.

Wolf Realty was in a modest storefront on a side street—74th near 3rd. Most clients found out about us via word of mouth or online listings. There were three agents in the office, including me, and each of us had a desk adjacent to the left wall, mine in the middle. Our boss, Andrew Wolf, had his own space in a separate room in the back.

No kid says to his parents, "I want to be a real estate agent when I grow up." Real estate could be lucrative if you get lucky, but it was usually a career that people fell into when another career didn't work out. Take my coworkers, for example. Claire was an empty-nester who'd only gotten her real estate license three years ago because she had no recent work experience and couldn't find a job doing anything else. Brian had worked as a film editor, shoe salesman, stagehand, waiter, editorial assistant, and dogwalker, and I doubted real estate would be his last career move. Andrew Wolf himself had only gotten into the real estate business after a few restaurants he'd owned had gone belly-up.

When I arrived, Claire and Brian were talking on their phones, though they seemed to be on social calls. There was a lot of down time at our job. The New York City real estate market was hot, but we were competing against online listings, and even Airbnb. We all feared that real estate agents, like travel agents, would become obsolete. On days like this, my career, my future, and the future in general, seemed incredibly bleak.

As I waited for my PC to boot up, my gaze drifted toward the sign I'd hung above my desk: GOD IS MY COPILOT. When I started going to A.A., my first sponsor had suggested that I keep inspirational reminders around me. Sometimes the sign seemed corny, even a little kooky, but I looked at it every morning anyway.

I began my usual routine, browsing new listings that had come in—nothing very interesting—and then got a text from Maria: *Steve and Kathy invited us over next Sat.*

Steve was an old friend/ex-boyfriend of Maria's from college, one of the friends she occasionally went hiking with. Steve and Kathy had two sons—one Jonah's age.

I texted Maria: *I might have an open house that day, but I'll try to move it.*

She responded: *Okay, I'll accept.*

I hadn't told her that I could definitely go, only that I'd try, but I didn't feel like correcting her.

Then I got a text from Rob McEvoy: *Brothaman!! On way to airport. Holy fuck, last night was incredible bro. That woman was insane. I can barely walk today!!*

I was pissed that he was leaving the city already—I'd thought he'd be in town for another day or two. And where the hell was his offer?

I wrote: *Wow, already? Thought you'd be in town longer.*

Then I got: *Yeah some shit blew up at LA office. Be back in town soon and we'll jam!!!*

And another: *And I'm still jonesing for that apartment. B in touch soon!*

"Fuck me," I said.

I felt like a total idiot for believing that Rob, notoriously unreliable Rob, would come through for me.

I read the text again. If he was really "jonesing" for it, why couldn't he make an offer now? It wasn't like he needed to go back to L.A. and talk it over with his wife: *Hey, honey, mind if I buy a fuck pad in Manhattan?* Was it possible he'd been bullshitting about his income and that he actually couldn't afford the apartment? I didn't get why he would bust my chops to this extent; then again, isn't that the way everybody rolled in L.A.?

I texted: *Sounds great, man! Safe flight!*

I figured there was no use probing for the truth. He was either full of shit or he wasn't, and there was nothing I could do to change that.

"How was it?"

Claire's voice startled me. She was standing next to my desk.

"Wow, somebody's edgy today," she said.

"I didn't have my coffee yet," I said.

"Isn't coffee supposed to *make* you edgy?"

"Good point," I said. "Then I guess it's just a side effect of losing a sale first thing in the morning."

I told Claire what had happened at the showing.

Then she said, "Yeah, I thought I had a hot one yesterday. She was a new divorcee, empty-nester from Westchester, looking to move back to the city. You know that oversized one-bedroom on 78th and 2nd?"

"The one with the cherry cabinetry," I said.

"Right," Claire said. "She loved it and she had immaculate credit and was preapproved and everything. She said she'd call me later in the day to make an offer. I didn't hear from her, so I called her this morning and—"

"She offered on another apartment," I said.

"How did you know?"

"It's like asking me, how do I know if I'm having the same recurring nightmare?"

Brian came over and said, "Oh, pa-leeze. What're you two complaining about now?"

"Notice how I'm not complaining to you," Claire said to him.

"Got an accepted bid yesterday," Brian said, "my second this week, third in two weeks, and I closed on that 69th Street co-op on Monday. But yesterday's was the biggie. I listed it last week, got the asking price, eight sixty-two. I don't think they'll have any problem passing the board either—a lawyer and a doctor."

Just what a struggling real estate agent wanted to hear about—somebody else's sale.

"Congratulations," I said, trying to muster up some enthusiasm.

Later, Brian went to lunch, and Claire left to meet a client. I should've made a few calls to potential buyers, but I wasn't in the mood. I was feeling generally depressed about my life. Aside from

Jonah, nothing had gone the way I wanted it to go. Although I knew I was just in a rut now, and I'd get out of it eventually, knowing this didn't make me feel any better.

I was looking through a file of my recent contacts when Andrew Wolf exited his office.

"How was that open house?" he asked.

"Open house?"

"The one on 95th."

"Oh, right," I said. "Competitive. Have a solid lead, but I'm not sure I'll close him."

"Well, I hope something comes through for you soon," he said. "You really need a sale, Jack."

After he made a couple of photocopies, he returned to his office and shut the door. I tried to do some work, but I kept ruminating about his last comment—*You really need a sale, Jack.* I couldn't help interpret this as a threat; it had sure as hell sounded like one. Andrew was well aware of my lack of success over the past several months and, although I was a commission-only employee, that didn't mean he couldn't fire me. During my six-plus years at Wolf Realty, I'd seen about ten agents come and go and, actually, I was currently Andrew's most senior employee, but I didn't know if this was good or bad. Andrew usually didn't fire his employees, but just a few months ago, Lisa Castillo, his former longest-term employee, had left the agency. Although Andrew had told us that Lisa's leaving was "a mutual decision," it was clear that she'd been encouraged to leave because of disappointing sales. It sucked that longevity at the agency didn't bring about job security, but I understood Andrew's position. He ran a small agency and he only made money when we made money. There were only three desks in his office, and he needed agents who weren't deadweights.

I knew if I was fired, there was no guarantee I could find another job. I could try to find work at another agency, or even go out on my own. But it would be difficult to hustle for clients, having to compete against the big agencies and Internet sites, and if I wasn't doing well at Wolf, why would I do any better someplace else?

Two things were clear.

I needed my job.

And time was not my friend.

# CHAPTER FIVE

I SPENT MOST of the day working the phones, trying to set up the rest of my week. I made several showings for tomorrow and the next day with two prospects and I felt reasonably good about both of them.

At 2:55, I picked up Jonah at school and we went to the Carl Schurz Park playground so he could play soccer with his friends. As always, I chatted with a few of the moms and babysitters I knew. Karen, Jonah's friend Noah's mother, was complaining to me and Ann-Marie, and Sylvia, Jeffery Katz's babysitter, about the Common Core math curriculum.

"I'm sorry, but I think the kids are falling behind. Noah has friends in other schools who already know all their times table, and my daughter is still having trouble with addition."

"I know, I think we need to do something," Ann-Marie said, "talk to the principal or start a petition."

"I don't think that'll do any good," Sylvia said. "The principal is so stuck in her ways."

Karen went on, complaining, and then she asked me, "What do you think?"

"Excuse me?"

Karen had asked me something, but I hadn't processed it.

"I asked you what you think about Common Core," she said.

Karen was the class mom.

"Oh, yeah, I'm totally anti–Common Core," I said. "I think it's putting a tremendous, uh, burden on the students."

I continued participating in the conversation, making appropriate comments such as, "I think a petition's a great idea," and, "As parents, we all need to be more assertive." But I felt distracted, disconnected.

After the playground, I went with Jonah and a few of his friends and their moms and babysitters for frozen yogurt at Sixteen Handles on 2nd Avenue. On the way home, Jonah and I swung by Agata & Valentina on 1st Avenue to pick up some groceries. We'd had Chinese a lot lately, and I thought it would be nice to have a home-cooked meal for a change.

I made a garden salad and one of my specialties—chicken cutlets and rice pilaf. Okay, so it wasn't exactly difficult to sautée a few chicken breasts and prepare packaged rice pilaf, but it's the thought that counts, right?

Maria came home and saw dinner on the stove.

"You cooked?" She sounded surprised.

"Yeah, just thought it would be nice to mix things up for a change."

"Great idea," she said.

She went into the bedroom to change out of her work clothes.

During dinner, Jonah told us all about what he'd learned in science class in school and about Pokémon Go. It was nice to have a pleasant dinner with my family. For the first time in a long time things seemed normal. Maybe if I continued to make an effort, things with Maria would improve. Maybe we could have a date night, talk more, and enjoy each other the way we used to.

"It's too bad they don't teach Pokémon on the fourth-grade exam," I said to Maria.

"Yeah, that's true." Maria suddenly seemed out of it.

"Are you okay?" I asked.

"I'm not sure," she said, wincing, as if she had a sour taste in her mouth. "I have to go lie down."

She headed into the bedroom.

Later, after I tucked Jonah in, I heard Maria in the bathroom, throwing up violently.

"Are you okay?" I asked, concerned.

She couldn't answer, but I caught a glimpse of her very pale face.

"Close the door," she said.

For the next half hour, she couldn't leave the bathroom. I made periodic offers to help her, but she insisted that I leave her alone.

Finally, she left the bathroom, looking like she'd been through hell.

"Jesus, you should lie down again," I said. "Can I get you something? Water? Ginger ale? Imodium?"

She stood near the bathroom, looking disgusted, holding her stomach.

Then she said, "I think it was the chicken."

"I don't see how that's possible," I said. "I cooked it thoroughly and it definitely wasn't spoiled. I remember checking the date on the package. I really think you should force yourself to drink some water."

"Did you clean the knife?" she asked.

"Of course I cleaned it," I said.

Actually, I *thought* I'd cleaned it, but I couldn't remember for sure.

"I mean before you made the salad," she said.

"Yes, of course I cleaned it," I said. "I mean I don't remember not cleaning it."

"So there's a chance you didn't clean it."

"I cleaned it, I'm sure," I said. "Besides, I'm not sick and Jonah isn't sick. It's obviously just a virus, or something you ate at work. It's going around. Four kids were absent in Jonah's class today."

"I know the difference between food poisoning and a virus," Maria said, "and this isn't a fucking virus. It must've been salmonella from the knife you used to cut the chicken."

I understood why Maria was upset, but I didn't like how she was taking it out on me.

"You don't have to curse," I said, "and are you actually accusing me of giving you salmonella?"

"I can curse whenever I want to curse," she said,

She was about to add to this when her face turned grayish-white. She rushed back into the bathroom, slamming the door.

"Why's Mommy so mad?"

Jonah had heard the door slam and came out of his room. He looked worried.

"She's just not feeling well," I said. "But she'll be fine, I promise."

"Okay," Jonah said and returned to bed.

I sat on the couch for a while, trying to relax. I felt bad for arguing with Maria, especially within earshot of Jonah, but the dynamic was typical. It seemed like whenever I made an attempt to try to improve my marriage or open up communication, it somehow backfired.

Trying to distract myself, I went online on my laptop. I checked Facebook—Rob had posted a selfie of himself with a big smile in front of the big clock at Grand Central Station—and I discovered that the Powerball ticket I'd bought the other day had no correct numbers. I was about to close the browser when I remembered Rob talking about that extramarital dating website; what was the name of it? Dangerous Hookups? No, Discreet Hookups, that was it.

For the hell of it, I checked it out.

The welcome page was the silhouette of a man sitting on a beach. As I dragged the cursor over the man, a silhouette of a shapely woman appeared next to him. Then above the couple the words appeared:

## MARRY FOR COMPANIONSHIP, CHEAT FOR HAPPINESS

I was about to close my laptop, but then I thought, *What the hell?* and clicked enter.

I read the testimonials with "real Discreet Hookups clients"—men and women, claiming about how Discreet Hookups had helped them to meet "sexy, exciting married people" and saved their own marriages. Then I browsed several articles about affairs with titles like "The Truth About Extramarital Affairs" and "Why Good People Cheat." All of the articles were skewed toward the attitude that life is short, so why waste it in a bad marriage? They cited probably inflated, distorted statistics claiming that seventy-five percent of all married men cheat on their spouses, and sixty percent of all women cheat. One article, written by some expert marriage counselor, claimed that affairs had saved the marriages of many of his patients. Another argued that the "stigma of infidelity" was an American phenomenon, and that in Europe, affairs were much more accepted.

Of course all the articles—and, let's face it, the entire website—left out the other side of the story, about how affairs destroyed marriages and families and caused pain for everyone involved. Most of the divorced people I knew in A.A. had cheated on their spouses and claimed that, aside from their decision to take their first sip of alcohol, it was the worst choice they'd ever made. But I couldn't blame the Discreet Hookups people for avoiding the depressing side effects of affairs. Would alcohol and tobacco companies warn consumers about the potential dangers of their products if they weren't forced to by the government? As long as there were no legal restraints about a dating service for infidelity, why get all moral with people and ruin the fun?

Admittedly, there was something titillating about the site. This wasn't an accident; it had been designed to get unhappily married guys like me intrigued.

I wanted to browse the photos, just to see what kind of people went on these sites. Of course there was no way I was going to register with my actual name, but there was an option to register as a guest. I didn't have to give a credit card number, just some basic information—height, body type, and my "limits" and "status." For status I chose "Attached male seeking females"; for limits I selected "something short term." I had to choose a user name. What the hell, I tried NYCRockGod, but it was taken. Brilliant minds? So I went with NYCRockGod2.

I guess I was expecting to see provocative pics of scantily clad women, but the women of "D-Ho" looked very average, like—well, like the moms I saw in the playground every day. Some weren't complete photos—they were taken from the neck down or their faces were blacked out—but most of them were unobstructed, normal photos, probably like the ones on any dating site.

Almost all the women had the same status: Attached female seeking males. Some claimed that their limits were "undecided," but most indicated that they were interested in "cyber affair/erotic chat." Most had chosen provocative names that included some combination of hot, sexy, honey, horny, or siren, but very few of the photos seemed to match the names.

Well, I'd gotten my glimpse into the world of extramarital dating websites. I wanted to give Maria some space, so I went for a walk around the neighborhood. I was thinking about my marriage, trying to figure out how things had gotten to this point. I wished we had a dog—for the companionship and to give my walks more purpose—but Maria was allergic. On the way home, I stopped at a deli and bought Maria ginger ale and Saltines. Back at the apartment, I checked on her. She was in bed, on her back, with the lights out. I thought she was asleep, then she stirred.

"How're you feeling?" I asked.

"Like shit," she said.

"I got you some ginger ale and crackers."

"I'll probably just throw them up."

I knew this was a bad time to get into it, but letting things fester wasn't good either.

"I'm not happy," I said.

She remained still for maybe ten seconds. I thought she might've fallen asleep. Then she jerked upright to a sitting position, and with a suddenly angry expression, she said, "And what's that supposed to mean?"

"I'm just telling you how I feel," I said. "I just think we both have to admit that we have problems. I mean, I think it's obvious that we've drifted apart, but I don't think it's anyone's fault. This isn't about blame, it's about acknowledging the way things are with us. I think we should—"

"Should what?"

She sounded livid, but I kept going.

"Figure out what we're doing," I said.

She lay on her back and stared at the ceiling.

"Come on, I know you're not happy either," I said. "How could you be?"

She wouldn't look at me.

I waited another minute or so, then left the bedroom.

Sleeping apart wouldn't bring us any closer, but I needed space. I took a spare blanket and pillow from the hall closet and lay on the couch, but I couldn't sleep. I kept shifting, mainly thinking about work and snippets of the stupid argument with Maria, muttering "Salmonella, Jesus Christ."

Then a realization hit—my marriage was over. This wasn't just "going through a little rough patch"—I'd been lying, telling myself that crap for years. The truth was we couldn't have a conversation anymore without it spiraling into an argument. What was

I supposed to do, suggest marriage counseling for the umpteenth time? I was in my forties, *mid*-forties. Did I really want to be in a sexless marriage for the rest of my life?

But I didn't feel bad for Maria or myself—I felt bad for Jonah. I didn't want him to be in the middle of this, but it wasn't good for him to have a ringside seat for a toxic relationship for the rest of his childhood either. That's what I had gone through as a kid and look what had happened to me. The last thing I wanted for Jonah was for him to have a repeat of my life.

I went in the bathroom and washed up, then returned to the couch. I just wanted to get a good night's sleep, but when I lay down I couldn't stop ruminating. I was imagining telling Maria that I wanted a divorce and the clusterfuck that would ensue.

Later, I dreamt that I was in prison, clanging on the bars, screaming to get out. Finally, the guard came, but the guard had morphed into Maria. She handed me a key chain with dozens of keys. I was trapped in the cell with an animal, or some kind of monster. I couldn't find the right key to fit the lock. The monster was about to bite my head off when I woke up, drenched in sweat.

I didn't have to be Freud to understand the meaning of the dream.

I had to find a way out.

# CHAPTER SIX

In the morning, Maria was still angry at me. As she got ready for the gym and work, she didn't make eye contact and spoke to Jonah about me in third person—"Your father will make you breakfast," and, "Why don't you ask your father if he'll sign that permission slip?"—then stormed out of the apartment.

Although Jonah didn't say anything, it was obvious by how he retreated into his room and started playing on his Nintendo Switch that he was upset. This was particularly disturbing as Jonah was acting the way I often responded to conflict—running away and hiding behind some kind of vice. Not that a kid's video game was a vice, but I feared that when he got older this behavior could morph into avoiding conflict by going to a bar and getting loaded.

I made breakfast for Jonah—well, poured Special K into a bowl.

As he was eating, I said, "Sometimes me and Mom don't get along, just like you and your friends don't get along, but that's okay. It doesn't mean we don't love you."

"I know," he said. "She hates you, not me."

"She doesn't *hate* me," I said. "She just gets angry at me sometimes. There's a difference."

He looked at me like he saw right through my bullshit.

On our way to school, he still seemed aloof. I was worried that he was still upset and I wanted to distract him. As we headed along York Avenue, a strong gust came, blowing leaves off the trees.

I snatched a falling leaf and said, "Got one."

Jonah and I had invented our "leaf catching game" when he was three years old, and we'd played it every fall since then. The goal was to catch as many falling leaves as you could.

He darted along the sidewalk and lunged, but a large leaf zigzagged just past his outstretched hand.

"Aww," he said.

I caught another and said, "That's two."

"No fair," he said, disappointed.

"Hey, remember, we're a team," I said. "No winners and no losers. When I win, you win."

"But I wanna catch one," he said.

"There's one, right up there," I said.

A big orange-and-red leaf was falling toward the curb. He reached up, getting ready to grab it, when a breeze came and steered the leaf toward the street. Jonah darted toward it, heading between two cars.

Then I noticed the taxi speeding down the block.

The leaf was blowing away faster now, toward the street, and Jonah was still chasing it, about to run out to the street.

"Jonah!" I screamed.

He stopped short as the cab sped past. I rushed up behind him, grabbed him by the arm, and yanked him back onto the sidewalk.

I squatted so our faces were at the same level and scolded him: "Don't you ever, ever do that again, do you understand me? Do you understand how dangerous that is? Do you understand what could happen to you?"

I was practically screaming. He looked terrified and was starting to cry. I was glad. I wanted him to be upset so he'd understand how serious this was. I was pretty shaken up myself.

"I'm not losing you." I shook him. "You understand? I'm not losing you. I'm not losing you!"

When he was full-blown hysterical, I hugged him and told him it would be okay and gave him tissues to blow his nose.

We arrived at school a few minutes later, and he had to go up to class by himself. At the door, I kissed him on top of his head and said, "Are you okay?"

"Fine, Daddy," he said.

"You sure? Because I don't want you to go to school if you're still scared."

"I'm not scared."

He seemed to be telling the truth. But, while he'd recovered from his crying fit, I was still upset myself.

"I love you," I said, "more than anything," and kissed the top of his head once more.

* * *

I knew if I thought about my marriage I'd sink into a depression. But I was good at blocking things out—always had been—and I focused on work.

I had a productive day. I placed a few new ads online, generated some new leads and followed up on some old ones, and did follow-up calls for a couple of upcoming open houses.

After school, Jonah and I kicked a soccer ball around for a while in John Jay Park. When we got back to the apartment, Maria was already home. Our apartment was 580 square feet, but it felt like 300. Maria was trying to avoid eye contact with me and vice versa. They say blood pressure is the silent killer, but I could feel mine rising just from being in the same room with Maria. I didn't know how we could go on like this—without me having a massive heart attack or going insane.

I waited until Jonah was in his room, out of earshot. Then I went into the kitchen, where Maria was making herself a bowl of yogurt with fruit, and said, "We have to talk."

"There's nothing to talk about anymore," she said.

"See?" I said. "That's why we have to talk."

She took her food with her into the living room and ate while watching a show on Food TV.

She was right, I realized—there was nothing to talk about anymore. I felt like I was stuck in a maze—a maze with no exit.

Later, when Maria went to bed, I announced that I had "some work to do." Then, in the living room, I logged on to Discreet Hookups.

I recognized some of the profiles from last night, but there were a lot of new ones, too. I wondered if the robots of Discreet Hookups had rotated the profiles to make the site seem less stale, or if it was to boost the morale of the users, to show they weren't alone—there was seemingly an endless supply of unhappily married men and women.

Then a pop-up appeared:

FUGITIVE_RED *has sent you a message!*

I was surprised; without a profile photo or any information about myself, I hadn't expected someone to actually *write* to me. She looked pretty in her thumbnail, and I clicked, expanding it.

She had long, straight red hair and pale skin. The second photo was a wider angle of the first, a full body shot. She was casually dressed in jeans and a light-blue tank top and seemed to be in a backyard. She was thin, maybe too thin, but I liked the way her hips curved. She looked like she was in her mid-thirties, forty tops. She wasn't smiling in the photo. She wasn't making any expression at all really; she was simply *looking* at the camera.

I opened the message:

FUGITIVE_RED: *Hey Rock God! Do you like music? I'm lonely tonight Wanna chat?*

Ugh, what had I been thinking? NYC RockGod2 probably came off as incredibly pretentious, stupid, or both.

I clicked through her photos again. She wasn't the prettiest woman on the site, but there was something compelling about her. She was into music—that got my attention—and the name Fugitive Red intrigued me. It sounded familiar somehow.

I checked out the rest of her profile. She listed her location as White Plains. Her status was "Attached female seeking males" and her limit was "Undecided." Under "Preferences and encounters I am interested in" she had written: *I'm unhappily married, looking for adventure. How about you?*

Her list of "What really turns me on," chosen from a checklist, included—Discretion/Secrecy, A Sense of Humor, Spontaneity, Says What They Want, and Asks What I Want. Under "What I am looking for," she had—Extended Foreplay, Lips/Tongues, Slow Hot Oil Massage, Role Play, Satin Sheets, Wine Tastings, Romantic Walks, Long Drives, Slow Kissing.

I reread her profile, then saw the notification below her picture: online now.

My pulse pounded as I thought, *But do I really want to do this?*

Then I reminded myself that my marriage was effectively over, so, seriously, what exactly did I have to lose? She was going to flip out when I announced I wanted a divorce; my life was going to go down the shitter whether she caught me online or not. So, what difference did it make? Why not have a little joy in my life for a change?

I tried to send a response when a message informed me that since I was only a guest member, my messages didn't have "priority status."

But if I became a full member I could send "elite messages," which were much more likely to be actually read. A full membership cost, naturally, $69. As a full member I could also initiate instant messaging sessions. The catch was that in order to send elite messages, I had to purchase credits that could be used to send messages.

The whole setup seemed shady to me—designed to make money for Discreet Hookups but not to actually connect people.

But thinking, *Well, I came this far, might as well go all the way,* I registered as a full member. I remembered Rob boasting about how the site was secure, and we had a Visa card that Maria never used, so there didn't seem to be much risk of her finding out.

My rationalization complete, I made the payment and also bought twenty dollars in credits. I just wanted to send this woman a message or two, get whatever was going on with me out of my system. After tonight, I'd probably realize how ridiculous all this was and never return to Discreet Hookups again.

I finished registering then returned and saw that FUGITIVE_RED was still online.

> NYCRockGod2: *Hey, sorry had to register Yes, love music*

I waited about a minute, got no reply. She'd probably given up on me, gone on to somebody else. After all, I didn't have a lot of information about myself on my profile and I hadn't even posted a picture so I probably seemed like a fake profile. All she could see was my basic information, which probably wasn't much different from everybody else's basic information. Then I heard a loud beep and saw:

> FUGITIVE_RED: *Hiii*
> FUGITIVE_RED: *nice to hear from you :) :)*

Shit, the sound on my laptop was at its highest level. I immediately muted it. I listened, making sure Maria wasn't coming, then sent:

NYCRockGod2: *Hey! I know you probably get this a lot, but this is my first time doing this :) :)*

Liking my message, I clicked send. It was honest anyway, and I figured honesty had to be a rarity on an extramarital dating site.

FUGITIVE_RED: *yeah actually new here too :) :)*

Shit, now I had a feeling my opening had been a cliché. Everyone initiating a chat session on an extramarital dating site probably claimed it was their first time, just like every convict in jail was innocent.

I wanted to respond with something clever, but my mind was blank.

FUGITIVE_RED: *Love music! I used to be in a band rock/punk band in school*
NYCRockGod2: *Wow you're kidding me, so did I! ? :) Do you play an instrument?*
FUGITIVE_RED: *Guitar, but I sing mostly*

Looking at her pictures again, I imagined her onstage—in some leather getup, in a punk band. The fantasy enhanced her pics, made her seem much sexier.

NYCRockGod2: *I play guitar too Love rock, punk Especially 70s/early 80s*
FUGITIVE_RED: *Me too! Love The Ramones, Blondie, The Clash, Sex Pistols Floyd Led Zepp*

It was like a list of my inspirations.

NYCRockGod2: *Wow, love ALL of those You have amazing taste! R u a musician???*
*I played n punk bands in high school and college Then was a studio musician and toured a little with bands*

She didn't respond right away; I feared it was because I sounded too into myself.

Then I got:

FUGITIVE_RED: *Wow, you sound incredible :) :)*

Whew.

NYCRockGod2: *Thanks. :) How bout u? Did you sing in a band?*
FUGITIVE_RED: *Yes small bands Nothing you've heard of, but I love singing That's the most important thing, right? Doing what you love.*
NYCRockGod2: *I always say the same thing!!*
FUGITIVE_RED: *:)*
FUGITIVE_RED: *How come u don't have a profile pic?? :( :(*

I'd expected her to ask this. I knew exactly which photo to use—one Maria had taken of me about six, seven years ago, on the Great Lawn in Central Park. I still had long, thick hair then, so it was sort of false advertising, but what difference did it make?

NYCRockGod2: *hold on!*

As I uploaded the photo, it occurred to me that this probably wasn't such a great idea, posting a photo of myself on a website for cheaters. What if a mom or dad from Jonah's school somehow saw it? Nah, I told myself. The odds were astronomical that anyone I knew would see the photo tonight, and if anyone did see it, that person would be cheating themselves and not be in any position to judge. Besides, I would delete the photo in a few minutes, right after I finished the chat session.

I sent:

NYCRockGod2: *K its up!!*

Several seconds passed, then I got:

FUGITIVE_RED: *wow, amazing pic! You're so sexxxxy!*

Did the ego boost hit? You bet it did. What forty-four-year-old guy who hadn't had sex in four and a half years didn't desperately need an ego boost? Okay, yes, she was commenting on a particularly good picture of me that had been taken a long time ago, but so what? I'd take all the compliments I could get.

NYCRockGod2: *Guess I was having a good hair day :)*
FUGITIVE_RED: *Hahahahahah yr funny!*

I looked at her pics again. Somehow, she seemed better looking now.

NYCRockGod2: *You look great in your pics too!*

A pause then:

FUGITIVE_RED: *You think I'm sexy?*
NYCRockGod2: *Very. :)*
FUGITIVE_RED: *Funny! My husband never tells me I'm sexy anymore*
NYCRockGod2: *Well that's ridiculously*
NYCRockGod2: *Ridiculous that is! you look amazingly sexy too :)*

Okay, so yeah, maybe "amazingly sexy" was overdoing it a little, but so what? It was fun to flirt with this woman, and I wanted to keep the high going.

FUGITIVE_RED: *I'm lonely right now Are you lonely?*
NYCRockGod2: *Yes.*
FUGITIVE_RED: *Is your wife home?*
NYCRockGod2: *Yes*
FUGITIVE_RED: *Can I ask you a personal question?*

Was she going to steer the conversation toward sex? Isn't that what inevitably happened on these sites?

NYCRockGod2: *Yes.*
FUGITIVE_RED: *why r u on here?*

Not exactly the question I'd expected.

NYCRockGod2: *Why is everybody on here?*

I was deflecting, or whatever the psychological term for it was, but I didn't feel comfortable talking about myself in person, no less to a stranger on the Internet.

But she persisted:

FUGITIVE_RED: *Bad marriage?*

The first step is admitting you have a problem.

NYCRockGod2: *Yes*
FUGITIVE_RED: *Me too My husband hasn't touched me in years*
NYCRockGod2: *Similar situation here But wife in my case :)*
FUGITIVE_RED: *:) You have really sexy lips*
NYCRockGod2: *Thank you!*

FUGITIVE_RED: *I bet women always tell you that*

Maria used to tell me my lips were sexy—maybe a decade ago.

NYCRockGod2: *No not really*
FUGITIVE_RED: *I bet your a gr8 kisser :)*

Maria used to tell me that, too.

NYCRockGod2: *Ha thanks!*
FUGITIVE_RED: *Sorry if I'm embarrassing you*
NYCRockGod2: *No its fine im not embarrassed at al*

Turned on, yes. Embarrassed, no.
My heart thumping, it was hard to think . . . or type.

NYCRockGod2: *I'm jus not used to this thas all*
FUGITIVE_RED: *Me neither :)*

Then the guilt hit. This had been fun and exciting to chat with a total stranger, but this wasn't me. I wasn't a cheater. And if I really wanted to get out of my marriage, this definitely wasn't the way to go about it.

NYCRockGod2: *Sorry have to go*
FUGITIVE_RED: *?????*
NYCRockGod2: *sorry!!*

I deleted my photo and logged out. A rush of relief hit, like I'd been dangling from a ledge and someone had pulled me to safety. Yeah, Maria and I had serious problems, but acting impulsively was a big red flag for me—I talked about this all the time at A.A. meetings—so it was hard not to feel as though I'd avoided a relapse. Chatting with a stranger was an exciting diversion, but that's all it had been—a diversion—and this wasn't the way I wanted my marriage to end. Getting caught on Discreet Hookups would make me look like the bad guy; was that how I wanted Jonah to think of his father for the rest of his life?

I was too hyped up to sleep. I had a snack in the kitchen—a couple spoonfuls of Jiffy—and reminded myself that there really was no danger of getting caught. The entire conversation had been anonymous; we hadn't even exchanged actual names, and now that my laptop was off, that woman was out of my life permanently, and it was like it had never happened. As long as I didn't make it into a big deal, it wouldn't be a big deal.

But, there was no doubt, chatting with FUGITIVE_RED had felt invigorating, like meeting a woman and going on a great first date and becoming insanely attracted to her all at once. Of course, I knew these emotions were fake; we weren't making an actual connection. All we'd done was exchange some flirty, flattering words. Besides, for all I knew she'd been lying about everything. Maybe she'd never been the lead singer of a band. Maybe that was just to impress me, to make me *think* we were connecting. Maybe she wasn't even married, and maybe that picture wasn't of her. Maybe I'd been chatting with a man, or even a teenage boy. Maybe he was texting his friends about it right now, laughing his ass off as he told them the story about the "horny old guy online" he'd just duped.

But I couldn't get myself to believe that FUGITIVE_RED wasn't a real profile.

It had to be legit.

I went into Jonah's room to check on him. He was sleeping soundly on his back with his head turned to the side. It reminded me of the way he used to sleep when he was a baby in his crib. I gave him a gentle kiss on the forehead and then went back to the living room.

Back on my laptop, I returned to Discreet Hookups, to FUGITIVE_RED's page. When I saw the green dot above her pic, indicating she was still active on the site, my pulse quickened. I wanted to IM with her again, feel that rush.

But then I caught myself and shut the browser before I had a chance to change my mind again.

# CHAPTER SEVEN

In the morning, after school drop-off, I stopped at the office briefly and then headed out to meet a potential buyer, Megan Conaway. Megan was in her mid-twenties and worked in marketing at *New York Magazine*, and was looking for a starter apartment—a large studio or junior one. Her parents were planning to cosign for the mortgage, and they had been preapproved, so this was a prime prospect.

I had a feeling Megan would like this 77th Street one-bedroom, though. It was on the fifth floor of a walk-up, but an elevator and doorman weren't requirements for her, and she'd told me she didn't mind being on the fourth or fifth floor. I had the key from the owner and, as we climbed the stairs, I told her about the building's financials. The apartment was listed for $475,000, with maintenance of $1,200, which I knew was in her ballpark.

When I opened the door, she said, "Wow, this is incredible."

The apartment had a lot of light and a big kitchen with a nice-size balcony.

"It really is a find," I said. "It just went on the market yesterday so you're pretty much getting a first crack at it. And the owner will make a deal with you if you want to keep any of the furniture."

I remained in the living room area, while she checked out the kitchen and the balcony.

"Oh my God, I really, really love it," she said.

I was in a relaxed mood, with much more confidence than I'd had at recent showings, and I didn't pressure her the way I might've yesterday or the day before. I remained near the door while she checked out the rest of the apartment.

She returned and said, "The bedroom's great, but the bathroom's a little small."

"It's true," I agreed, "it is small."

No pressure. If she didn't love the place and want to make an offer, it would be no big deal. I'd show her something else.

She asked me some questions about the building's financials and the co-op board. I answered all of them honestly and matter-of-factly.

"The co-op board isn't easy," I said. "They've rejected people in the past. That said, I think they'll like you a lot. And you want a tough co-op board. You don't want to live in a building that lets people do whatever they want to do to their apartments and that has Airbnb people coming and going."

Rather than pushing for a sale, I told her she could take all the time she needed. Then, lo and behold, *she* suggested another appointment to take measurements and to show her parents the place. I could tell she was excited and would likely make an offer.

Later in the morning, I had two other showings and they both went well. I didn't know if they'd lead to sales, but there was no doubt that I wasn't nearly as stressed out about my job as I had been lately. I'd try as hard as I could to sell a few apartments, but if it didn't work, I knew it wouldn't be the end of the world. I could always find another job, or figure out another way to make money.

At my office, Claire and Brian were away, and Andrew was busy on the phone. I downloaded the Discreet Hookups app to my phone and went to my messages. I wasn't actually going on to chat with FUGITIVE_RED again; I just wanted to see if her profile was still there. Well, this was what I told myself anyway.

Her profile hadn't been removed, but she wasn't online. After I browsed her photos—the same ones I'd seen and knew so well—I did some work. I didn't have any more showings scheduled for today, but I had a lot of phone calls to make, and I wanted to contact the seller of the 77th Street apartment to make sure I could schedule another showing for Megan. Throughout the day, I kept returning to FUGITIVE_RED's page, to see if she was online. She wasn't. I was becoming increasingly convinced I'd been played.

I went out and grabbed a slice of pepperoni pizza for lunch. I ate it NYC style—fast, standing up. Staring at a mirror above the counter, I noticed I had dark circles under my eyes and the "lines" in my forehead looked like what they actually were—wrinkles. My sideburns were too long and my eyebrows were noticeably unruly. I definitely needed to do a little grooming. Then I took another bite of pizza, I imagined all the fat going right to my stomach and love handles, and spit the mushed-up food into a napkin.

As I headed back to my office, I decided it was time to start taking better care of myself. No more pizza or deli sandwiches or Chinese takeout—I was going to eat more salad and fruit and home-cooked meals and start taking a bagged lunch to work. And I'd hit the gym more often, too. I was paying eighty-six bucks a month for a membership at New York Sports Club, but I couldn't remember the last time I'd worked out. A month ago? Two months ago? I had to stick to it, lose ten or fifteen pounds. I had to start dressing better, too, paying more attention to my appearance. I'd always dressed simple, casual, but what had happened to my "look," my sense of personal style? When I was a musician, I used to wear trendy tee shirts, funky necklaces, bracelets, and had both ears pierced. Now, as a middle-aged real estate agent on the Upper East Side, I was in clothes from H& M and the earring holes had closed up. What the hell had happened to me?

Claire was at her desk, talking to a young couple, potential buyers, and Brian and Andrew were out of the office. When Claire and the couple left, I had the office to myself.

FUGITIVE_RED still wasn't active. I decided I'd send her a message, figuring if it was a fake page after all, the worst thing that could happen was that I wouldn't get a response. Then I saw the green dot appear on FUGITIVE_RED's profile.

I bought another hundred dollars of credits on my Visa card, then sent:

NYCRockGod2: *Hey!*
FUGITIVE_RED: *hi*

It was hard to judge another person's mood online, but the lack of caps and no exclamation point made me feel like she wasn't enthused. Was she upset that I'd logged off last night? If so, she'd responded immediately, so how angry could she be?

NYCRockGod2: *I'm really sorry about last night. My apartment got crowded*

Figured "crowded" was a more polite way to say: "my wife had walked in."

After a long pause, she sent:

FUGITIVE_RED: *ha no worries Totally get that!*
FUGITIVE_RED: *I was pretty nervous too Guess that's why you took down your pic huh?*
NYCRockGod2: *Yeah*

Like last night, I'd felt an oddly strong connection to this woman I'd never met, whose name I didn't know. Was it just because of my situation, because I was in an unhappy marriage? Or did we have a real connection?

FUGITIVE_RED: *Makes sense You don't want your wife to catch you online! I totally get that :)*
NYCRockGod2 : *I told you I haven't done this before and now you know I was telling the truth right? :)*
FUGITIVE_RED: *I appreciate your honesty*

Paranoia hit.

NYCRockGod2: *are you home now?*
FUGITIVE_RED: *Yes*

I pictured her sitting on a deck, overlooking an idyllic backyard covered with colorful fall leaves.

NYCRockGod2: *It's a beautiful day but I heard it's going to get cold this weekend*

Ugh, what was I doing, writing to her about the weather? Could I sound any more banal?

FUGITIVE_RED: *yeah im looking forward to the winter I hope we get a lot of snow this year where r u?*
NYCRockGod2: *my office*

Leaving it vague. Figured, let her imagine me sitting at a big mahogany desk with a panoramic city view.

FUGITIVE_RED: *Nice! What sort of work do you do?*

I paused, wondering if I should reveal a personal detail. Then I thought, What I did for a living wasn't really *personal*, was it?

NYCRockGod2: *I'm a high end real estate agent*

Okay, yeah, I was trying to pump myself up a little, stoke her fantasies, make her think she was chatting with some big-shot mogul.

FUGITIVE_RED: *Wow very cool!*

Cool wasn't a word I'd ever use to describe my job.

Then I thought, *Why am I sugarcoating it*? Like I always preached in my A.A. speeches—*be transparent.*

NYCRockGod2: *Actually I'm full of shit Im just a basic real estate agent and wish I was doing something else with my life*
FUGITIVE_RED: *ha you're funny! :) But it's sad that you want to do something else I mean if you want to do something else why not just do it?*

She made it sound so simple.

NYCRockGod2: *Thank you for saying that. I totally agree!!!*
FUGITIVE_RED: *You said u play guitar right? Why did you quit?*

Angry, I typed:

NYCRockGod2: *My wife wasn't exactly supportive*

About to click send, I hesitated. Maybe bashing Maria didn't make me look good?

*Eh, whatever,* I thought, and I sent it.

FUGITIVE_RED: *WOW*
NYCRockGod2: *Sorry! I didn't mean to bash her like that I know I'm responsible for my own decisions, including marrying her*
FUGITIVE_RED: *I'm with you! I feel like my husband stifles me too That's why I'm dying to escape!!!*

We continued chatting. She asked where my office was; I wrote her that I lived and worked on the Upper East Side. Then she told me about the big house she lived in in White Plains. I didn't handle property in that area, but it sounded sprawling, and I figured it had to be worth around 1.7 mil. I wondered if the money was hers or her husband's.

Then we discussed college for a while—my time at Oneonta, hers at Oregon State—she grew up in the Pacific Northwest. She didn't go on to explain why or when she had moved East; again, I didn't feel it was the right time to ask.

I got so caught up in our chat I was amazed when I realized that over an hour had gone by. It was also amazing how titillating it felt just to chat with her. Our conversation wasn't at all raunchy; her words didn't excite me, the mystery did—wondering what she was thinking and feeling. Was she into me? Was she fantasizing about me? The unknown was arousing, the questions more exciting than the answers. She'd awakened a flirty, fun side of my personality that had been dormant for years.

Claire and Brian had returned to the office.

> NYCRockGod2: *I should really get back to work :(*
> FUGITIVE_RED: *K, no worries*
> NYCRockGod2: *Can't wait to chat with you again sometime!*
> FUGITIVE_RED: *That would be great! BTW I'm Sophie :)*

I hesitated. On the one hand, our names were the simplest, most basic information about ourselves—if we'd met in person, we would've introduced ourselves immediately—yet in the world of online extramarital dating revealing our names felt like a huge deal, as if it would somehow signify a whole new level of intimacy.

> NYCRockGod2: *Jack :)*

I felt like I'd jumped off a cliff, but I didn't care. I wanted to keep falling.

FUGITIVE_RED: *Nice to meet you, Jack :)*

I hated ending the session, but Claire was looking over from her desk, as if wondering what I was doing online that had me so entranced, and I didn't want her to get suspicious. I wrote to Sophie that I'd love to chat again later if she was around. I added that I'd try to be online around eleven tonight, and she responded that she'd try to be free then, too.

I tried to distract myself with work—emailing, texting, making my daily follow-up calls to potential buyers. It was hard to not think about Sophie, though. How had some kind words from a total stranger had such a pronounced effect on me so quickly? Had I been more lonely and starving for attention than I'd realized? I noticed a major change in my whole attitude. Normally, when I was talking to clients, I was curt and professional and didn't have a lot of excitement in my tone. But today I had a lot more energy and I sounded much more positive and confident, and I could tell it was having an effect. A couple of people who might've blown me off normally arranged for times to go out to look at apartments.

I guess there was something to the power of positive thinking because a few minutes later Megan Conaway called and made an offer on the 77th Street apartment. Although the offer was $15,000 below the asking price, I knew the sellers hadn't gotten any offers and were eager to make a deal. I immediately called the sellers and, sure enough, they accepted the offer. I called Megan back with the news, and she was thrilled, and so was I at my first sale in months. I didn't know if chatting with Sophie, and the surge of optimism and excitement this had given me, had anything to do with getting the sale, but it felt like it had.

Claire and Brian congratulated me. Andrew Wolf had been working in his office, but when he heard the commotion, he came out and asked what was going on.

"Jack got a sale," Claire said.

"Which apartment?" Andrew asked.

"One-bedroom on 77th," I said.

"Nice," he said. Then added, "Well, let's get a few more like that, and you'll be back in business."

Andrew was a nice guy—he was a good father, had two beautiful daughters—but he could also be a big-time jerk. *A few more like that?* Making me feel like I was, what, auditioning for my own job?

"I'll do my best," I said, smiling.

At two thirty, I happily left my office and headed toward Jonah's school for afternoon pickup.

It had warmed to about sixty degrees and the sun was shining brightly. I took out my cell to call Sophie and tell her about the good news. Then I remembered that I didn't have her phone number; I'd never even heard her voice. She was a virtual stranger, but, oddly, I already felt so close to her.

I picked up Jonah after school and took him to his karate class. Afterward, remembering my vow to eat healthier, we stopped at Fairway on 86th and picked up vegetables, brown rice, and a couple of pounds of Alaska salmon. I'd been eating way too much meat and cheese and fried food lately. I wanted to start over, get all the junk out of body that felt like it had been building up inside me for years.

When we arrived at the apartment, surprisingly, Maria was there, too, in the bedroom, changing out of her work clothes. It was only four thirtyish and she usually didn't get home until past six.

Ordinarily, I would have been excited to tell her about the possible sale I'd made, but she was still giving me the silent treatment, and I knew that making up before she decided she wanted to make up was practically impossible.

As Maria talked to Jonah about his day and helped him with his math homework in his room, I started cooking dinner. When I was sautéing the salmon, the apartment got smoky and the smoke alarm went off.

"Shit," I said.

I stood on a chair under the alarm and waved a dish towel for maybe ten seconds until the alarm shut off.

Maria, who'd come out of the bedroom, muttered something.

"Did you just call me a jerk?" I asked.

"No," she said.

I knew what I'd heard.

"Because it sounded like that's what you said," I said.

"Well, you're good at making things up," she said as she went into the bathroom.

Jonah, nearby, had overheard this.

I was furious. Again she was starting with this crap, right in front of Jonah? I didn't want to live like this anymore.

Jonah and I had dinner alone.

"Where's Mommy?"

"Resting," I said.

"Oh," he said.

Maria and I avoided each other for most of the evening. I thought about going to an A.A. meeting, but I wasn't in the mood. When Maria finally went to sleep, I logged on to Discreet Hookups.

Like the other times, I felt a rush, but this was more intense. I didn't just want to get online; I *needed* to get online.

I went right to Sophie's page, felt the disappointment when I saw the message: FUGITIVE_RED is offline.

Paranoid thoughts crept in: *What if she had disabled her account? What if I never heard from her again?*

As my thoughts continued to spiral, I imagined how devastated I'd feel if I never chatted with her again. Of course I knew, rationally, that all of this was ridiculous—I was acting like some heartbroken high school kid about a woman I'd never met—but I couldn't deny how I felt.

It seemed ridiculous to just sit at the dining room table, staring at the laptop, hoping for her green dot to appear. I tried to distract myself by reading Facebook posts and scrolling through Instagram, but I couldn't let more than a minute go by without switching back to the Discreet Hookups page to see if she was there.

At 11:15, she still wasn't there. I was cursing to myself, shaking my head, wondering what I could have written to scare her off. Had the mention of my son freaked her out? Yeah, probably.

Then at 11:31 the notification appeared: FUGITIVE_RED is online.

I actually said, "Yay," but, thankfully, not too loud.

> NYCRockGod2: *Hey!*

I felt relaxed and free, like a huge burden had been lifted.

> FUGITIVE_RED: *Hey!!*

Two exclamation points—that had to mean *something.*

> FUGITIVE_RED: *How was your day?*

When was the last time Maria had asked me how my day was?

> NYCRockGod2: *Awesome. I sold an apartment.*
> FUGITIVE_RED: *That's so amazing!! Yay! I'm so happy 4 U!!*

Her enthusiasm felt great.

I gave her more details about the sale and she seemed genuinely happy for me. It felt good to smile again. It also felt nice to communicate with someone who wasn't calling me an "idiot."

Then I asked her how her day was.

FUGITIVE_RED: *Not as good. I don't want to upset you I'm very emotional right now :(*
NYCRockGod2: *You don't have to apologize for emotion.*

Could I sound more like an alcoholic?

FUGITIVE_RED: *Sometimes he hits me I've put up with it for nine fucking years. I don't know why I don't just leave, run away. I've tried, but I can't. I just can't get away.*
NYCRockGod2: *You can't blame yourself. Sometimes it's not easy to get out of a bad situation.*

Platitudes, I know, but at A.A. meetings I was used to counseling people in domestic abuse situations. Also, it had always been much easier for me to help solve other people's problems than to work on my own.

FUGITIVE_RED: *When I was single I didn't understand why unhappily married people stayed together I thought if you aren't happy why not just get a divorce? But then when you get married you find out how much more complicated it is*
NYCRockGod2: *Yeah I totally get that!*
FUGITIVE_RED: *Do you like Van Gogh?*

I loved Van Gogh. Could this woman be any more perfect?

NYCRockGod2: *Yesssss!!!*
FUGITIVE_RED: *Same. :)*
NYC RockGod2: *He's my favorite artist! I mean I know that it sounds like a total cliché because everybody likes Van Gogh, but his art really speaks to me*

Ugh, I wished I'd reworded that—I sounded like some pretentious fuck—but I'd already clicked send.

FUGITIVE_RED: *That's why I chose my name FUGITIVE RED :) There was an article a few weeks ago in the NYT magazine They say the reds in his paintings have faded*

I'd read that article, too.

NYCRockGod2: *Right fugitive reds!!!*
FUGITIVE_RED: *They were bright and vibrant for a short time then faded*
NYCRockGod2: *I read that article too Yes!*
FUGITIVE_RED: *To me that's what love is*
NYCRockGod2: *You think love fades?*
FUGITIVE_RED: *Yes People meet for a short time have great connection and maybe that's all there is*
NYCRockGod2: *Interesting maybe I agree!*
FUGITIVE_RED: *Can I ask you a personal question?*
NYCRockGod2: *K*
FUGITIVE_RED: *Are you in love with your wife?*

I paused, considering how to word my response. Then I sent:

NYCRockGod2: *No*
FUGITIVE_RED: *I'm sorry That sounds rough :(*
NYCRockGod2: *It is what it is*

I was tearing up a little, as I sometimes did on the podium at A.A.

FUGITIVE_RED: *So now you have all my baggage? If you want to run now's your chance.*

I never ran from baggage, even baggage I should've run from. Call it my fatal flaw.

NYCRockGod2: *I'm not going anyway*

NYCRockGod2: *Anywhere I mean :)*
FUGITIVE_RED: *:)*
FUGITIVE_RED: *I wish I could see u right now I want to look into your eyes*
NYCRockGod2: *Me too*

I was hoping she wouldn't ask to Skype. That seemed too risky.

FUGITIVE_RED: *We seem so right for each other*
NYCRockGod2: *I know! we have everything in common*

Pause, then:

FUGITIVE_RED: *I have an idea*
NYCRockGod2: *K*
FUGITIVE_RED: *Maybe we should meet up Just to see what it's like*

My pulse accelerated. Although I knew this could lead to nothing good, the idea of meeting her, actually *seeing* her, was turning me on.

NYCRockGod2: *What do you mean?*

Of course, I knew exactly what she meant; it was just hard to think clearly.

FUGITIVE_RED: *Just meet and you know be with each other.*

I imagined a glimpse of us in an elegant Midtown hotel room, attacking each other. Why not do it, just go for it? I hadn't had sex with Maria in years and my marriage was on life support. What was the alternative, living the rest of my life without ever having sex again?

NYCRockGod2: *Thats probably not a good idea.*
FUGITIVE_RED: *Why not? You think I'm sexy don't you?*

I thought she was incredibly sexy. It wasn't just her looks; it was how she made me feel. And it was true—we did have everything in common; she truly got me. I know, I know—I barely knew this woman. But it didn't matter—the feelings felt real.

NYCRockGod2: *Yes.*
FUGITIVE_RED: *So if we don't find out what it's like, we'll never know. And isn't not knowing worse than anything?*

It was hard to argue with this logic, especially when it felt so good chatting with her. How amazing would it feel to actually *be* with her? To *experience* her?

FUGITIVE_RED: *Come on, let's just go for it. How about Friday eve? My husband has plans and I can say I'm going into the city to meet a friend.*
NYCRockGod2: *I really don't think it's a good idea*
FUGITIVE_RED: *???*
NYCRockGod2: *I just don't think it's a good idea. I mean we're both still married. And I have a kid*
NYCRockGod2: *I'm sorry :( :(*
FUGITIVE_RED: *You don't love her so that's why you went on here, right? To hook up discreetly with a married woman?*

Was that why I went on? Or did I just want attention, or a distraction?

NYCRockGod2: *My situation's complicated.*
FUGITIVE_RED: *Everyone's situation complicated. But it would be more complicated if we were single*

Now I was confused.

> NYCRockGod2: *??*
> FUGITIVE_RED: *We're both married and unavailable so it's not complicated at all. Don't you see? You can trust me, I can trust you. We both have just as much to lose!*

Jesus, now she sounded like Rob McEvoy. Worse, the skewed logic made sense.

Wanting her, I wondered if I was just overthinking all of this. Why couldn't I be Mr. Casual like Rob? He'd probably had dozens of affairs and claimed he was in a happier marriage because of it. I'd never cheated on Maria, but had it made us happier? Was it true that an affair could save a marriage? And I wouldn't be having multiple affairs, I wouldn't be *philandering*. It wouldn't even be an *affair*; it would be a fling. Everybody had a fling once in a while, right? Only in America people treated it like a big deal. In other parts of the world, like in France, everyone "took a lover" every once in a while. If I were French, I could be just like Rob—have carefree flings. My father, I'm sure, had had flings, and anyone who traveled on business had had at least one fling. I was a forty-four-year-old man trapped in a sexless marriage for God's sake. Didn't I deserve some happiness?

> FUGITIVE_RED: *I don't want to pressure you into anything If you don't want to do it, no worries :) We could just say goodbye and go on with our lives*

Although we'd just met, the idea of never communicating with her again seemed much worse than any alternative. I knew I'd become emotionally attached to her, but until that moment, I didn't realize how involved I'd actually gotten. I was in deep, and the quicksand wasn't holding. This wasn't an actual exit—it only seemed like one.

NYCRockGod2: *Okay, let's go for it!*

I knew I'd just made an awful decision, but the rush of excitement felt too good to pass up.

What else was new?

# CHAPTER EIGHT

FUGITIVE_RED: *Great!!! How's Friday? 6 pm??*

Actually Friday—two days away—was perfect. Maria was always exhausted from her work week on Fridays, and I usually hit an A.A. meeting then went out to a diner with my friends.

NYCRockGod2: *Friday @ 6 works! But where?*

I was worried about the logistics of going to a hotel, having to use a credit card.

FUGITIVE_RED: *Great! I have a townhouse in the city 32nd between 2 and 3 We can meet there I'm so excited!!*

I felt the adrenaline rush I always felt when I couldn't stop myself from doing something.

NYCRockGod2: *Wait I'm little confused Thought you lived in White Plains?*

Had I caught her in a lie?

FUGITIVE_RED: *I do*
FUGITIVE_RED: *I mean we do*
FUGITIVE_RED: *We have two residences actually*

*Ah.*

NYCRockGod2: *Ah*

But now I was curious how they could afford two residences—especially a second residence that was a townhouse that could cost a few million dollars. Did they own the townhouse? Either way, they had to be wealthy.

I was glad, though. A townhouse sounded much safer than going to a hotel and leaving a paper trail of bills.

Well, unless . . .

NYCRockGod2: *What if your husband shows up?*
FUGITIVE_RED: *He won't. I'll arrive before you No one will see us I promise!*

It sounded like there wasn't much risk, but I knew I wasn't in the best state of mind to be a good judge.

Then I had an idea:

NYCRockGod2: *Do you want to talk on the phone first? Would be nice to hear your voice. :)*
FUGITIVE_RED: *I thought you wanted to meet me :)*
NYCRockGod2: *I do!!!*
NYCRockGod2: *I just thought it would be nice to talk that's all*

A long pause. I thought I'd screwed up, turned her off, made her think I wasn't interested.

Then she sent:

FUGITIVE_RED: *We can talk, but wouldn't it be sexier to keep it more mysterious?*

She was right. We were going to meet anyway, so what was the point of talking?

NYCRockGod2: *Okay!*
FUGITIVE_RED: *:)*
FUGITIVE_RED: *I have to go my husband's coming home soon But I'm so excited Jack!! Can't wait till I can actually see you and feel you hehe :) It'll be so, so amazing I can't wait!!*

Feel me? God, I was turned on just imagining what this meant.

NYCRockGod2: *Can't wait too! :)*

* * *

The next two days were amazing. I wasn't wrought with anxiety, the way I'd been, well, for years. I felt attractive, sexy, fun, and I was looking forward to the future rather than dreading it. Yeah, okay, I'd made an impulsive, risky decision; but maybe, for once, this would work out for me.

Most of my daily routine hadn't changed at all. I went to work and spent time with Jonah after school. When Maria came home, we avoided each other. I could tell she was still upset about our arguments earlier in the week and expected me to eventually apologize, the way I'd done in the past, but I was through playing these games, always being passive, trying to keep the peace. It was liberating to feel like I'd finally gotten past this negative pattern, that I had started to take control.

When I wasn't working or parenting, I was in my own head, daydreaming about Sophie. I imagined her standing in front of the foot of the bed, undressing. Not a striptease—there was nothing overtly erotic about my fantasy. Just matter-of-factly unbuttoning her blouse, one button at a time, and then letting the blouse fall to the floor. Then unclasping her bra, revealing her small, firm breasts, and letting the bra fall. Finally, taking off her jeans and panties, letting them fall to the floor, and then standing naked in front of me.

In the bathroom—at home and at work—I masturbated to this fantasy. I hadn't felt so sexed up since I was a teenager.

While the chats with Sophie clearly had a profound effect on my overall mood, making me more upbeat, energetic, and optimistic, I didn't realize the full influence she'd had on me until Thursday after work, when I took my Gibson guitar out from the back of the hallway closet, dusted it off, tuned it, and began strumming.

I played one of my favorite R.E.M. songs—"Superman." I hadn't played it in years, but when I started playing I felt like I'd never stopped. I had natural musical talent, perfect pitch, and I was as good as I'd always been. The only thing I'd forgotten was how relaxed playing music made me feel, like I'd taken a break from existence. I know this will sound nauseating, but I disappeared into the music. Jack Harper didn't exist anymore—he was just a vessel, a conduit between the guitar and the music. Why had I given this up? Or, better question, why had I let Maria convince me I should give it up?

After R.E.M., I played some old U2 and Nirvana, then one of my old original songs: "City People." I remembered all of it, as if I'd just walked onto the stage for a gig downtown twenty years ago. I sang: "City people, lose control . . . City people, no place to go . . . "

Okay, so I wasn't exactly Dylan, but the song had been a crowd pleaser.

"You play guitar, Daddy?"

Jonah had come out of his room.

I stopped playing and said, "Yeah. Of course I do."

"Wow, you're really good, Daddy," he said. "Can you teach me how to play?"

"I'd love to," I said.

Jonah sat next to me on the couch, and I showed him how to play the basic chords. He got the knack of it right away and seemed to have some genuine talent.

When I was demonstrating a chord for him, Maria arrived. Seeing me playing a guitar seemed to surprise her.

"What're you doing?" she asked.

The question seemed loaded. I interpreted it to mean, *Why* are you playing guitar again?

"Just giving Jonah a little guitar lesson," I said. "I think he's a natural."

"Listen, Mom," Jonah said excitedly, and then he played the chords he'd made.

"That's great," Maria said, but she didn't seem to be paying attention.

Deciding to not let this go, the way I'd let things like this slide in the past, I said, "Is something wrong?"

"Just a long day at work," she said, on her way into the bedroom.

"Damn it," I muttered.

Jonah seemed concerned.

"Not you, buddy," I said. "You're doing awesome. I think you're gonna be a rock star someday."

Jonah grinned and continued practicing.

* * *

On Thursday night, Maria went out for drinks with work friends. I was excited because it gave Sophie and me an opportunity to have an IM session. I know, I know, sneaking around was incredibly immature, but the thrill of having a secret chat session was impossible to resist, and I'd been looking forward to it all day.

Jonah was engrossed watching TV, so I went into the bedroom, locked the door, and logged on to Discreet Hookups.

Sophie was already online, as I'd messaged her earlier in the day, letting her know that my wife had plans this evening and that I'd be "free to chat."

NYCRockGod2: *Hey!*
FUGITIVE_RED: *Hey sexxxy!*

A woman who thought I was sexy—what unhappily married forty-four-year-old man didn't want to hear that? And sexy with three X's no less.

FUGITIVE_RED: *I'm so excited, it's been hard to sleep*
NYCRockGod2: *Ditto!*
FUGITIVE_RED: *:)*
FUGITIVE_RED: *Can I tell you something important that you need to know??*

Uh-uh, was a bombshell coming? I'd had a gnawing feeling that all of this seemed too good to be true—there had to be *something wrong* with her. Was she going to tell me she was a man? Had an STD? An arrest record?

NYCRockGod2: *Sure.*
FUGITIVE_RED: *I hope you don't think this is too weird*
NYCRockGod2: *(crossing my heart)*

After a long pause:

FUGITIVE_RED: *It has to do with how I like to have sex*

She had my attention.

NYCRockGod2: *Oooh tell me*

I'd been fantasizing about sex with Sophie for days, but I'd kept it to myself. It felt good to express myself, to be open.

There was a very long pause, so I knew a long message was coming. Somehow the anticipation of the message made it feel even more erotic.

> FUGITIVE_RED: *I'm a submissive. I like to be restrained during sex.*

Pause, then:

> FUGITIVE_RED: *I like to be tied up, spanked hard. Would you enjoy doing that to me?*

I had once tied up a girlfriend in college. It had excited me, but I'd never suggested it to Maria because I knew she'd be horrified, or at least offended.

> NYCRockGod2: *Yes!*
> FUGITIVE_RED: *Yes you'll be my domme?*
> NYCRockGod2: *Yes I'll be yr domme!*
> FUGITIVE_RED: *Mmmm That REALLY turns me on I'm so wet right now Jack!*
> NYCRockGod2: *Then lets go for it!*
> FUGITIVE_RED: *R u sure you're okay with it?? I don't want to offend you if you're not into it totally understand :)*
> NYCRockGod2: *No, I want to tie you up Not offended at all!*

It felt great to feel like myself, untethered.

> FUGITIVE_RED: *Awesome! Oh I like it rough too . . . VERY rough. I want you to call me bad names Will you call me bad names Jack?*
> NYCRockGod2: *I'll do anything you want me to do, Sophie*

Long pause. Then:

FUGITIVE_RED: *Tell me what you want to do*

I tried to think.

FUGITIVE_RED: *Still there???*
NYCRockGod2: *I like kissing And holding you*

Ugh, was that the best sexting I could do? I hesitated because I wasn't sure how graphic she wanted me to get.

FUGITIVE_RED: *That's nice but you don't have to keep this PG 13 :)*

*Well, if that's what she really wants . . .*

NYCRockGod2: *OK I want to pin you down so you can't move*
FUGITIVE_RED: *Mmm I want that . . . Tell me more*
NYCRockGod2: *I want to fuck you so hard*

I was getting into it now; I liked this.

FUGITIVE_RED: *Yesssss please fuck me Jack MORE GRAPHIC please!*
NYCRockGod2: *I want to pound you and fuck you so hard with my big hard cock*

A long pause. The delay got me even more turned on. I was imagining *her* getting turned on, concocting an erotic reply.

Finally I got:

FUGITIVE_RED: *Better OMG yessss please fuck me hard and slap me in the face really hard and tell me how bad I am*
NYCRockGod2: *You're so bad Sophie*

FUGITIVE_RED: *Slap my ass harder*
NYCRockGod2: *I'm slapping it harder*
FUGITIVE_RED: *OMG Will you tie me up too?*
NYCRockGod2: *Yes*
FUGITIVE_RED: *OMG Love that!!!!*
NYCRockGod2: *Yes I can't wait to tie you up and slap your face like you deserve*
FUGITIVE_RED: *OMG I want you to tie me up while you're fucking me so hard*
NYCRockGod2: *OMG*
FUGITIVE_RED: *OMG you're getting me so fucking wet right now My pussy is so fucking wet for you Jack!!*

I typed, *Mmm you just made me come so hard for you*, but I deleted it. I didn't think it would turn her off—I didn't think *anything* could offend this woman—but I didn't want to risk it.

So instead I sent:

NYCRockGod2: *God I can't wait to see you tomorrow*
FUGITIVE_RED: *I can't wait too! I wish it was tomorrow already This is going to be SO FUCKING AMAZING JACK!*

* * *

I got up before dawn and I was so excited and I couldn't fall back asleep. It didn't matter, though, because when I finally got out of bed around seven, I felt fully rested.

I had arranged for Jonah to have a play date after school with his friend Leo—Leo's nanny would pick up Jonah and Leo from school, and then Maria would pick up Jonah after work from Leo's—so I planned to go to meet Sophie directly from work. Now

I just had to decide what to wear. Usually I barely thought about getting dressed in the morning; I put on whatever was clean and wasn't too wrinkled and I was out the door. But today I wanted to look my best.

I put on beige slacks, a black button-down, and a black sport jacket. I looked good, but did I look too good? I usually didn't wear sport jackets to work so it would create a possible red flag for Maria. Also, I didn't feel like myself; I felt like I was trying too hard to impress and I reminded myself that there was no reason to try so hard—Sophie was already into me.

So, keeping it casual, but not too casual, I went with jeans and the button-down. Underneath I was wearing the boxer briefs that I'd kept in the back of my underwear drawer for years because they were way too tight on me but, hell, I felt sexy in them and, okay, yes, I liked how they showed off my package.

After I dropped Jonah at school, I went to the office. I'd purposely cleared my schedule for the entire day, knowing I'd be too hyped up to focus on work. I tried to do some of the paperwork on my last sale, but I kept getting distracted by the fantasy of Sophie undressing and flashing back to snippets of our sexting.

My bliss must've been evident because Brian leaned into my cubicle and said, "You got one sale and now you're retiring?"

"Ha ha," I said, playing along, like I thought it was funny.

Later, Andrew Wolf said to me, "Why you all dressed up? Got a hot date?"

I hadn't realized that a button-down constituted getting dressed up, but I guess for me it did.

Trying to ignore the heat, or at least sweat, on the back of my neck, I said, "Ha, no, just have an apartment to show later."

"This is good," Andrew said. "I like this—this new attitude of yours. Putting on a shirt to come to the office, showing some new professionalism. But don't go ahead and rest on your laurels now. You're on a roll. Keep it up."

"I will," I said.

Normally the vaguely demeaning subtext of his comments would've pissed me off and ruined my whole day, but today I refused to let the negativity affect me. I was in such a great mood today that nothing could bring me down. After all, I was meeting Sophie later—Fugitive Red herself! This was going to be the best day of my life.

Trying to stick to a seemingly normal routine, I had a banal text exchange with Maria. I reminded her that I was going to an A.A. meeting later, then out to dinner with friends and that she'd pick up Jonah at Leo's apartment.

She replied: *KK*

The afternoon dragged. As I tried to work, I couldn't stop checking the time on the lower right-hand corner of my monitor. Although I didn't have to meet Sophie until six o'clock, I left my office at about four fifteen.

The townhouse was in Kips Bay, about forty blocks from my office. I could've taken the subway or bus, but I had time to kill and lots of pent-up energy so I walked instead. I was so absorbed in my fantasies—imagining what it would be like to see her for the first time, and hold her, kiss her—that time got disjointed and I just seemed to wind up in midtown and I barely remembered walking there. I still had time to kill, so I went to a coffee bar and checked out some of the newer rock bands on YouTube and Spotify. I used to feel plugged into the business, but over the past few years I'd fallen behind. I was eager to get back into music for real, though, perhaps even suggest jamming with Sophie sometime. I imagined Sophie and I going upstate together for a weekend, getting a cabin by the lake, and spending the weekend jamming, laughing, and having amazing sex.

I continued downtown.

At ten to six, I arrived on the corner of her block on 32nd Street. I wondered if Sophie had arrived at the townhouse already. We hadn't exchanged cell numbers so I couldn't text her, and I didn't have her actual email either. I considered messengering her via Discreet Hookups but decided against it. We already had made the plan, so what was the point? I did check to see if she had messaged me though, in case she'd had to change the plan for some reason. She hadn't messaged me, so I assumed this was it—she was there.

On 32nd Street, I passed a schoolyard and was approaching the townhouse. Paranoid, I looked around in every direction, to make sure no one I knew happened to be passing by. In New York that sort of coincidence was incredibly unlikely, but I had to look anyway.

Then I thought, *What the hell am I doing?*

For a few minutes, I just stood there totally confused, as if I'd passed out and regained consciousness. The idea of having a safe, guiltless affair was ridiculous. I wasn't a philanderer; I wasn't Rob McEvoy. I couldn't go off and casually cheat on my wife and manage to pull off that kind of deception. I was a horrible liar. Maria probably already suspected something was going on, and if I actually cheated on her, she'd know right away. An affair wouldn't save my marriage; it would destroy it.

And how could I do this to her, the mother of our son? I had my issues with her, but she'd stood by me through my darkest times, and this was how I was going to repay her?

Then I reminded myself how my marriage actually was on a daily basis, how I hadn't been happy in years, and how invigorated I'd felt while chatting with Sophie online. Thinking about it this way, it seemed crazy *not* to go. Besides, nothing had to *happen* today. This was just a first meeting—like a first date really. I could check her out and if anything seemed off about the situation, I could always bail. If things went great and we wound up having sex, it didn't necessarily mean my marriage would be *over*. It could be a onetime thing, a fling, and it could force us to deal with marital issues head-on. I could rededicate myself to my marriage, convince Maria that we needed counseling, or I could decide that I'd done everything I could possibly do to try to save the marriage and move on. Either way, the important thing I had to remember was that I was in total control—I was the driver of my life, not the passenger.

I believed all of this—well, maybe for ten seconds or so. Then I decided I was full of shit.

An affair was a huge mistake that I didn't want to make. I had to do the mature, adult thing and go home to my family and try to work things out the right way. But I couldn't just take off, not without giving Sophie some kind of explanation.

I continued down the block, proud of myself for finally making the right decision, and headed up the stoop to the front door of the townhouse. I'd apologize to Sophie, tell her that it had been a blast getting to know her, and that if things didn't work out in our marriages, I'd love to get to know her better, but right now this was the right thing to do. She'd be disappointed, but she'd understand.

My mind was made up; I felt so mature, so logical. Why couldn't I have had this revelation a week ago?

As I'd expected, the door was open, slightly ajar. I entered, blown away by how gorgeous the place was. I'd expected a townhouse worth millions to be nice inside, but somehow, from my chat sessions with Sophie, I'd expected the place to have an offbeat, Bohemian vibe. Instead it was full-throttle upscale. A large foyer with a winding staircase going up. Going by the new floors and new crown molding, the place seemed to have undergone a renovation recently.

"Hello?" I said.

As I went farther inside and smelled perfume—her perfume, I figured—suddenly I wasn't sure I'd be able to resist her, after all.

"Hello?" I said again.

No answer.

I continued through the downstairs of the townhouse. The place was nice, all right—way nicer than I'd expected. The dining room had an elegant table that could easily sit ten people, and the kitchen had been totally redone with an island with a sink and new appliances. Brian at my agency had sold a similar property, also in Kips Bay, for close to four million last year and this one was in better shape. It could get six and change, maybe seven.

I checked the kitchen, but she wasn't there, and then, looking up, I noticed that a light was on upstairs.

"Sophie . . . Sophie, are you there?"

Still nothing.

As I headed up the spiral staircase, the scent of her perfume was getting stronger and I was getting weaker. I knew what was going to happen next. I'd go into the bedroom and she'd be there, waiting for me. I flashed back to our sexting, the things she'd said she wanted to do with me. I'd try to be strong; I'd try not to give in. I'd explain to her all the reasons why this was a bad idea, why it would screw up our lives.

But what if I couldn't resist? I'd never had self-restraint. Who was I kidding?

The second floor had a wide hallway and my feet creaked the long floorboards. I passed a bathroom and what looked like a guest bedroom.

"Sophie?"

I continued to the end of the hallway, toward another room. The door was a few inches ajar and a light was on.

When I first began performing live music, I'd suffered from awful stage fright. Sometimes the anxiety got so bad that I couldn't even move, no less perform. Though my terror never fully subsided, I managed to deal with the issue well enough to get through my gigs.

I felt the same way now. My breath got short and my pulse throbbed, but I forced myself to fight through it.

I entered the bedroom and sure enough she was lying in bed. Jesus, a woman I liked, whom I'd connected with, was waiting for me in bed. I couldn't turn back now; I'd come too far.

The scent of her perfume was so intense, so overwhelming, that at first I wasn't really aware of anything else. Then I saw that there was something weird about her mouth—her jaw was sagging—and something was wrong with her face, too. It was too pale, and her eyes were wide open—and she was wearing a bright red tie.

Then I realized she wasn't wearing the tie.

Somebody had strangled her with it.

# CHAPTER NINE

I STARED AT her for a long time—thirty seconds, a minute, or it could've been longer. Time was distorted; it was hard to be sure about anything. My legs were weak and I felt unsteady, like I was trying to balance myself on the deck of a boat in rough water.

Then I thought I saw her chest move.

Snapping into action, I loosened the tie and tried to give her mouth-to-mouth. I'd taken a CPR class before Jonah was born, but under pressure, I couldn't remember how to do it. Were you supposed to breathe five times? Three times? And when were you supposed to pump the chest? Anyway, her lips were stiff and cold and whatever I was doing obviously wasn't working. I tried to loosen the tie, but it was wound too tight. Going by how cold and stiff her lips were, I'd probably made a mistake; I hadn't seen her chest move and she'd been dead all along. After a couple of breaths, I backed away again, shaking.

Then I saw the blood on my hands.

I was confused for a few seconds; where the hell had blood come from? Then I saw some blood on her head, near the pillow. I must've gotten the blood on me when I gave her CPR.

I rushed to the bathroom and rinsed the blood off my hands, watching the pink water spiral down the drain. I scrubbed my hands, too, to get rid of any perfume scent.

Then I went out to the hallway. Several seconds went by, maybe longer, and I just stood there. In shock, I guess. Then a terrifying thought hit: *How do I know that the killer isn't still here?*

I listened, didn't hear anything, then realized how pointless this was. If someone was here, what was I going to do, get into a conversation?

I went down the stairs as fast as if I'd jumped from the top of the landing. But at the front door I stopped, telling myself, *You can't just leave.*

A woman had been killed; a woman whom I *knew* had been killed. This was a crime scene now. If I ran away, it would be like a hit-and-run. Even though I was innocent, if I left now I'd be committing a crime. Besides, my prints and hair fibers and whatever else were probably in the house, maybe even on her body. From the CPR, my saliva was on her mouth. And what about the blood? I probably still had some on me.

No, I couldn't leave now. I had to do the right thing and call the police.

In the vestibule, still trembling, I punched in 911 from my cell.

"Nine one one, what's your emergency?"

My lips started to move, then I ended the call.

From the moment I'd seen the body till the moment I'd heard the operator's voice, I'd been reacting, not really *thinking*, but now it all clicked—I realized what deep shit I was in.

The woman I'd met online and had arranged to meet for a sex date had been strangled to death. When the police came, I'd be questioned; I might even be a *suspect*. Then Maria would find out that I'd met the woman online—on Discreet Hookups no less—and any hope for a "good divorce" would be officially shot. There would be no convincing lie to tell, no way to explain it all away.

Although nothing had actually happened—I didn't kill this woman and I didn't have an affair with her—there was no way she'd believe this. She'd want a divorce and, if I was a murder suspect, I'd almost certainly lose custody of Jonah.

I hated myself for making the bad decisions that had gotten me to this point, for fucking up my life all over again.

Then I heard a voice inside me, shouting, *Run! Get the hell out!*

But I couldn't run—running would only bury me deeper.

On Discreet Hookups, there were records, chat transcripts, of all my interactions with Sophie. Even if I deleted my account and the police never found any record of the chats, I wouldn't be safe. Sophie had told me that she'd kept our relationship a secret, but what if this wasn't true? What if her closest friends knew all about us?

I called 911 again and, as calmly as I could, said, "I want to report a dead body," and I told her the address on East 32nd Street.

"How did the person die?" the female operator asked.

"Murdered." I was so scared I was shivering. "I mean, I think she was murdered. I mean, strangled. Or maybe hit on the head."

"Help is on the way," the operator asked. "Are you still inside?"

"Yes," I said.

"Is there anyone with you?"

"No."

"Is it possible for you to go outside?"

"Yes."

I left the townhouse.

"I want you to go outside," the operator said.

"Okay, I'm outside," I said.

The cool fall air taunted me, like the air in a prison yard.

"Help will arrive soon," the operator said. "Can you stay on the line with me?"

"Yes," I said.

As the operator continued to talk to me, trying to keep me calm, it registered that Sophie was dead, actually *dead*. I didn't actually know her, but it felt like I'd known her, like I'd lost a friend. I saw flashes of the bright red tie around her neck, the blood on my hands, and her wide-open eyes, and queasiness hit, like I was discovering her body all over again.

Who the hell had done this to her? *Why?*

The answer to question one was so obvious that if I hadn't been so busy, worrying about my own situation, it would've occurred to me immediately.

*Her husband had killed her.*

I was still in shock and scattered and it was hard to think clearly, but her husband—it had to have been him. She'd said he was abusive, that there had been problems in their marriage for a long time. Besides, it was *always* the husband. He must've followed her here and—

Shit, the front door. I remembered it had been ajar when I'd arrived. I'd assumed Sophie had left it like that, but her husband could've forced his way in and dragged her into the bedroom. He killed her and then took off quickly without bothering to close the door. But he must've left at least a couple of minutes before I'd arrived, or I would've seen him.

Unless . . .

I glanced at the house; curtains covered the windows downstairs so I couldn't see inside. Was it possible that he was still in there, hiding somewhere?

Then I heard a siren, increasing in volume, and a few seconds later saw the police car turn onto 32nd Street. It stopped in front of the townhouse. Two officers got out—a young, muscular Latino and a blond, stocky woman. Although I knew there was nothing funny about any of this, as the officers approached me, I realized I was smiling. A nervous smile overcompensating for panic and fear, but, still, probably not the best first impression to make to the police at the scene of a murder. My expression could have easily been misinterpreted as a crazed, shit-eating grin.

"We got a call about a possible homicide," the woman said.

"Yes, that was me." Shit, that's not what I'd meant to say. "I mean, I made the call. She's inside, second-floor bedroom."

"You discovered the body?" the Latino asked.

I looked at his name tag: Jimenez. The woman was Riley.

"Yes," I said.

"Who are you?" Jimenez asked. "Neighbor?"

"Friend," I said.

"Does the vic live in the house?" Riley asked.

"Yes," I said. "I mean, sort of. It's a, um . . . second residence."

"There anybody else in the house right now?" Jimenez asked.

"Maybe," I said. "I don't think so. The door was open when I got here. Maybe he left."

"He?" Jimenez asked.

"I think her husband killed her," I said.

I knew I was talking too much, but I was nervous and couldn't help it.

"Why do you think that?" he said.

"Because she said he was abusive, he was beating the shit out of her."

"When did she tell you this?"

"She didn't actually tell me it, she implied it, and . . . it just makes sense, okay? He probably followed her here, or knew she was going to be here."

"She told you her husband was going to be here?"

"No, he wasn't supposed to be here, but he came anyway."

I realized I had no evidence to suggest her husband had killed her; it was all just speculation.

Riley walked away up the sidewalk a little, talking into her radio, saying something I couldn't hear.

"What's your name?" Jimenez asked.

"Jack," I said.

"Jack what?"

"Harper."

He was writing in a little pad.

"And you discovered the body?"

"Yes," I said. "I . . . I tried to give her CPR . . . She was already dead."

"You sure she was dead?"

"Yes," I said.

Then I thought, *Was I?*

"I mean I think so," I said. "I didn't know there was blood until after I gave her CPR. So I washed the blood off my hands. I mean, I was shocked, and just wanted to get it off me, so . . ."

"You washed the blood off before you called nine-one-one?"

"No," I said. "I mean yes. Like I said, I was in shock. I was surprised."

He took some more notes then asked, "How do you know the victim?"

"Like I said, I'm a friend."

"And you just stopped by to say hi?"

"No, she invited me."

Although I was telling the truth, I felt like I was lying.

"Did you touch anything else in there?"

"Else?" I asked.

"Besides her."

"I . . . I'm not sure. I . . . I mean probably."

"You're not sure or probably?"

"Probably?"

"Did the vic live here or not?" he asked.

"No," I said. "I mean, yes. It was a second residence."

Another police car pulled up. Riley went to talk to the cops—an older black guy and a Latino, younger than Jimenez. Then Riley called Jimenez over and the four cops huddled.

Maybe a minute later, Jimenez came over to me and said, "Wait with the other officers, please. We'll have more questions for you, I'm sure."

With their guns drawn, Jimenez and Riley entered the house. Meanwhile, I was trying to come up with a way to explain why I was here that wouldn't ruin any chance of getting even partial custody of Jonah. I could say Sophie was showing me the house for a possible listing, but if the cops discovered the Discreet Hookups transcripts, I'd be fucked.

An ambulance arrived and two male EMS workers came over to where I was waiting with the other officers.

"We're in there right now," the older officer told them.

After about five minutes, Jiminez and Riley exited the house. Riley spoke to the EMS workers and they entered the house.

"So why did she invite you over?" Jimenez asked me.

I could tell it was the second time he'd asked me this. I'd been distracted—by my panic and by watching Riley.

"What do you mean?" I asked.

"You her boyfriend or what?"

"Oh, no not really. But I came here to meet her, yes."

"She let you in?"

"No, no of course not. She left the door open for me."

"Why'd she do that?"

"Because she said she would."

"When did she say she would?"

"Look, it's a weird situation, okay?" I was terrified to tell the truth, but I knew there was no way to sugarcoat it. "I . . . I met her online."

Jesus Christ, I was starting to cry. I couldn't help it—the emotion, all of my pent-up disgust with myself, was gushing out. But I was worried the cops would misinterpret it. Did crying make me look upset or guilty?

"Where online?" he asked.

Trying to get ahold of myself, I didn't answer.

He said, "Facebook? Twitter?"

"Discreet Hookups," I mumbled.

"What?"

I knew he'd heard me; he just wanted to hear me say it again, maybe for humiliation's sake.

"Discreet Hookups."

"What's that, some kind of dating site?"

"Yes," I said. "I mean, no. I mean, not really."

"Wait, I've heard of it," he said. "It's one of those cheating sites, like Ashley Madison."

"It's not really like that," I said.

His look said, *Yeah, right*. In his mind, I was a cheating scumbag and nothing I could tell him would change that.

But I tried: "I mean, I didn't go on the site to cheat. This whole thing, it wasn't serious, okay? I mean, we just got to know each other and . . . and we decided to . . . meet. Just to hang out and say hi, you know?"

"Not serious, huh?" he said. "A woman's dead and that's not serious?"

"That's not what I mean," I said. "I mean, we weren't *doing* anything. We weren't in any kind of relationship."

I saw Jimenez's eyes shift downward briefly, obviously noticing the wedding band on my left hand, and then his gaze met mine again.

"Look, I had nothing to do with any of this, I swear on my life," I said. "Obviously I'd rather no one knows I was here."

"Lemme be clear with you about one thing," Jimenez said. "We want to find out who killed this woman. We don't give a fuck about your marriage."

I should've expected this reaction.

"Of course," I said. "I totally get that. Obviously what happened here is more important than anything related to me. I'm sorry I even said that. I'm just really nervous right now."

If I wanted any chance of Maria not finding out about any of this, I had to be as helpful as possible with the cops, not antagonize them.

"When was the last time you talked to the vic?" Jimenez asked.

I had to think for a moment, then said, "In person? Never. It was totally an online thing. That's when she told me about her husband. He's the guy you should really be talking to."

"Why? She told you something about her husband?"

"She told me she was in a bad marriage."

"What does that mean? If every guy in a bad marriage killed his wife, there'd be no wives left."

"It was an abusive marriage—she was scared of him. I'm telling you, you have to check out her husband."

"What's his name?"

"I don't know."

"Do you have an address or phone number?"

"No, but check her cell phone, I'm sure you can find it there."

He made a note in his pad as he asked, "So tell me again how you discovered the body, Mr. Harper?"

I told him what had happened. Although I was still in shock, I managed to explain exactly what had happened since I'd left my apartment to go meet Sophie. I was very forthcoming and factual and to the point. I needed them to arrest her husband, or whoever had killed her, as soon as possible. Maybe if there was a quick arrest the whole story would go away and Maria would never find out that I had been involved. I was praying that there wouldn't be a lengthy investigation and that the police didn't have to talk to me again.

While I was answering Jimenez's questions, an ambulance and a few other police cars pulled up in front of the townhouse. One was snazzy and black; it looked like a Charger, and a youngish guy with slicked hair in what looked like a designer suit got out. I figured he was a detective. He was chomping on gum and looked arrogant as hell. Something about him reminded me of Rob McEvoy.

I was explaining to Jimenez how I came right downstairs and called 911 when he cut me off in mid-sentence, saying, "Hold on," and went over to talk to the guy in the suit. As Jimenez talked to him, I saw the guy look over in my direction a couple of times. Then the guy came over to me and said, "Your name's Jack Harper."

He said this as a statement and, although he was staring right at my eyes, I felt like he was looking through me.

"That's right," I said.

"And you were fucking the victim," he said.

Again, not asking. Again, reminding me of Rob.

"No," I said. "It wasn't like that at all."

"Then what was it like?"

"I just explained it to—"

"Explain it again."

I felt like I was being interrogated. My lips were quivering and it was hard to speak.

"We just met . . . online."

"What were you doing here?" He was already losing patience.

"We arranged to meet, but I wasn't going to go through with it. I swear to God. I was planning to call the whole thing off."

He couldn't care less, probably wasn't even listening to me. "How did you get into the building?"

"We arranged it . . . She left the door open for me."

"You got here before her?"

"What? No, she was already here. I told you, she was dead when I got here."

Maybe I imagined it, but I thought I saw a sarcastic smile crease his face. Then he said, "Can you come with me, please?"

"Where am I going?"

"Can you come with me, please?" He meant it.

I followed him to the Charger. He opened the back door and asked me to get in.

"Why?" I asked, and he said, "Just get the fuck in."

When I got in, he slammed the door and headed back toward the townhouse. Now I was officially scared shitless. Did he actually think I *killed* her? This was insane. I wondered if I should ask, hell, *insist* on calling a lawyer. But if I got a lawyer involved, it would cost money and how would I keep it a secret from Maria? I felt like everything was spiraling out of control, going from bad to worse. I imagined glimpses of the possible scene at home—Maria screaming and cursing at me, Jonah hiding in his room, terrified. The scene was so vivid; it felt like it was already happening.

I told myself, *Relax. Okay, just relax.*

I was probably exaggerating, jumping to a lot of conclusions. I was still in shock, too, which had to be skewing things. Maybe this was all routine. Just because he'd asked me to get in the car didn't actually mean anything. He was a cop, just doing his job. I discovered the body so of course he had to clear me as a suspect. Once he found out more information, got all the facts, he'd let me go home and that would be the end of it. In a few minutes he'd probably return, ask me a few more questions, or maybe just tell me her husband had been arrested and I was free to go.

Crime-scene workers and more cops came and went. Neighbors and news crews had congregated on the street in front of the house. When the EMTs carried the body, covered by a sheet, out of the house, the horror of the situation slammed me again. The vision of the red tie around that poor woman's neck, how it had contrasted with her pale skin, already felt permanently imprinted in my consciousness, and I knew I'd be haunted by it for a long time, maybe for the rest of my life.

I watched the ambulance with her body pull away toward 2nd Avenue until it was out of view. Detective Prick was back in the townhouse. How long had he been here? It seemed like at least an hour. I wondered what he was doing, if he was still investigating, or if he was just trying to make this as difficult as possible for me. Maybe he was planning to keep me waiting all night. It was already almost eight o'clock. If I came back after midnight, Maria would get suspicious, or at least ask me where I was. I'd need to coordinate with my friend Roger from A.A. to back up any explanation I came up with. Maybe I could say a bunch of us went back to his place to watch a movie, or mov*ies*. That seemed somewhat plausible. But what if Prick was planning to take me back to a precinct? Couldn't he legally hold me for questioning for twenty-four hours or longer? I had no idea how the law worked in these cases and I didn't want to have to consult with a lawyer to find out. I just wanted to get out of here, go home, and try to put this whole nightmare behind me.

At around eight fifteen, Prick finally left the townhouse, exchanged some words with Jimenez and another officer, and then returned inside without even glancing in my direction.

A few minutes later, when Jimenez was within earshot, I knocked on the window.

When he opened the door, I asked, "How much longer do I have to stay here?"

"Just stay where you are, okay?" he said.

It was clear to me now that they were treating me like a criminal. Prick went in and out of the house a couple of more times and didn't bother to even glance in my direction, acting like he'd forgotten about me. Jimenez passed me again, got into his squad car with the female officer he'd come with, and drove away.

It was nine o'clock and I'd been in the car for almost two hours. I had to piss badly. I was about to ask another officer how much longer I'd have to wait when Prick appeared again and headed in my direction. He opened the car door and said, "Get out."

As I got out, I said, "Look, I really don't understand why—"

"Shut up," he said.

Two officers came over to me and the older, graying one said, "Okay, let's go."

"Where am I going?" My pulse was pounding.

"Manhattan South, 35th Street," the other cop said. He was younger, had a thick Brooklyn accent.

I looked back toward Detective Prick—yeah, like I'd get any support from him—but he was gone, probably back in the house.

"This is crazy," I said. "I discovered the body, that's it."

Gesturing with my arm, I accidentally hit the officer on the side of his shoulder.

"We gonna have to cuff you?" the younger officer asked.

I noticed all the neighbors, watching me being taken away. Afraid someone would recognize me or, much worse, photograph or videotape me, I pressed my chin against my chest and stared at the ground. I'd never felt more humiliated.

They put me in the back of the squad car and drove me to a precinct across town on 35th near 8th Avenue. I knew I could, or even *should*, call a lawyer, but I was still most concerned about the possible consequences with Maria. If I had to wait for a lawyer, I would get home late, even tomorrow morning, and how would I explain that? I didn't want any drama; I just wanted this to blow over. With any luck, there would be an arrest soon and I'd be released with no hoopla. I didn't care if I had to stay in an unhappy marriage for the rest of my life. I just wanted the cops to find Sophie's killer, and I wanted my old life back.

Like a mantra, I whispered to myself, "Stay calm, stay calm, stay calm."

Maybe I was whispering louder than I realized because the younger cop, not driving, looked back over his shoulder and glared at me.

At the precinct, I finally was allowed to pee, then they took me right to an interrogation room. I asked how long this was going to take, and the older cop said, "I'd make myself comfortable."

They left me alone in the room. There was a table, two chairs, nothing else. I sat in one of the chairs for maybe twenty seconds, then got restless and started pacing. Shit, it was past nine o'clock. For all I knew they were planning to keep me here all night. I wondered if they'd found Sophie's husband yet. Once they did, it wouldn't take long for them to figure out that he'd killed her. What had I been thinking, getting into the middle of this mess? She'd obviously been in a crazy, volatile situation with her husband. Any sane person would've run away, but I'd sprinted right toward her.

I waited for about an hour and no one came into the room, even to give me an update on how long I had to wait. At one point, I opened the door and peeked out to the hallway. A cop saw me and said, "Back into the room, please."

Finally, at about ten thirty, Detective Prick strolled in. There was no hello or apology. He didn't even make eye contact.

This time I decided not to speak until I was spoken to. I was sitting in the seat facing the door, and he commanded, "Sit in the other seat."

I switched seats. I had to pee again badly, but this was the least of my concerns. The small room already reeked of his cologne.

"Tell me what happened," he said, "from the beginning."

"Why am I being interrogated?" I asked. "All I did was find her body and call the police. I should be commended."

He smirked, as if he found that amusing, then said, "Look, I just want to know what happened. At this point you're a witness, not a suspect."

*At this point*. What was that supposed to mean?

"Fine," I said.

As calmly as I could, I summarized what had happened over the past several days, from meeting Sophie online, to discovering her body tonight in the townhouse. Prick was looking at his phone as I spoke, occasionally tapping the keyboard. He seemed like he was taking notes, but for all I knew he could've been texting with his girlfriend. Meanwhile, I was focusing on my tone. I wanted to sound calm, logical, forthcoming, and I thought I was doing an excellent job of it. I didn't see how he could possibly think I was a suspect. After I finished talking, I expected him to ask me a few follow-up questions and then tell me I was free to go. Instead, when I was describing how I'd called 911, he cut me off, saying in a very gruff tone, "Did you touch the body at all?"

"Yeah, I already told the cop," I said. "When I saw her, I rushed over and loosened the tie around her neck and tried to, you know, revive her. I did mouth-to-mouth, but she was already dead. I mean, I did my best, but it was clear she was dead. That's when I called 911."

"You own a red tie?" he asked.

"*What?*" I said.

"It's a simple question. Yes or no?"

"If you think I—"

"I asked if you own a red tie."

"No, I don't own a red tie, and I had absolutely nothing—"

"Are you sure?"

Was I sure? I was so anxious I couldn't be sure of anything.

"I feel like you're interrogating me again," I said.

"I think we both want the same thing," he said, "a fast arrest in this case. So the more you cooperate, the faster we can get to the truth."

"I have a tie that's mostly red," I said, "but it wasn't the tie around her neck. If that's what you think, you're—"

He cut me off with: "According to your story, you were only in that room for, what, about a minute? Less? You were panicking, adrenaline out of control. But yet you're telling me you took a good look at the tie."

"It wasn't my tie," I said firmly.

"There were actually four ties," Prick said. "We found three more in her pocketbook."

"So if she had three ties in her pocketbook doesn't that seem to indicate that the fourth tie was hers?"

"Somebody could have put the ties there," he said.

"I only saw the one tie," I said.

"I didn't say *you*, I said *somebody*. Do you have any idea why she would've brought four men's ties to a meeting with you?"

Remembering our chat last night about bondage, I said, "Yeah, I guess that makes sense."

"What make sense?"

"The ties were probably to . . ."

I really didn't want to get into this, make it part of the official record of the case, but I didn't know how to avoid it.

"To . . ." he asked.

"To be tied up with," I said. Then added quickly, "It wasn't my idea, it was hers, and we weren't going to actually *do* it. I told you I was planning to—"

"Go home, I know." His tone oozed sarcasm.

"Seriously, what're you trying to do here," I asked, "question me or humiliate me? You should get her husband down here. He's the one who did this."

"So this is a kink of yours," Prick said matter-of-factly. "You like to tie chicks up when you bang them."

"That was *her* idea, not mine."

"You pick up chicks online all the time on these sites?"

"I didn't pick her up."

"Then what do you call meeting a married woman for a booty call? Maybe you're the type of guy who leads a double life, Mr. Harper. You're this normal guy on the outside, dark as hell on the inside. You like rough sex, but sometimes it gets too rough. Sometimes you lose control."

"*What?* This is insane."

"Maybe she wasn't into it. She panicked, wanted to leave, but you had a problem with that. So you grabbed a vase, hit her over the head with it. Maybe you didn't mean to kill her, but she wound up dead. So you wrapped a tie around her neck and—"

"This is bullshit."

"—and called nine-one-one. Figured you'd frame her husband for it."

"I didn't kill her," I said. "I'm telling you the absolute truth. And I'm not gonna sit here and get interrogated for something I didn't do."

I had to calm down. I knew how desperate and defensive and, yeah, guilty I must've sounded.

"How do you know she was murdered?" Prick asked.

Was he serious?

"What do you mean?" I said. "I told you, I found her body."

"So, I didn't tell you she was murdered," he went on. "When you walked into the room and saw her on the bed, why did you think murder right away?"

"She had a tie around her neck," I said. "I knew she didn't strangle herself. And then I saw the blood."

"I thought you said you saw the blood later, after you gave her CPR."

"I did," I said. "But I saw the tie. It looked like someone had done it, so I tried to save her."

"Were you arguing?" he asked. "She threaten to call your wife? 'Cause, you know, you're better off telling me the truth up front. Because we're going to talk to the people at this website you hang out on . . ." He smiled with one corner of his mouth then spewed, ". . . *Discreet Hookups*. We're going to get a hold of every word you two wrote to each other."

I flashed back to our sexting, the things I'd written to Sophie about wanting to tie her up and slap her in the face. She'd prodded me to make these requests, but I'd still made them. Could the police really try to use this as evidence against me?

"Did you talk to her husband yet?" I asked.

"We will," Prick said.

"Well you should, right now, instead of wasting your time talking to me. She said she was in a bad marriage . . . abusive."

"She told you her marriage was abusive?"

"She told me he'd hit her. I could tell she was afraid of him. Look, that's why I was planning to call the whole thing off. I didn't want to get in the middle of something."

This wasn't really true—I'd chickened out because I didn't want to mess up my own marriage—but I thought I sounded convincing.

"So you were planning to break up with her, but you showed up at the townhouse anyway because . . ."

"Because I realized it was a bad idea," I said. "Look, I'm being honest with you about everything, I swear. Just talk to her husband. Maybe somebody saw him coming into the townhouse with her. You can solve this case in two seconds instead of wasting your time talking to me."

He glared at me, with a suddenly venomous look, then said, "You want to talk about wasting time? Keep telling me how to do my job, I'll waste a whole shit load of your time. I'll put you in front of a judge, book you for obstruction."

I didn't want to argue with him—I just wanted to go home. So, as calmly and as patiently as I could, I answered all his questions—new questions and questions I'd already answered. At first, I felt like he was just living up to his name, and was trying to make things as difficult as possible for me, just for the hell of it. But then the questions started to seem more perfunctory, and I started to think that he was just doing his job, trying to be as thorough as possible, and he didn't necessarily believe I was a suspect.

At eleven thirty, he stood and said, "That should do it . . . for now."

"Can I leave?" I asked.

He left the room.

I knew this was a total power trip. He wasn't out there working. He was probably out in the hallway bullshitting with other cops about their fantasy football teams or whatever.

When he finally returned, about forty-five minutes later, he said, "You can go now, but I need all your numbers and don't leave the city. I might need to get back in touch."

"I just want you to know," I said, "this whole night has been devastating. I never met Sophie, but she seemed like a great person. I hope you find whoever did this . . . fast."

He was staring at me, like he was trying to look through me.

Then he took my information, inputted it into his phone, and said, "Oh, almost forgot." He handed me a business card. "Maybe there's something you forgot to tell me. Something she said, something you saw, or maybe you want to just call to say hi." He smiled widely, in a fake way, and said, "I had a great time tonight, Jack, hope you did, too. Sorry, but you don't get a kiss goodnight."

I watched him walk away.

On my way out of the precinct, I looked at the business card.

Prick's name was Nick Barasco.

# CHAPTER TEN

IN FRONT OF the precinct a few reporters fired questions to me about Sophie Ward.

"Sorry," I said without stopping. "Don't know anything."

I saw one news camera. I didn't know if it was recording, but I avoided it, looking away, just in case.

I hailed a cab on 8th Avenue. About fifteen minutes later I was home.

It seemed like I'd been gone for months. If everything worked out and the case was solved quickly, I vowed to do everything I could to work out my problems with Maria. If I couldn't convince her to go into counseling, I'd go to therapy on my own. The problems in our marriage were probably mostly my fault anyway. I had a history of blaming others for my misery and maybe I'd been demonizing Maria, making her into the antagonist, when I'd been the one fucking up, not her. It takes two to mess up a marriage, so I had to take at least equal responsibility. Maybe it was true that she didn't want to work on things, and had taunted me with threats of a nasty divorce, but she'd gotten that way for a reason. It was because of me—because of *my* behavior. She wasn't the only one who'd checked out of our marriage—I'd checked out, too. I'd become distant, more absorbed with Jonah and my own dissatisfaction with my career decisions. I could've buckled down and tried to fix our marriage, but I hadn't. The truth was, she was a great mother, and had been supportive of me for years.

She deserved better than to live with an unhappy husband sneaking around behind her back, arranging to meet a woman on an extramarital dating website. I'd put her through a lot, and she'd always stuck with me, and I didn't want to subject her to another round of misery.

I went into Jonah's room and kissed him on top of his head and whispered, "I love you so much, kiddo," and then I got ready for bed.

Maria was asleep when I entered the bedroom, but when I lay down next to her, she stirred. Then she rolled over onto her back and stared at me for a few seconds, probably just trying to orient herself, then said, "Where were you?"

Seeing a flashing of myself trying to give Sophie mouth-to-mouth, remembering the feel of her stiff, cold lips against mine, I said, "A.A."

"So late?"

"Bunch of us went out to a dinner and then watched some Netflix at Roger's."

She seemed to buy the explanation. Or at least half-asleep she did.

"G'night," she muttered, then turned the other way.

My head was spinning. I felt a sinking in my gut every time I thought of Sophie's wide-open eyes and her sagging jaw, or being driven away in the squad car, or sitting in the interrogation room. I hoped the police had arrested her husband already, or at least brought him in for questioning. As long as my name was left out of it, I'd be happy.

At three in the morning, I was still awake, obsessing.

Eventually I conked out.

* * *

When my eyes opened, I heard Maria's and Jonah's voices coming from the living room. I managed to delude myself into believing that it was like any other Saturday morning. I'd cook Jonah breakfast—pancakes or French toast—and then take him out bike riding or to shoot some hoops in Carl Schurz Park.

Then reality hit as I remembered the nightmarish events from last night. Although I'd only slept a few hours, I wasn't tired—adrenaline maybe. I looked outside. It was bleak, cloudy, looked like rain. I hoped this wasn't a bad omen.

Jonah was sitting Indian-style in front of the TV, watching Pokémon.

"Morning," I said, and he said, "Hi, Daddy."

Like any other Saturday.

Well, not exactly.

"Good morning," Maria said.

She sounded irritated—not unusual. But there was another tone in her voice—suspicion? Maybe I was just imagining it.

"Is there coffee?" I asked.

"Just made some," she said—I thought—flatly. "You want a cup?"

"That would be great," I said. "Thanks."

I sat on the couch next to Jonah, and then Maria brought me the coffee.

"Are you okay?" she asked.

"Fine." Did I sound too defensive? "Why?"

"I don't know, you just seem very . . . distracted."

"Guess I'm just tired, that's all."

"So what time do you want to get going?"

"Going?" I was lost.

"We're going to the barbecue at Steve and Kathy's today, remember?"

Shit, I'd totally forgotten that we'd been invited to Steve and Kathy's in Westchester.

"That's right, sorry," I said. "I guess I'm still half asleep. My brain isn't functioning yet."

"Well, I can be ready to leave in about an hour. Maybe we can take an eleven o'clock?"

I wondered if I should just cancel. Wasn't I supposed to stay in town? But I'd have to give Maria a good excuse or it might seem suspicious.

"You know, I feel a little under it today," I said. "I mean, just from staying up so late."

She absorbed this, then said, "So you don't want to go?"

"I'm not sure. Um, let me think about it, see how I feel in a few minutes."

Maria went down the hallway toward our bedroom. I could tell she was angry at me, and I couldn't blame her—I'd been acting so aloof lately, lost in my own world.

Then I thought, Wouldn't it be better to be up front about everything right now? I could be honest, tell her how Rob McEvoy had told me about Discreet Hookups and I went online, just to see what it was like, because I was unhappy and frustrated with how distant we've been, and I talked to a woman and I got curious, so we exchanged a few notes, and I got a little carried away with my fantasies. But that's all it had been—fantasies, harmless fantasies. In the end I'd decided that my marriage was too important to me to risk. That was what happened, wasn't it? Maybe she'd see the whole thing as a positive, how my demons had reared up again, tempting me, but I'd resisted. She'd be proud of me, see it as a sign of my progress, my becoming a new, better man.

Who was I kidding?

But I had to open up to her, at least hint at the shit storm that was coming down the pike so it wasn't a total surprise. What choice did I have?

I joined her in the bedroom. She was undressing, in her panties, getting ready to take a shower. I noticed how beautiful she was. The curves of her hips used to be a big turn-on for me, but her back was more toned now from all the time she'd been spending at the gym the past several years. When was the last time I'd told her she was pretty? Maybe if I complimented her more often she wouldn't lash out at me as much and we wouldn't have had marriage problems. See? It *was* all my fault.

"There's something we need to talk about," I said.

"Okay," she said, picking up from my tone that it was something important.

I hesitated, realizing I could regret this. Why confess if I didn't have to? Sophie's husband could be under arrest already, and I would be left out of it completely. Besides, could I really convince Maria that I hadn't gone over to the townhouse last night with the intention of sleeping with Sophie when I wasn't even sure I believed this myself?

Maria was still waiting for me to answer.

"I just wanted to tell you that I think I can go up to Steve and Kathy's, after all," I said.

She seemed confused, as if she didn't quite believe that this was what I'd come into the bedroom to tell her.

I went into the kitchen and started making French toast. Jonah was going on about how excited he was about the day trip. Steve had two sons and his youngest, Tyler, was a year older than Jonah. Steve had bought Tyler a trampoline for his latest birthday, and Jonah couldn't wait to play on it.

"How high can I jump?" he asked.

"Maybe all the way to the moon," I said.

"No, I can't," he said. "I can only jump about three feet, see?"

He demonstrated.

"You never know," I said. "If you put all your strength into it and reach up really high . . ."

Having breakfast with my son was a nice distraction. I almost forgot about my problems, and then I thought that maybe this *was* the problem—that I'd been obsessing, driving myself crazy. Maybe if I stopped worrying so much, my problems would just go away.

The strategy seemed to work. In the shower, I started feeling more confident that everything would be okay, and when I was toweling off, I convinced myself that the whole thing was over. Sophie's husband had to have been arrested by now and my name would be left out of it. Part of me realized I was in some kind of weird denial state. I wasn't even as upset about Sophie's death as I should've been, and it was all going to hit me later.

When I came out of the shower, Maria was busy getting Jonah ready, so, standing near the kitchen, I checked local news stories on my phone.

My legs buckled a little when I saw:

WOMAN SLAIN IN KIPS BAY

So it hadn't been a nightmare, as I'd been hoping. It had actually happened.

I skimmed the first couple of paragraphs then slowed when I got to the best possible news: the police had been talking to Sophie's husband, Lawrence Ward, who was considered a "person of interest" in the case. The only mention of me was: "An online friend, Manhattanite Jack Harper, discovered the body Friday evening at approximately six p.m. and contacted the police."

*An online friend.*

That had to have come from Detective Barasco, that asshole. He had to put my name in the paper? What if Maria saw it, or somebody at work? I wasn't prominently mentioned in the article, but my name was still *there*, for anyone to see.

Rationalizing, I decided it wasn't *so* bad, or at least could be worse. While the description was loaded, implying sleaziness, as least there was nothing about me as a possible suspect in the case. If everything went well, her husband would be arrested soon and the police wouldn't bother looking into Sophie's browsing history.

I did a search for "Lawrence Ward White Plains." I didn't know what I was expecting him to look like, but I was surprised by his appearance. He had gray hair, a lanky build; he looked innocuous, not like a wife beater, but, then again, abusers didn't have to look the part. He was a CFO of a pharmaceutical company, which explained how he was able to afford two residences. In our chats, Sophie hadn't told me her last name, so I hadn't Googled her at all yet. I found her Facebook page, saw her photos. The photo I had seen on Discreet Hookups was there, as well other photos of her, mostly at charity events and other socialite-type gatherings. She didn't seem as, well, fun as she had in her chats, but this was Facebook, so it made sense that the photos represented who she was supposed to be, and not who she actually was. One thing about her resonated for me, though—her glassy blue eyes. They were so lively, so soulful. It seemed impossible that she was gone forever . . .

After I got dressed, I went into the living room and picked up Jonah and put him on my shoulders and spun him around. He was laughing hysterically. Then I went over to Maria and kissed her on the lips and said, "I'm sorry things have been so rough with us lately. I love you."

The words sounded odd; I couldn't remember the last time I'd told her that I loved her.

She stared at me, confused, then without much emotion said, "Love you, too."

She still seemed lost, maybe a little suspicious, but I hoped I was just imagining all of this.

* * *

We caught the 11:01 train from Harlem to Katonah. Jonah was playing on his Switch, Maria was reading on her Kindle, and I was staring out the window.

"Are you okay?" Maria asked.

I was terrified and I guess I wasn't doing a very good job of hiding my emotions.

"Yeah," I said, "my eyes are just irritated. Allergies, I guess."

I went into the train's bathroom, barely aware of its urine stench, and sobbed for a few minutes. Then I splashed my face with cold water and returned to sit with Maria and Jonah.

"You sure you're okay?" Maria asked, not looking up from her Kindle.

"Yeah," I lied. "I'm fine."

* * *

Steve was waiting for us at the Katonah train station, standing next to his double-parked SUV. He'd always been overweight, but he looked heavier than the last time I'd seen him—a year or so ago—and his hair looked thinner and grayer. This had happened before—not seeing him in a while and noticing how he'd let himself go. Some people move to the suburbs to escape the grind of the city and for a more relaxing lifestyle, but going by Steve's declining appearance, the burbs had been as stressful as a presidency.

"Hey, how are you guys?" he said. "Great to see you."

He kissed Maria on the cheek and gave her a big hug, then he shook my hand with his usual dead-fish grip.

After he gave Jonah a high five, he said, "Tyler's psyched to see you. We have a trampoline in the backyard now."

"Awesome," Jonah said.

We all got in the SUV—Maria sat shotgun next to Steve. They did most of the talking—catching up about the kids, and gossiping about friends from college. Meanwhile, Jonah was engrossed in the game on his Switch, and I was distracted by my nervous, paranoid thoughts.

I'd never really understood why Steve and Maria's relationship hadn't worked out. Maria had once told me that it was because "we knew we were wrong for each other," but they'd always seemed to have a great connection. I'd never had any reason to be jealous, but sometimes I wondered if Steve still pined for Maria and was jealous of me and my marriage. It wasn't anything he'd ever said or done; it was just a vibe I got from him, or an occasional glance. He liked me, but he also seemed to be perpetually sizing me up, as if trying to figure out if I was worthy.

When Maria and I met, Steve and Kathy were already together. For several years, they'd lived in the city, on the West Side, and we often went out to movies or had dinner at each other's apartments while the kids played. Steve and I became friendly as well. We had coffee sometimes and occasionally he invited me over, sans Maria, to watch football and basketball. Neither Maria nor I had ever become very friendly with Kathy, though, who'd always seemed cold and standoffish.

When Evan, their oldest son, reached elementary school age, Steve and Kathy moved to Westchester for "the schools." This logic had never made much sense to me since there were excellent schools in Manhattan, but in their case, Kathy had grown up in Westchester and had never liked the city, so I'd figured that was part of the reason for the move.

We didn't get together as couples as frequently as we used to. This was partly due to distance and the logistics of coordinating the work schedules and the kids' schedules.

In South Salem, we turned off the main road onto a narrow, windy road called Savage Lane. They lived in a contemporary four-bedroom house, built in the 1980s, on about an acre, that would probably go for about $600,000. Whenever we visited, it was hard not to feel envious of their space. The living room alone was practically the size of our apartment in the city, and there was a big wraparound deck with a woodsy view. Yeah, I loved the city, and there were things I could never give up, but lack of space had been a problem for Maria and me, maybe our biggest problem. What would things have been like if we'd moved out of the city when Steve and Kathy had? Would we have fought less, stayed closer, continued having sex? Would I have had an emotional affair with a woman on the Internet?

If Steve and Kathy were any indication, moving to the suburbs might not have changed much for us. I knew that the move had stretched them financially, and lately they'd been digging into their savings and getting help from Kathy's family. Kathy came from money—grew up in Greenwich—but it couldn't have been easy for either of them to be in their early forties and getting support from her parents. All of this had to be putting a strain on their marriage, and maybe if they hadn't left the city, Steve would've stayed in shape and his hair wouldn't have turned gray quite as fast.

Choosing another path in life doesn't necessarily solve your problems—sometimes it just leads to a new set of them.

Jonah rushed off with Evan and Tyler, eager to play on the trampoline, and Steve and Kathy invited Maria and me onto the deck for coffee. I got into a conversation with Steve about his accounting job—his company was in the middle of a merger. A few times, I checked my phone for news, but I stayed as focused as possible.

Meanwhile, Kathy and Maria were chatting about their kids. I noticed that the awkwardness between them was worse than usual. There were long silences, and when Kathy asked Maria questions, she'd give one-word replies followed by more silence. On the train up here, Maria had seemed quiet and distant, barely talking to me or Jonah. She'd livened up with Steve, but what did that mean? She always liked talking to Steve.

I couldn't help feeling paranoid. Did Maria suspect that I'd met someone else, but she just hadn't confronted me about it yet? It was very much like Maria to internalize her feelings, especially her anger.

Later, Steve invited me down to the basement to look at the new renovation. He'd put down new carpeting, bought a ping-pong table.

We were playing ping-pong, just volleying, when he asked, "So is everything okay with you and Maria?"

Shit, was it *that* obvious?

Trying to stay cool, I said, "Yeah, everything's fine." I paused, catching my breath, then asked, "Why?"

"I don't know, I just noticed some tension between you two."

While I considered Steve to be one of my good friends, he had known Maria much longer than he'd known me, and I knew his allegiance was to her, not to me. Had Maria asked him to find out what was going on with me, so he could report back to her? It was possible, but either way I definitely didn't feel comfortable confiding in him.

"We're okay," I said. "Just been going through a little rough patch lately."

"Join the club," he said. "Kathy and I have been in counseling for six months."

So maybe this was why he'd asked me about my marriage—to have an excuse to talk about his.

"Sorry to hear it," I said.

"Don't be," he said. "Actually Kathy's been unhappier than me lately. As you know, we moved up here because she wanted to move up here, because she's not a city person. I mean, I would've been fine raising the kids in the city. But now she says she's bored. I want her to go back to work, the kids are old enough now, but she doesn't want to, so what am I supposed do?"

"That's rough," I said.

"Eh, what can you do?" Steve said. "It might work out, it might not, but at least I know we're doing everything we can. Things were going to come to a head eventually anyway, so it feels good to deal with it."

He hit a nice backhand shot that made me lunge. I managed to return it, but it set him up for a slam.

As I retrieved the ball, he said, "So what about you? Are you guys going to counseling?"

"Maria's against it."

We were volleying again.

"Yeah, that sounds like Maria," Steve said. "She's never been the most introspective person in the world. But what can you do? You can't force somebody into therapy. I know a guy at my country club, dragged his wife kicking and screaming into therapy and it was a total disaster. You do what you can, and if it doesn't work out, you get a divorce."

"You make it sound so easy," I said.

"I never said it was easy, but what's the alternative? The last thing you want to do is stay in a bad marriage for the rest of your life."

Had Maria told him our marriage was bad?

"I wouldn't say our marriage is *bad*," I said.

"Oh, I didn't mean it like that," he said. "I mean, difficult marriage, a marriage with issues. As our therapist told us—a good marriage needs work, but not hard work. But whatever you do, don't start screwing around."

I swung at an easy shot and missed.

"Want to switch paddles?" he asked.

"I don't think it'll help when I can't hit the ball," I said.

I retrieved the ball from between two boxes, then wiped off the cobwebs on my pants leg, and started playing again. I didn't want to get paranoid, but it was hard not to. Was I that easy to read? Was I emitting a vibe, walking around with a big A—the Scarlet Letter of adultery—stamped on my forehead? Or had Steve seen the *Times* or another article today about this and was all of this just some kind of mind fuck?

Trying not to sound too defensive, I said, "Why do you think I'd screw around? I mean, I'm just curious."

"I'm not saying you would," he said. "I'm just warning you against it, that's all."

"Have you?" I asked, trying to shift the conversation away from me.

"No, and I never would," he said. "But there was a couple up the road from us. The wife was cheating, having an affair with a teenage boy. Talk about bad decisions. Meanwhile, everybody thought the husband was cheating with this divorced woman who used to live next door to us. Anyway, point is, cheating is never the right decision. When your marriage is in trouble it's always so much better off if you take the high road."

Where was Steve last week, before I went on Discreet Hookups?

"Well, I'm not a cheater," I said.

"That's good to hear," Steve said. "Maria can be stubborn and opinionated, as we both know, but she's a great woman. I know if she was my wife, I wouldn't let her go."

I hit a ball off the side of my paddle at it ricocheted against the wall.

"I think that's enough ping-pong," Steve said. "I need another beer."

We went upstairs. Kathy was in the kitchen, alone, preparing salad. Through a window, I saw Maria in the backyard, talking on her cell. She had a serious, businesslike expression. Was she talking to her cousin Michael, the divorce lawyer? Maybe, while I was playing ping-pong, she'd read about me online, found out I'd been involved with Sophie Ward.

"You okay, Jack?"

I turned around, startled; I hadn't heard Steve come up behind me.

"Yeah, fine," I said. "Just, um, enjoying the country view."

When Maria finished her call, I went outside to intercept her before she came in.

"Hey," she said, "how was ping-pong?"

Normal question, but she seemed distracted.

"Great," I said. "Who were you talking to?"

"Oh, just my boss," she said. "The system was down this morning, but it sounds like it's up-and-running again. Let's go eat, I'm starving."

The rest of the afternoon, Maria seemed aloof to me, and I wasn't myself either. I'd be okay for a few minutes, then I'd get paranoid, thinking that Steve and Maria, or even Kathy, were giving me knowing, judgmental looks, or I'd get an image in my head of the red tie wound around Sophie's neck and her mouth sagging open and feel like I was reliving the horror.

What made things even worse was that I had no way to mourn. I couldn't start crying or even tell anyone what I was upset about. Assuming the police made a quick arrest in the case, I'd have to go back into therapy to unburden myself, or I'd have to keep it a secret forever.

After lunch, we all hung out together, making small talk about the kids mostly. No one was talking much, though, and it was hard to keep the conversation going. I asked Steve if he could drop us off at the train station in time to make the 4:31 back to Manhattan. We'd originally planned to leave a couple of hours later, but things were so awkward that neither he nor Kathy seemed particularly upset to see us leave earlier.

"Okay," Steve said, going right to the closet to get his coat, "but we better hustle if we want to make the train."

During the train ride back, Maria still seemed cold and distant. Jonah was absorbed, reading Pokémon manga, so I said to Maria in a hushed tone, "Are you angry at me about something?"

"No, what makes you think I'm angry?"

"Well, you've been acting weird all day so I'm just wondering if you're actually angry or if I've just been misreading you."

She held my gaze for a few seconds, then said, "It's always about you, isn't it?" and looked away.

She'd made cryptic, melodramatic comments like this to me before when we were arguing. But this time I didn't even know what we were arguing about.

"Did I say something I wasn't supposed to?" I said. "Did I insult you somehow? If I did, it would help if you let me know so I can apologize."

"I don't want to talk about it."

"If we don't talk about it, how am I supposed to know what's wrong?"

She was looking away again and with Jonah right there I didn't want to push it any further.

The rest of the trip we barely spoke. Jonah was getting cranky and acting out, so Maria and I were focused on him most of the time.

At 125th Street we took a cab downtown. Maria still seemed upset, avoiding eye contact. She'd acted almost exactly this way once before, I recalled. It was when my drinking was at its worst and she confronted me and told me that if I didn't get help she was going to leave me and make sure I never saw Jonah again. Terrified, it had forced me to get my ass into A.A. I was afraid that when we got home she was going to hit me with a similar ultimatum—sit me down and accuse me of having an affair and threaten to leave me and take Jonah. If she did confront me in any way, I planned to deny everything. Although I was sick of the deception and wanted to be honest from now on, I couldn't risk that she'd blow up and start with the divorce threats again.

Entering our building, I should have known something was wrong when Robert, our doorman, looked right at me when I said hi, but he didn't say hi back the way he normally did.

Then, in the mirrored wall adjacent to the elevator, I saw why.

# CHAPTER ELEVEN

"MISS ME?" DETECTIVE Barasco asked, smiling.

Terrified, I didn't answer and I could barely think. My only clear thought was, *This is it—the end of my marriage.*

"Aren't you going to introduce me to the family?" he asked, oozing cockiness. "Eh, I'll do it myself." He extended his hand toward Maria and said, "Nick Barasco, NYPD."

I swear, he was looking in her eyes like he was trying to pick her up.

As he shook her hand, he was smiling at Jonah, saying, "Hey, and it's nice to meet you, too. What's your name?"

Jonah, hiding shyly behind Maria, didn't answer.

"Yeah, I know, I'm having that kinda day, too," Barasco said. Then he said to me, "Got a few minutes to chat?"

I needed to give Maria some explanation for why an NYPD detective wanted to talk to me, but I was too flustered to think of one.

While I was hesitating, Maria asked, "What's this all about?"

Barasco started to speak and I interrupted quickly, "There was an incident involving a potential client."

Under pressure, it was the best lie I could come up with.

"Really?" Maria asked. "What kind of incident?"

"It's sort of complicated," I said. "Why don't you and Jonah just go and wait upstairs?"

I could tell Barasco, the sadistic son of a bitch, was amused by my desperate attempts to save my marriage. For him this was entertainment.

"You didn't tell me anything about this," Maria said.

"I forgot," I said. "Jonah is tired, just go up."

"You're gonna have to tell her the truth eventually, Mr. Harper."

"The truth about what?" Maria asked.

"It's nothing," I said.

"There was a homicide last night," Barasco said.

"A homicide?" Maria sounded shocked.

"What's a homicide?" Jonah asked.

"I think it would be better if we had this conversation upstairs," Barasco said. "Besides, I need to use your john."

In the elevator, Barasco didn't speak. I was aware of Maria staring at me, but I focused my attention on Jonah, saying, "When we get home, I want you to go right into your room and do your homework."

"But I'm hungry," he said.

"You'll have dinner later. First, I want you to do your homework."

On our floor, Maria and Jonah got out first and then Barasco held out his hand in the "after you" gesture, and I left the elevator ahead of him. God, I hated this guy. He was like the old-school cop from hell—the kind of cop who decides who's guilty and then starts building a case, instead of the other way around. Meanwhile, I was still trying to figure what I was going to say to Maria, how I could possibly explain this all away.

As we were entering the apartment, I glanced at her and I could tell she was already fuming. Her eyes were narrowed to slits, her nostrils flared.

"Why can't I have dinner now?" Jonah asked.

"Because you can't, that's why," Maria said, and she took Jonah into his room as he continued to protest.

"May I?" Barasco asked, glancing toward the bathroom.

"Go right ahead," I said.

While he was gone, I paced, desperately tried to get my thoughts together, to come up with some kind of plan.

After about ten minutes, Barasco exited the bathroom. I caught a whiff of the putrid odor wafting out.

"Sorry, had Indian for lunch," he said.

He didn't sound sorry; he sounded proud.

In a hushed tone, I said to him, "Why do we have to do this here with family home? Why can't we go back to the precinct?"

"Look," he said, "I know you're worried about your wife finding out you were fucking around—"

"I wasn't fucking around."

"Sorry, but when you pick up women online and arrange booty calls, that's fucking around."

"What's going on?" Maria had just returned to the room.

"Nothing," I said.

"What do you mean, nothing?" Maria turned to Barasco. "Why do you want to talk to my husband about a homicide?"

"A woman was murdered last night," Barasco said. "Sophie War—"

"Look, I can explain, okay?" I said. "It's going to sound bad, but it's not as bad as it sounds because nothing happened."

"What's going on?" Maria glared at me.

"Nothing," I said. "Nothing at all."

"You knew this woman who was killed? Stacie—"

"Sophie," Barasco said.

"It was just a friendship," I said.

"A *friendship*?" Maria sounded angry and confused.

"Look, I know you two are going to have a lot to discuss when I leave," Barasco said, "but right now I'm afraid I don't have time to watch the fucking *Young and the Restless*." He smirked at his dumb joke, then he looked at Maria who was still looking at me. "If you want to leave, maybe take your son somewhere, then come back and discuss this later, that might be a good idea."

"What kind of friend was she?" Maria asked me. "How do you know her?"

Caught off-guard, I hesitated, then said stupidly, "What?"

"Who's Sophie?" she asked.

I couldn't lie, not with Barasco there.

"I met her online," I said.

"Online?" she said. "You mean Facebook?"

"No, um . . . uh . . . a different website."

"What website?"

When drinking was at its worst, I did a lot of things I'll never stop regretting. I insulted employers, got into bar fights, and was pretty much a total asshole on a daily basis. But I'd never felt more pathetic and ashamed than I did when I said, "Discreet Hookups."

"Discreet Hookups?" She sounded shocked, humiliated, and enraged.

"If the name isn't self-explanatory, it's a site for cheaters," Barasco said.

"I've never cheated on you," I said to Maria.

"I can't . . ." She had to get a hold of herself. "I can't fucking believe this."

"You're really going to have to have this conversation later on," Barasco said, smirking. "Right now I have to—"

"I want to know the truth," Maria said to me. "Were you cheating on me or not?"

"No," I said, looking right at her eyes, trying not to blink. "I swear to God, I never even spoke to her. It was just a flirtation, that's it, that's all it was."

Maria continued to glare at me, not blinking.

"I need to ask you some questions now, Mr. Harper," Barasco said.

"What kind of questions?" Maria asked.

"He discovered her body," Barasco said. "He was . . ." He looked at me, then continued, "Let's just say, *involved* with her in the days prior to her death."

"I wasn't involved."

Ignoring me, he said to Maria, "At the very least, he's an important witness in this case, maybe the most important witness."

"*Very least?*" I said. "What's that supposed to mean?"

"It means whatever you want it to mean."

"I told you everything I know yesterday so talking to me again's a total waste of time. Besides, I saw in the news you brought her husband in, so you got your guy."

"We released Lawrence Ward earlier today."

"What?" I couldn't believe this. "Why?"

"Because we had nothing to hold him on."

"Nothing to hold him on? He killed his wife."

"He has an alibi—he was at a work meeting in Stamford at the time his wife was murdered."

"How do you know that?"

"We have witnesses who vouched for it."

"The witnesses are lying," I said. "She was terrified of her husband. He killed her. It was him."

"Look, Mr. Harper, I suggest you—"

"You have to talk to him again," I said. "Fuck his alibi."

"Mommy, I'm hungry."

Jonah had just come out of his room.

"Maybe you should take him out to eat," I said to Maria. "Let me take care of this alone."

Maria gave me a loaded hateful look, as if warning me that she wasn't through with me yet, and then said to Jonah, "Put your jacket on, we're going out to dinner."

"Why?" Jonah asked.

"Just put your fucking jacket on," Maria said.

"Hey, don't curse at him," I said.

"Don't tell me what the fuck to do," she raged at me. "You fucking cheater!"

With my eyes closed, I asked myself, *How did this happen? How did we get here?*

When they were gone, I launched into Barasco, saying, "This is ridiculous, barging into my apartment on a Saturday, trying to cause trouble for me, traumatizing my son, for absolutely no reason. I did the right thing. I discovered the body, I called the police. What exactly did I do wrong?"

He waited a couple of beats, then leaned in and said, "You fuck me, I'm gonna fuck you back—harder."

"Huh?"

He took out a small pad and a pen.

"Where were you all day today?"

"Westchester."

"I told you not to leave the city, then you take off?"

"I didn't *take off*. I went to a barbecue at a friend's house."

"I told you not to leave town."

"Westchester's New York; New York is town. Besides, I thought the case was solved anyway. You had her husband, I read about it in the news."

"New York City is *town*, Manhattan is *town*. When I tell you not to leave town and you leave town, that's taking off. You know I can have you arrested for this."

As he stared me down, I realized that arguing with an NYPD detective who already had his suspicions wasn't going to improve my situation.

"Look," I said, "if I felt I was guilty of anything, I'd get a lawyer. But I don't want to have to get a lawyer and drag this thing out. I'm willing to tell you everything I know if you promise to respect my privacy as much as possible."

"You think I give a fuck about your privacy?"

Now he sounded like Maria. Maybe *I* was the problem, not them.

Going for a calmer, more diplomatic tone, I said, "So what do you want to ask me? I told you everything I know last night when you kept me till one a.m."

"Sit down," he said.

He settled on the couch, and I reluctantly sat on the love seat adjacent to him.

"Let's talk about Discreet Hookups."

"What about?"

"I'm trying to get a hold of your chat transcripts from Sophie," he said. "We don't find anything on Sophie's phone or her laptop or any other devices. Can you provide them or should I get a warrant?"

Panic hit. I remembered the things I'd written to Sophie, how caught up I'd been, how it all would seem. If he got a hold of those transcripts and shared them with Maria, my marriage would go from nightmare to something worse.

"I deleted them," I said. "She probably deleted them, too."

"Why did you delete them? Oh, right, because you were cheating."

"I wasn't cheating . . . I was just flirting."

He rolled his eyes a little and said, "Did you communicate with Sophie Ward in any other way aside from via the Discreet Hookups website?"

"No," I said. "I didn't even have her email address and we never even exchanged phone numbers."

"If you won't play ball, it's okay," he said. "I'll just get a warrant. These days information never disappears."

He was probably right—there could be cookies, or whatever, on my laptop. Should I destroy my laptop or my hard drive? But how would that look if I did that?

"Why did you need the transcripts?" I asked.

"You're right," he said, overdoing the sarcasm. "She was killed, and I'm a detective investigating her murder, but there's absolutely no reason at all why I should investigate that."

"You're just trying to hurt me," I said, "hurt my marriage, because you think I'm withholding information or something. But I'm not—I'm being one hundred percent honest and cooperative . . . I'm just saying, if you do this, I'll sue you. This is totally illegal."

I had no idea if it was illegal or not. But Barasco didn't exactly seem concerned.

"How come you didn't tell me you called nine-one-one twice?"

"I didn't call twice," I said. "I called . . ." Then I remembered—hanging up the first time, trying to figure out how to handle the situation. "Oh, yeah," I said. "I did call twice. I got disconnected the first time, so what?"

"How much do you think Sophie Ward weighed?"

"Weighed?"

"Yeah," he said.

"I have no idea." I also had no idea what he was getting at.

"Come on," he said, "take a guess."

"I don't know," I said. "Maybe a hundred twenty, hundred twenty-five. But why—"

"You picked her up, didn't you?'

"What do you mean, *picked her up*? You mean at a bar?"

"No, I mean you actually *picked her up*. You carried her from the hallway and put her in bed, right?"

"I didn't carry her anywhere," I said. "I found her in bed."

"Are you telling me the truth," he said, "or are you forgetting something, like when you forgot to tell me about the two nine-one-one calls?"

"Look, if this is what this is about," I said. "If you're going to be accusing me—"

"I want to know what happened yesterday and I don't want any more bullshit."

"I told you what happened." I realized I was practically screaming and this wouldn't get me anywhere. In a calmer voice, I continued, "Don't you have DNA? I mean she was strangled, right, so there must be skin, DNA, in her fingernails. That's what happens when people get strangled, isn't it?"

"You tell me," Barasco said.

"Did you check her fingernails or not?" I asked.

Ignoring my question, he said, "You know so much, maybe you should be the cop and I should be selling real estate . . . That might've helped us, if she was strangled, but actually strangulation wasn't the cause of death."

He paused, waiting for my reaction.

"I don't get it," I said. "When I got there, the tie was around her neck."

"We believe she died of a head injury," he said

"I have no idea what you're talking about," I said, aware of how stilted I sounded. I was trying so hard to act natural that I was coming off sounding phony, like I had something to hide.

"There was wall damage in the foyer," he said, still watching me closely. "We believe she was thrown against the wall, or fell hard against it, and then she was carried upstairs."

Now I got why he'd asked me about her weight; he'd been trying to get me to slip up.

"Don't you get it?" I said. "He was trying to make it look like I killed her."

"Who was?"

"Her husband," I said. "He somehow found out I was meeting Sophie at their place on 32nd Street, so he hired somebody, you know a hit man, to follow her into the city. Maybe the hit man was supposed to kill both of us, but I arrived late. Anyway, the hit man killed Sophie downstairs then maybe he called Sophie's husband and said, 'What do I do? She's dead downstairs.' Then maybe her husband said, 'Carry her into the bedroom, make it look like the guy she's meeting did it.' I have no idea what actually happened, okay, I'm just saying, when you think about it, it all makes sense. The hit man carried her upstairs and wound the tie around her neck. Then he left, probably a minute or two before I got there."

I thought I sounded convincing and my theory made at least some sense, but Barasco seemed incredulous.

"That's very impressive," he said. "Yeah, I watch cop shows on TV, too. But, just so you know, we've found nothing to back up this idea that her husband's some crazed, jealous maniac. Actually we took him in last night because when a woman is killed, you always have to look at her husband first. But Lawrence Ward's a respected guy, a CFO."

"He was hitting her."

"Nobody's telling me that except you."

"It's in our chats."

"The chats that she doesn't have and that you deleted?"

"I'm not making it up, I swear."

"There was no history of domestic violence, no restraining orders."

"She was scared," I said. "She was hiding it."

"Or she was lying."

"No, *he's* lying," I said. "And if somebody's lying about one thing, he could be lying about everything, right?"

"According to the friends and neighbors we've spoken to, there was no recent tension between them. We spoke to her family members, her brother and sister, and no one ever heard of any conflict between them at all."

"I guess she didn't tell them. Like they say, you never know what's really going on in a marriage, but she was seriously scared of that guy. She wasn't lying. Why would she lie?"

"Wild guess. She might've told you things were rough in her marriage to suck you in. If she told you her husband was a saint, would you still want to fuck her?"

"No." I was shaking my head. "It wasn't like that. There was real concern, real fear."

"So let me get this straight," Barasco said. "She didn't tell her brother and sister about her husband beating her, but she told you, a stranger on the Internet?"

"We had a connection," I said. "I know it sounds crazy because we never met . . . But I think she felt safe with me. Or at least comfortable telling me, because of our connection."

"Your connection." Barasco repeated it back to me for effect. Then he added, "I don't want to say you're gullible, Mr. Harper, but okay, I'll say it—you're gullible. I mean, you meet a chick online, she says she wants to screw around, and you think she's telling you the *truth*?"

"She wasn't 'some chick,'" I said. "She was a sweet, sincere woman, and yes, I believed her."

"Just like you believed it was her first time meeting a guy online?"

"Yes, I believe it was her first time meeting a guy online," I said. "I mean, if she wanted to lie to me, why not lie to me about everything?

Why give me her real name?" I felt like I was making sense so I started talking faster, with more confidence. "I didn't tell her about my past relationships so why would she tell me about hers? She'd want to get to know me first before bringing up something like that."

For the first time, I felt that if Barasco didn't one hundred percent believe me, at least he was listening.

"I'm telling you," I said, "she wasn't lying about her husband. *That* was all real."

"Did Sophie tell you about meeting other guys on Discreet Hookups?"

"No, she didn't."

"So you really think you were her first, huh? You think she wasn't a serial cheater and met other guys?"

Was he right? Had there been others? Maybe I wasn't special to her at all. Maybe I was just another conquest.

"What difference does it make?" I asked.

"Maybe she met another guy, and he got jealous or possessive," he said. "I mean, if you say you didn't kill her, then someone else did, right?"

"Sorry, yes, that is important," I said. "But no, she didn't mention any other guys."

"Did she mention anyone else she was scared of? Threatened her in some way?"

"No, she didn't mention anyone she was afraid of except her husband."

"But her husband has an alibi so we have to look at other options. You see where I'm coming from, right?"

"How did you know he didn't hire somebody to kill her?" I said. "You know, like a hit man. Are you looking into that?"

"We're looking into everything, Mr. Harper."

For the next half hour or so, Barasco continued to question me, mainly rehashing questions he'd already asked yesterday and today. Maybe he was trying to get me to slip up or give him new information. I remained as patient as possible, continually telling myself that this was probably all routine, that he probably questioned all his witnesses extensively, and just because he was treating me like a murder suspect didn't necessarily mean I was one.

I tried my hardest to believe this was true.

Finally, when he realized I had no more information to give him, he put the pad away in his inside jacket pocket and said, "Well, that should do it for now, but this investigation is ongoing . . . obviously. I'll probably have to talk to you again later or tomorrow."

"That's fine," I said, "but I'm telling you, her husband did it."

"If he did, I'll find out about it. Nobody gets away with murder, Mr. Harper, at least not on my watch."

He held my gaze for a good five seconds, like a warning, then left the apartment.

# CHAPTER TWELVE

When Maria and Jonah returned from dinner, Maria didn't say anything to me. She seemed barely aware of my existence as she busied herself with getting Jonah ready for bed.

I knew her wrath was coming. It was only a matter of when.

Jonah was brushing his teeth and Maria was in Jonah's room, unmaking his bed.

"Before you say anything, I'm sorry," I said. "I know we've had problems lately, but nothing justifies putting you through all this."

Without looking at me, Maria spewed, "We'll discuss it later."

I agreed though that this was obviously going to be an involved conversation and we were better off having it when Jonah was asleep.

Jonah, God bless him, was in his usual great mood. He was yapping excitedly about his friend Andrew's birthday party at Chelsea Piers and, for tonight at least, seemed oblivious to the tension between his parents.

At eight thirty I checked on Jonah and saw he was asleep. Maria had gone into our bedroom and shut the door. When I entered, I saw her sitting on the foot of the bed, talking on her cell phone. She looked up at me, and I could tell how angry she was. I took a deep breath, gathering strength. We'd had some big arguments during our marriage, and I knew this would be another one of them. But I was willing to do whatever it took to convince Maria that I could be a great husband and to not give up on me.

"I have to go," she said to whoever she was talking to. From her tone I assumed it was one of her friends from college—probably Anne or Tasha.

Seizing the chance to speak first, I said, "I know how angry you are at me right now and I know you don't want to go to marriage counseling. But I just want you to know I'll do anything you want to make up for this. I'll delete my Facebook and Instagram accounts, I'll never send any emails without you screening them, I'll never go online again. I just want a chance to get your trust back, that's all I want. Tell me what I have to do and I'll do it."

"I don't think that's possible," she said.

"What's not possible?" I said. "I'm telling you, I'll do anything you—"

"I want you to move out," she said.

This was different from the times when she threatened to leave me for dramatic effect, to get a rise out of me. There was a rigidness and finality and coldness in her tone, as if she'd made a decision and there was nothing I could say to change her mind.

Though I understood the gravity of the situation, I pretended to not take it seriously, saying, "Come on, let's just talk about it. There's no reason to—"

"It's over," she said. "There's nothing you can say."

She wouldn't look at me. She was biting on her lower lip, staring at the dresser.

"I know you're upset but—"

"I don't want to talk about it," she said. "I just want you out of here."

"Why?" I said. "I didn't do any—"

"Please, just stop it!" she screamed. "Fucking stop it!"

Knowing it would be impossible to talk to her when she was this upset, I said, "Fine, we'll talk about this later or tomorrow morning."

"We're not talking about anything," she said. "I'm through with you. Through with you, you lying, cheating son of a bitch!"

"You're not being logical right now."

"Bullshit!" she yelled. "Bullshit, bullshit, bullshit!"

"I told you the truth."

"The truth," she said mockingly. "Oh, and that means so much coming from you."

I knew this was a dig about my past, the lies I used to tell her when I was drinking.

"I know I've screwed up before," I said, "but this is different."

"Oh, really?" She fake smiled. "You go on some cheating website and you expect me to believe you changed, you're a new man?"

"I was acting out," I said. "I know it's no excuse, but we've been having problems, and I didn't know how to solve them so—"

"You picked up a woman online and she wound up dead."

"I didn't pick her up," I said. "It was just flirting, and I know that's bad, too—"

"So if the detective sends me your chats," Maria said, "are you telling me all I'll see is harmless flirting?"

Remembering the things Sophie and I had written to each other, I said, "It'll look worse. It'll look a lot worse. But things aren't always like they seem."

She stared at me, holding my gaze, as if trying to see into my brain.

Then she said, "Why should I believe anything you tell me anymore? How do I know you're not lying to me to me right now? How do I know you *didn't* kill that woman?"

This hurt, the way you'd expect it to hurt when your wife accuses you of murder.

Looking right at her, I said, "You know I didn't do that."

She wouldn't look back at me.

"Get out," she said.

"Look," I said. "Let's talk about this later, when we're both calmer—"

"Fuck later! I want you out of this apartment, out of our lives!"

"*Our* lives? What's that supposed to mean?"

I knew exactly what she meant, of course.

She walked away, into the living room.

I followed her, saying, "I can't control what you do, but if you think I'm just going to walk out on Jonah, you're out of your mind."

"Just leave," she said. "Get the hell out of here!"

"Then tell me," I said. "Why did you say 'us'?"

"I'm not supposed to discuss this with you," she said.

"What do you mean, not suppose—" I cut myself off, realizing what she was getting at, and all of the implications. "Wait a second," I said. "You were talking to your cousin Michael, weren't you?"

"What if I was?"

"What did you do, call him when you were out? Holy shit, did Jonah overhear—"

"Jonah didn't hear anything," she said. "I was very vague."

"I can't believe you," I said. "Why? Why're you doing this? What the hell's wrong with you?"

She smiled in a self-satisfied way, like she felt she was, what, getting some kind of revenge?

Then I made a big mistake. I was so frustrated I cocked my fist. I wasn't going to hit her, of course. I just did it as a reflex, because she'd gotten me so upset, made me feel so helpless.

I lowered my fist almost immediately, but it was too late. She'd seen what I'd done.

"Changed my fucking ass," she said, and then she marched melodramatically into the bathroom and slammed the door and locked it.

I was still angry at myself, but it wasn't *all* my fault. Anybody threatened with the possibility of losing a child was liable to lose control.

I was craving a drink. I used to think that alcohol relaxed me—what alcoholic didn't believe that? The reality that when I was drunk I was a belligerent asshole never occurred to me when I wanted a jolt of liquor. I did my deep breathing, my creative visualization, and settled on the couch. Within a few minutes I actually felt relaxed, and I didn't have to go off the wagon to get there.

I was actually glad that Maria had gone into the bathroom. Today had been an extremely stressful day for both of us. It would be much better to have a discussion about our marriage tomorrow, when we were calmer and less emotional.

When she came out, I noticed she had her cell with her, which got me paranoid—had she been texting her cousin Michael in there? Wisely, I didn't say anything, though. She went into the bedroom and shut the door. Rather than joining her, I decided that it would be best to spend the night on the pullout.

I turned on the TV—Jimmy Kimmel interviewing Justin Timberlake. I hated how happy they both seemed. It was hard to focus and, after a little while longer, I zapped the TV and killed the lights.

The apartment was dark except for some faint orange lamppost light from outside. Lying there, staring at the ceiling, my mind churned. I was ruminating about Sophie's bulging eyes, my nonexistent marriage, and the questioning from Barasco—pleasant stuff like that. I needed to lawyer up in a big way, but how was I supposed to start hiring lawyers? I didn't want to burn through thousands of dollars, and Maria and I had a joint bank account, so if I hired a divorce lawyer she'd find out about it. The last thing I wanted to do right now was give her a reason to have even more animosity toward me.

Then I started sobbing. I'd been so distracted by the police investigation and the drama at home that I hadn't a chance to mourn for Sophie. I barely knew her—had it really been just a week? ten days?—but I'd somehow become attached to her. I felt like I'd lost a relative, or a best friend.

Thinking about everything I'd done to fuck up my life, I continued to cry until I eventually passed out.

* * *

"Daddy, are you up yet? Daddy?"

I opened my eyes and saw my favorite sight in the world—Jonah's smiling face.

I kissed him on the forehead, feeling in that moment like the luckiest guy in Manhattan, then said, "I'm up now, kiddo."

"Did you sleep here all night?" he asked with amazement. Ah, to be eight years old. I wished I could be so easily impressed.

"Yeah, I did," I said.

"How come you didn't sleep with Mommy?"

Wanting to change the subject, I said, "Why are you up so early?" I glanced at the clock on the cable box. "It's not even eight o'clock yet."

"I don't know," he said. Then, as if he'd suddenly gotten the greatest idea in the world, he said, "You want to play NBA 2K?"

You gotta love kids' energy.

"Now?" I said. "Can't I have my coffee first?"

"Pleeease," he said in the manipulative, impossible-to-say-no-to tone all kids master. "We haven't played in sooo long. Pleeease."

"Okay," I caved.

"Yay," he said. "Just three games."

"Three games?" I said.

"Okay, two games."

"One game," I said.

"Three games," he said.

"Two games," I said.

"Deal," he said.

I laughed. The kid was a natural negotiator; I just hoped he didn't go into the real estate business.

As he was loading the game, it hit me that today was Sunday—*Sunday*. Holy shit, I had two open houses this morning and I was completely unprepared.

I grabbed my phone and emailed and texted reminders to potential buyers. I could think of four possibilities for the one-bedroom on 74th near York, and a few for the studio on 89th between 3rd and Lex, but I knew I was forgetting some people. The good work energy I'd had over the past several days was gone, and I was flustered, and had reverted to feeling off my game. I only had about fifteen minutes to get to the first showing.

"We'll have to play later," I said to Jonah.

I started putting on the clothes I'd worn yesterday and had left in a pile on a chair.

"Daaad."

He was trying to play the guilt card. On another day that might've worked.

"I'm sorry," I said. "I promise, when I get back later, I'll play three games with you, okay?"

"But you promised you'd play now."

"I can't now," I said, raising my voice, though I didn't want to.

He threw the Xbox remote down on the rug, so hard it bounced.

"Hey!" I shouted.

He rushed away into his room.

"Come on," I said.

Maria came from the bedroom, eyes widened, already enraged, looking for a fight.

"Why are you yelling at Jonah?"

"He threw the Xbox remote, and I didn't yell. I just raised my voice."

"Are you completely losing it?" she asked. "Can't you control yourself at *all* anymore?"

She was doing it to me again—twisting everything, making *me* into the one with anger issues.

"Okay, let's just drop it," I said.

"Oh, I'll drop it all right." She had a weird, sarcastic grin. "That's *exactly* what I intend to do."

Was she implying divorce again? In a rush, I didn't feel like trying to unravel one of her cryptic threats.

"Fine, whatever," I said, just to end it.

She returned to the bedroom.

I finished getting dressed, put on my shoes, and left the apartment. Getting away for a while would be the best thing—if Maria and I had spent the morning around each other's stress, a meaningful discussion would have been impossible.

* * *

When I arrived at the building on 74th Street, I saw a tense young couple waiting in the lobby. The anxious-looking woman was holding pages from the real estate section of the *Times*.

"Sorry, had a closing downtown," I said, wanting to give off the vibe that I was a successful real estate agent, out wheeling and dealing bright and early on a Sunday morning.

I rode with the couple—Dan and Jen—in the elevator, giving them the usual spiel about the general amenities in the building—a roof deck, a bike room, a laundry room—and how it's "new on the market," although it had actually been on the market for three months.

"Really?" Jen asked. "I thought I saw it listed a couple of weeks ago, but we were away and couldn't see it."

Damn, busted already.

"Oh sorry," I said. "I meant *fairly* new. But hardly anybody has seen it yet."

They didn't seem convinced. Already I felt desperate.

In the apartment, I did my best to stay upbeat, boasting about how spacious the place was and how there was a possibility of creating a second bedroom by putting up a wall in the living room.

"We're going to need that," Jen said. "I'm expecting."

"Wow, congratulations," I said. I was surprised because she wasn't showing.

"It's still five months away," she said, "but we'll definitely need that second bedroom."

I thought I had an in. I mentioned that I was a dad myself and that my son went to school on the Upper East Side. This created a great bond between us as I answered all of their questions about the school and the playgrounds in the area. Then I went into my spiel about how the building was very accommodating regarding putting up walls and how the apartment was ideal for it because the alcove they would section off had its own window and heating/air-conditioning unit. They seemed to really like the apartment, too—they were discussing where they would put their furniture, and how to decorate the apartment, which was always a positive sign. Dan had a few questions about the building's financials and seemed satisfied with my answers. I was confident that the discussion would segue into how they could go about making an offer and was already thinking about my commission on the deal—maybe ten thou after the agency's cut—when Dan went to check out the bathroom again and called Jen in to discuss something.

They remained in there for a couple of minutes, conferencing in a hushed tone, and I started to get paranoid, fearing they were having second thoughts.

When they finally returned, I said, "Do you want to go and take a look at the bike room in the basement? I don't know if you guys ride, but it's a great space down there."

"It's okay," Dan said. "Do you have a card?"

Sensing the blow-off, I gave him my business card. Obviously something had soured them.

"So what do you think?" I asked, trying to revive the upbeat vibe.

"We're concerned about the size of the bathroom," Jen said. "Especially with the baby coming and all."

"Oh," I said. "It's actually an above-average-size bathroom for a one-bedroom."

"It's smaller than our bathroom in the studio we live in right now and with a baby it'll be impossible. And we won't be able to give the baby baths with that old shower door."

Dan was near the front door, texting, obviously ready to leave.

I knew I'd lost them on this apartment, but I tried, "Actually, if you take down the shower doors and put up a curtain, it'll make the whole bathroom look more spacious."

"Thank you, we'll think about it," Jen said.

I knew this meant no.

"I have some other listings, a few great apartments right here in this neighborhood," I said. "If you have some time later this afternoon, I'd be happy to show them to you."

Actually I didn't have any other apartments in particular in mind, but I could come up with some possibilities. It didn't matter because Dan was already in the hallway, calling for the elevator. I'd done something to sour him, probably come off as pushy and desperate,

"We have a few other appointments later," Jen said. "But if you could text me the links to those places, that would be great."

They left and I sensed I'd never hear from them again.

Exuding positive energy was so important in selling real estate, and becoming a murder suspect hadn't improved the situation. While an upbeat attitude wouldn't have expanded the bathroom or closed the sale, I certainly wasn't helping myself.

The rest of the open house was pretty much a bust. I hung out at the apartment for two hours as nine people drifted in. No one showed serious interest and most were "professional open house goers," whom I recognized from previous open houses. They went to open houses every Sunday, claiming they were serious buyers, but they were really just lookers. I had no idea what people got out of spending their free time going to open houses, but addictions came in many forms.

At a little before noon, I walked uptown to the other open house on 89th. This showing had a better turnout and generated a few leads, but I still felt like I was off my game. I wasn't myself—I was an actor playing Jack Harper and was watching this make-believe Jack Harper hide his fear and desperation, trying his best to come off as relaxed and confident, and failing miserably.

It had been cloudy earlier, but had turned into a sunny, chilly day, dried leaves swirling on the sidewalk like a mini tornado. I checked my phone, hoping there was news about the arrest of Lawrence Ward. I had a flashback to discovering Sophie's body, the red tie around her neck, and, in front of a Mexican restaurant, people having Sunday brunch, I began sobbing. As the tears gushed, all I could think about was how connected I'd felt to her, how happy she'd made me feel. Now she was gone forever, and maybe those happy feelings were gone forever, too.

Distracted by my desperation to sell an apartment, and sadness about Sophie, I'd forgotten to eat. Morbidly, I realized that with Sophie gone, I had no reason to get into shape anymore, so I stopped at the Shake Shack on 86th Street. I ordered a cheeseburger, fries, and a chocolate shake. The woman took my order, and then I scanned my Chase banking card.

"Sorry, that card didn't go through," she said. "Got another one?"

"What?" I said, acting surprised to hide my shame, the way everyone did after a card was rejected. "That's impossible. I just used that card."

This wasn't true, I quickly realized. I actually hadn't used the card since yesterday.

"It doesn't work," the woman said. "Got another one or not?"

There was a long line, about twenty people, behind me.

From my wallet, I took out a Visa card and swiped it.

"Nope," the woman said.

"What the hell?" I said. "You sure something isn't wrong with your machine?"

"The machine's fine."

I tried my AmEx and it got rejected as well.

"This is ridiculous," I said.

"People are waiting, sir."

I got off the line and went outside. I could understand one card not working, but three? I already had an idea what was going on, but I didn't want to believe it was true.

I called Chase, got through to the fraud department.

"Hey," I said to the man who'd answered, "I think there may be a problem with my account."

I gave him my information, and then he said, "You currently have a zero balance."

My first thought: Detective Barasco was behind this. But that didn't make sense.

Then I thought: Maria.

That made more sense, but would she actually shut me out of the accounts?

When I approached my apartment and saw the news trucks and swarm of reporters, I knew "the best" was still far, far away.

There were maybe ten reporters and when they saw me approaching, they rushed toward me, shouting questions about Sophie. It was too overwhelming to process all of it, but I picked up words here and there—"person of interest," "murder," "suspect."

"Excuse me, I have to get by," I said. "Excuse me, excuse me, excuse me."

Finally, I made it into the lobby, but a couple of reporters were still trailing me.

One, a blond guy, said, "Mr. Harper, when did you meet Sophie Ward?"

The other reporter, a dark-haired woman, said, "How long were you two shacking up?"

I turned and shouted at them, "I'm not answering any questions so just leave me the fuck alone, okay?!"

My voice had boomed, louder than I'd intended. I realized I sounded, well, crazy.

After a pause, the woman asked, "Do you have anger management issues, Mr. Harper?"

Shaking my head, muttering to myself, I went toward the elevators when Robert, the doorman, cut me off. "Sorry, man," he said. "I'm not supposed to let you up there."

"What?" I said. "What're you talking about?"

"The locksmith came by before, changed your locks."

"What?" I waited a beat. "Are you serious?"

"I thought it was weird, I mean, on a Sunday morning and all, so I checked with your wife. She said I can't let you up there anymore."

"That's crazy," I said. "It's my apartment."

"She said the lease is in her name, which my boss said is true, so I don't know what to tell you, man. Maybe you can call her, I dunno, try to work it out."

"You can't stop me from going up there."

"Don't make me call the cops, man," Robert said. "I'm just looking to have an easy, quiet Sunday morning. I don't want trouble."

The reporters had been eavesdropping and were busy scribbling notes.

"Hey, both of you, go away," I said, as if directing a couple of overeager dogs. "I said, away!"

I went over toward the mailbox area for a little privacy and called the apartment. The call went right to voice mail. I tried Maria's cell—also voice mail—but this time I left a message.

"Look, I don't know what's going on here," I said, "but this isn't the way to handle this. We have a kid, you have to be mature, and I didn't do anything wrong. I don't know what you think happened, but I didn't fuck that woman—" I saw the reporters eavesdropping again and I said, "Go away. Now." The reporters moved back into the main part of the lobby. Then back into the phone I said, "Call me back."

I ended the call and texted her: *Left you VM Please, we need to talk.*

I waited, staring at the phone, but she wasn't texting back.

I texted: *You can't keep me away from Jonah This is wrong You can't do this!*

After a couple of minutes, she still didn't respond, and I said, "Fuck this," and I got on an elevator.

Robert, who was with the reporters by his desk, saw me and rushed over and said, "Hey, yo, you can't do that," as the doors shut.

On the twelfth floor, I went to our apartment, saw a new lock so didn't even bother with my key. I pushed the bell a few times and banged on the door a couple of times.

"Come on, Maria, open up! Can you just open up?" I banged again. "Please, I just want to talk to you, okay? I'm not mad. I just want to have a mature conversation, okay?"

I heard Jonah: "Why won't you let Daddy in?"

I couldn't make out Maria's response.

"Maria, dammit," I said. "Open the door—open the fucking door right now."

I knew I was losing control. Not being allowed to talk to my son, hearing how frightened he was, had pushed me too far.

Leading with my shoulder, I rammed the door. In the movies it looked so easy to break down a door; in real life, it seemed impossible. The door was fine, but my shoulder was bruised. This didn't stop me from trying again, though . . . and again. I don't know how many times I tried, or what exactly I was screaming, or how much time went by. At some point neighbors came out of their apartments, including Linda, an older woman who lived next door. She was trying to calm me down, get me to stop, but when I get focused on something, I get carried away, and nothing can make me stop.

"Hey, calm down! I said calm down!"

Well, nothing except maybe an NYPD cop. There were two cops actually—the bigger one cuffed me.

Only when the cops were pushing me along the hallway, and I saw Linda's cowering expression and noticed how she was backing away into her apartment as I approached, did reality kick back in, and I knew what a huge mistake I'd just made.

# CHAPTER THIRTEEN

*I'M RIDING IN the back of a squad car.*

I repeated this statement to myself in my head, trying to process it, but the repetition didn't make it feel any more real. What was I doing here? How did I get here? The sequence of events that had gotten me here, to maybe the lowest point of my life, unspooled in my brain, like a movie on super fast-forward, but this made everything seem more confusing, not less. I felt sorry for myself, yeah; mainly, I felt bad for Jonah. He'd always been much closer to me than to Maria; he was probably so frightened and confused right now. I was his dad, but I was also his confidant, his hero, his best friend. I needed to talk to him, assure him that I was fine and that everything was going to be okay.

"I didn't do anything wrong," I said. "I was just trying to get into my apartment. How's that a crime?"

I'd made similar pleas to the cops in the elevator and as they led me out of the building, but they were still pretending not to hear me.

"I need to talk to my son," I said. "I'm allowed one call, right? I'll make the call on my own cell, just let me make the call. Come on. *Please.*"

"You can make a couple of calls when you get to the station," the burly Hispanic officer who was sitting shotgun said.

"Do you guys have kids?" I asked. "If you do, put yourself in my place, have some empathy, for fuck's sake. My son's home right now, he's scared. I was just trying to see my son, to let him know I'm okay."

Nothing.

"Hey!" I shouted wondering if maybe the problem was they couldn't hear me through the glass. "I'm talking to you! Hello?"

The Hispanic cop said, "Hey, asshole, shut the fuck up back there."

I knew blowing up again wouldn't get me anywhere. I reminded myself that I hadn't done anything wrong—nothing major anyway. This was New York City, not Thailand; there was a limit to how long they could hold me. In a couple of hours, tops, I'd be released. By then, hopefully, Maria would be more reasonable. Right now she was upset, felt betrayed, but when she found out that I hadn't actually done anything, she wouldn't lock me out forever.

They took me to the 19th Precinct on 67th Street. I'd been there once before, years ago, after Maria and I were robbed and had to file a report.

This time was a little different.

The cops led me to the back of the precinct. I asked again if I could make my call now, but the cops ignored me.

*Whatever*, I figured.

This was probably routine. They'd hold me for a while, then let me go. Hopefully, by then, Maria would be more reasonable, let me into the apartment to see Jonah, and we could either work on repairing our marriage or agree to split amicably.

Then an officer led me to a room marked: Booking. A female officer, a muscular blond, sat at a desk.

"Whoa, what's going on?" I asked the officer who'd led me to the room.

He didn't answer.

I asked the same question to the blond cop.

"You're being booked," she said.

"For what?" I said. "I didn't do anything."

"Resisting arrest."

"Oh, come on, that's ridiculous. I was just trying to go home and see my son. How is that a crime?"

The woman nodded in faux sympathy, as if she'd heard similar protests from every person she booked and that there was nothing I could do to sway her or to change the situation. Still, driven by nervous energy and, well, terror, I continued to beg her to "just listen," and to please let me go home to my son.

Didn't work, of course.

I had to check all of my personal items—including my wallet, cell phone, and useless apartment keys.

They gave me a receipt.

After I was fingerprinted, the officer who'd led me into the booking room led me out.

"What happens now?" I asked.

He didn't answer, just led me toward a holding cell where another detainee—a scruffy guy—was seated, hunched over, with his head hanging down over his spread-apart legs.

Then, to my right toward the main part of the precinct, I saw a familiar face: Detective Barasco.

He was looking at me with his usual smirk. I didn't know what the smirk meant, if it was just his natural expression, or if he reserved it just for me, but one thing was very clear:

I needed to lawyer up.

* * *

Barasco tried to question me, but I refused to answer any of his questions without an attorney present. Just making the demand boosted my morale, gave me the illusion at least that I was taking control of this situation, that I wasn't a victim.

"Fine," Barasco said, "you can hire a lawyer. We'll just detain you until he gets here."

I knew the threat of detainment was to try to coerce me to talk without a lawyer, but I was more concerned about the word "hire." I couldn't afford a lawyer—at least one that cost a lot of money.

"I'm not sure which lawyer I'm going to use," I said.

"Oh, you have a stable of lawyers, huh, O.J.?" That sarcastic smirk again.

"Seriously," I said. "Do you have a list or something?"

"It's not like choosing a doctor out of a benefits book," Barasco said. "If you don't know a lawyer already, you can get a friend or family member to recommend one. Or, of course, there's the Legal Aid option."

I knew that Legal Aid was free. With no access to my bank account or credit cards, "free" sounded like the right price.

"Fine," I said. "I'll use Legal Aid."

"As you wish," Barasco said, seeming almost gleeful about it. "But it's Sunday, so you're not gonna reach anybody till tomorrow."

"So you'll release me till then?"

"You wish," Barasco said.

"Okay, so what happens to me then?"

"You wait for your lawyer," he said.

"Here?"

"No, they're not set up for that here. They'll process you into the system at Central Booking."

"Come on, that's crazy," I said. "I'm not a criminal."

"You wanted a lawyer," he said. "Sounds like you think you're a criminal to me."

I felt he was manipulating me, maybe because he *was* manipulating me. He was trying to get me to talk without a lawyer, forgoing my right, figuring I'd rather do anything, even incriminate myself for murder, than spend a night in prison.

"No worries," I said. "Take me wherever you want to take me."

* * *

They took me downtown to Central Booking in Chinatown.

After a brief medical exam, I was taken to a large holding cell to wait with about ten other prisoners. Despite the humiliation, it wouldn't have been so bad if this one scruffy addict-looking guy didn't smell like feces. I tried to stay as far away from him as possible, which in an approximately two hundred square foot cell wasn't easy. At some point, a man brought me lunch—well, an American cheese sandwich on semi-stale white bread. Even if I had an appetite, I wouldn't have eaten it.

I expected to get harassed, like what happened on movies and TV shows. But everyone was exhausted and left me alone. Like we were all on a long overnight bus ride.

I couldn't sleep, though.

Another thing Hollywood gets wrong—you get three calls, not one.

In the morning, I called home and got our voice mail. I tried Maria's cell and the call also went to voice mail, but this time I didn't hang up. I knew she had to be home, getting Jonah ready for school, and was screening my calls.

I said, "Hey, it's me. Just want to let you both know how much I love you. Maria, this is silly. I'm sorry for all the pain I've put you through. We have to talk and work this out. It just requires a conversation—a calm conversation."

With my third call, I contacted work and, as I expected, got Andrew Wolf's voice mail.

Going for the calmest, most relaxed voice I could muster, I said, "Hey, Andrew, it's Jack. I have a, um, personal issue I have to deal with today. Family-related. Anyway, the open houses Sunday went great, some hot prospects for sure, and I'll see you bright and early tomorrow. Okey-dokey, talk to you soon. Bye-bye."

Bye-bye? Okay, maybe I'd overdone it a bit, but I was glad I'd taken care of that. Now I just had to get the hell out of here.

* * *

At noon, my lawyer still hadn't arrived. I was exhausted and starving—the "food" was as inedible as you can imagine—and I was ready to agree to talk to Barasco without an attorney if it meant getting out of here soon.

Then, finally, at around three o'clock, a young, slim black guy in a suit approached the guard. The guy looked like he was twenty-five, tops.

As the guy spoke to the guard, I thought, *This can't possibly be my lawyer.* Then the guard opened the cell to let him in and said to the guy, "Here he is."

"Marcus Freemont, Legal Aid, how you doing?"

He extended his hand and we shook.

The guard escorted Freemont and me to a private room where we could talk. The room had a desk and two chairs, nothing else.

"Are you sure you're here to see me?" I asked.

"You're Jack Harper, right?"

"Right."

"Then I'm not here to see you, I'm here to represent you. Sorry, man, I had a shit load of cases downtown . . . Would you like to sit?"

I sat on a chair and he sat across from me, in the chair behind the desk.

Opening his briefcase and taking out an iPad, he said, "Sorry I was a little late. Got caught up in court downtown and got up here as fast as I could."

"When can I get out of here?" I asked.

"Soon as possible," he said. "How's that for a lawyerly answer?"

"Can I ask you a question?"

"I think you just did."

He smiled; I didn't.

"How old are you?" I asked.

He looked up from the iPad. "Thirty-three, why?"

"Oh," I said. "You look younger."

"I get that a lot," he said. "Good genes. My mother's Jamaican. She looks like she could be my sister."

Nice guy, but I wasn't exactly in the mood to chat.

"Have you handled similar cases?"

"Depends which case you're talking about."

"What I'm in here for," I said, "resisting arrest."

"Yeah, I can help you with that," he said. "I don't think they'll hold you too long. The murder case is a whole other thing."

"I didn't kill her, I just discovered the body."

"As I was saying. If you get arrested for murder, or need a lawyer to rep you during questioning, I highly suggest you don't use me for that. I'm just being up front with you. I have too many cases on my desk to put in that kind of work, and I don't think you need a half-assed lawyer, do you? If you need names, I can email you a list of lawyers in New York. They're not cheap, but they're good at what they do. In the meantime, if I were you, I'd keep my mouth shut. Have you been interrogated?"

"The other night, yes, and a little today."

He shook his head. "That was probably a mistake."

"I thought I was a witness, not a suspect," I said.

"I hear you," Freemont said, "just don't make the same mistake twice." He looked down again at his iPad. "Let's talk about what happened yesterday."

As I told him what happened at my building, he took notes. Or at least I thought he was taking notes. For all I knew he was tweeting.

But he must've been paying attention because when I finished explaining, he said, "I understand police officers weren't injured and no one else was injured. Is that correct?"

"Yes," I said.

"Well, it sounds like the resisting arrest charge is just some trumped-up bullshit," he said. "Since you have no priors, I'm confident I can get the charge dropped."

He must've seen my concerned expression.

"What's wrong?" he asked.

"I think you need to know something."

"Not the words I like to hear, but I'd rather hear it from you than them."

I paused, trying to figure out how I wanted to explain this.

Went with: "It has to do with my arrest record."

"So you have an arrest record."

"Technically . . . yes."

"Technically yes sounds like yes."

"It wasn't a major thing," I said. "I used to drink and there was an incident . . . a long time ago."

"How long?"

"Eight years ago. Seven actually. I was at a club downtown and I got into a fight. Well, not a fight—an *altercation*. I didn't start the fight, I was just there and I had to defend myself."

"You hit somebody?"

"Pushed—the manager of the club. Well, that's what they told me anyway. I blacked out and didn't even remember everything that happened. There were, well, conflicting accounts. Most people said it was total self-defense. He fell, but he was okay. Minor concussion, few stitches. Anyway, I was arrested."

"Charged with . . . "

"Assault. But my lawyer at the time got the charge reduced, and I didn't have to do any time. Like I said, I was drunk. Not that that's an excuse but . . . Look, what happened yesterday is ridiculous. I wasn't resisting arrest, I was trying to go home."

"I hear you, I'm just saying the prior complicates things. I'm sure they know about it, or *will* know about it. On the plus side, seven or eight years is a long time ago. Assuming what you told me is true and the previous charge was reduced, I don't think they'll hold you for resisting arrest, especially when it sounds like it's a trumped-up charge. But you'll get a court date, and it'll be hard to get them to drop the charge unless they want to drop it. There's a chance we'll have to fight it."

"Whatever," I said. "I'll do whatever you say. I just want to get out of here and see my son."

He was tapping on the iPad, probably taking notes. Then he said, "You mentioned you used to drink."

"That's correct."

"Are you—"

"In A.A., yes."

"Whatever you do, do not mention that under any circumstances. It can only work against you."

I knew exactly where he was coming from. A friend in A.A. had once told me that if you're an alcoholic and you get pulled over for speeding the worst thing you could do is mention you're in the program, as it only makes the cops assume you've been drinking again or at least are some kind of degenerate.

"My lips are sealed," I said.

After Freemont told me to "let me do the talking," he called the guard over, and then the guard led us into a plain room with a desk and a few chairs, similar to the one I'd been in the other night at the downtown precinct.

"The detective's a prick," I said.

"Barasco?" Freemont said. "Never met him before."

"You'll see," I said. "First, he'll make us wait here. Power trip."

As if on cue, Barasco entered, smiling.

Freemont gave me a look: *Guess not.*

"Talking about me?" Barasco asked.

I was about to say something, but Freemont put his hand on my arm to shut me up.

"I'm Mr. Harper's attorney."

"I know who you are," Barasco said, smiling.

Barasco remained standing, as there were no more chairs. He was holding a folder.

"If something funny's going on, please fill me in," Freemont said. "I could use a laugh."

"Well, just yesterday your client told me that only guilty people need lawyers, and today, lo and behold, he gets one." Then he said to me with a smirk, "By the way, you look a little scruffy. What, forgot to shave this morning?"

Again, Freemont's hand had to silence me.

"My client is simply exercising his right to counsel."

"Yeah, exercising his right and getting into more trouble on a daily basis."

"I didn't—" This time I cut myself off.

"Given that my client has never served time for any prior crime, and that no one was injured today, in particular no police officer, we request that the current charge be dropped immediately."

With the smirk that I was officially sick of, Barasco said, "Look what I just got my hands on."

He plopped the folder onto the table.

"What is it?" I asked.

"Read for yourself."

I opened the folder. There was a stack of maybe twenty pages. I glanced at the first one:

> FUGITIVE_RED: *Hey Rock God! Do you like music? I'm lonely tonight Wanna chat?*
> NYCRockGod2: *Hey, sorry had to register Yes, love music*
> FUGITIVE_RED: *Hiii*
> FUGITIVE_RED: *nice to hear from you :) :)*
> NYCRockGod2 : *Hey! I know you probably get this a lot, but this is my first time doing this :) :)*

Furious, I said to Barasco, "Where did this come from?"

"What is it?" Freemont was confused.

"Your client's cheating records," Barasco said smugly.

"I never cheated," I said.

"You can't deny it," Barasco said. "You're holding the evidence."

"You didn't answer my question," I said. "Where did you get this?"

"From Discreet Hookups," Barasco said. "What you have there is a complete record of every interaction you had with, what was her online name? Oh, yeah, Fugitive Red."

"Son of a bitch," I said, leafing through the pages. Yeah, it was all there.

"Part I found most interesting and, let's face it, most relevant, is when you talk about how you wanted to tie her up and hit her."

"You're taking that out of context," I said.

"The vic in this case was beaten and tied up," Barasco said. "I think that's as much in context as you can get."

"We need a chance to review this before we can discuss it any further," Freemont said.

"I think your client knows exactly what's there," Barasco said.

"She made me say those things," I said.

"Yeah? You were forced, huh?"

"You can tell if you actually read it. She coerced me, egged me on. We got caught up, that's all."

He grabbed the papers and found a page. "You wrote to her, here it is—'I can't wait to tie you up and slap your face like you deserve'."

"She wanted me to say that," I said.

"She asked for it, huh?" Barasco said.

"My client will not talk about this anymore, period," Freemont said.

Terror hit. I thought I might pass out.

"You didn't show this to my wife, did you?" I said.

"What if I did?" Barasco said.

I stood facing Barasco. "You fucking asshole! You're just trying to fuck up my life, you sadistic fuck!"

My saliva sprayed onto Barasco's face, but he didn't seem to notice, or care.

Freemont had gotten up, too, and came between us.

Grabbing my wrist, Freemont said, "Calm down. I said calm down."

"Yeah," Barasco said, "looks like I was *way* off base even suggesting the idea that you might have a problem with violence. I mean, you're not giving me any reason to even contemplate such a thing."

"Sit down," Freemont said to me.

I was still livid, but I complied.

"Okay, you don't want to talk about the transcripts, we won't talk about the transcripts," Barasco said. "Let's discuss the other matter that your client has attempted to hide from us—his assault charge."

I couldn't hold back, said, "I didn't hide any—"

But Freemont cut me off with, "That's a previous incident from years ago that isn't related to this case."

"I think it's related," Barasco said.

"I'm talking about resisting arrest," Freemont said. "I'm requesting that you drop the current charge."

"That's possible if your client cooperates with my murder investigation, emphasis on *if*." Barasco looked at me and said, "Oh, so I had a little chat with your wife. She just got a restraining order against you."

Was Barasco lying? Or was he just trying to rattle me? It was hard to tell.

"I just want to see my son," I said. "He's probably terrified right now."

"Good luck with that," Barasco said. "When she divorces you, she'll get full custody and maybe you won't even get visitation given your recent behavior. Oh, and I think after this incident, your neighbors might have a different opinion on who the crazy one in your marriage is."

While I still suspected Barasco was bullshitting, the idea of this happening—of not being able to see my son—felt too real and horrific to ignore. I wanted to lean across the table and tackle Barasco and beat the crap out of him. I actually *saw* myself, tackling him, pummeling him in the face.

But I managed not to budge.

"Do you have specific questions for my client pertaining to the current resisting arrest charge?" Freemont asked.

"As a matter of fact I do." Barasco looked at me. "What did you say to your wife to make her want to change the locks? Did you threaten her?"

"Never," I said.

"That's not what she said."

Freemont cut in with, "What exactly did his wife say my client said?"

"She said he said he was going to 'beat the living shit' out of her."

Had Maria actually lied to Barasco? It didn't make sense. It made more sense that Barasco was lying, trying to goad me into incriminating myself.

"I don't see how any of this pertains to the current charge," Freemont said. "My client had a right to go up to his apartment. There was no existing restraining order prohibiting him from entering the apartment. He was surprised that he couldn't get in and raised his voice to get his wife's attention."

"He was banging on the door, causing a disturbance," Barasco said.

"He feared for his son's safety," Freemont said. "He was trying to get into his apartment, which has no relation to the resisting arrest charge. Are the police officers reporting any injuries?"

"Were you drunk today?" Barasco asked me.

"Another irrelevant question," Freemont said.

"I disagree," Barasco said. "There's a pattern here. He's gotten violent and drunk before. Maybe he was drunk the night he murdered Sophie Ward."

"I didn't murder her," I said.

Freemont gave me a look that screamed, *Shut up*. Then he said to Barasco, "Regarding yesterday's incident. If the arresting officers suspected he'd been drinking, why didn't they give him a breathalyzer?"

Good question. For a Legal Aid lawyer, Freemont seemed to know his shit. I could've done much worse.

Barasco said to me, "Maybe you got drunk on Friday, too. Is that what happened? You drink before your date?"

Freemont said, "My client won't answer any more questions pertaining to the Sophie Ward murder case at this time."

"Afraid he won't be able to keep his story straight?"

"Can we please stick to the matter at hand?" Freemont said.

After glaring at me for several seconds without saying anything, Barasco got up and left.

"Thanks," I said to Freemont. "That was—"

"Don't," Freemont said.

A guard came and led me back to the holding cell.

Maybe a half hour later, the guard returned and said, "Harper."

Ecstatic, I followed the guard to the front of the precinct where Freemont was waiting. After I filled out some paperwork and received my personal items, Freemont and I left the building. Smoggy city air had never seemed so fresh.

"Thank you so, so much," I said.

We walked along Bayard toward Canal, passing Thai and Chinese restaurants and storefronts with neon "Bail Bonds" signage.

"You were right." Freemont was all business. "Detective Barasco does have a hard-on for you."

"Because he's an asshole," I said.

"He's just doing his job," he said, "which in this case is to be an asshole. Anyway, I have the feeling you haven't heard the last from him. If you get arrested, I highly recommend you hire a good criminal attorney, somebody experienced with this sort of case."

"But I'm one hundred percent innocent."

"Even if the evidence is circumstantial, he might try to bring charges," Freemont said.

"Why? Just to fuck with me?"

"Put yourself in his place," he said. "That area, Kips Bay, doesn't see a lot of homicides. And, let's face it, Sophie Ward was a white woman, and white lives matter when it comes to murder cases. He's under enormous pressure to make an arrest—fast."

"I didn't kill her," I said. "I swear on my life I didn't."

The scent of fried food everywhere reminded me that I was starving.

"Where are you staying tonight?" Freemont asked.

"What time is it?" I hadn't turned my phone on yet.

"Little after ten," Freemont said.

"I don't know," I said.

"Whatever you do," he said, "don't, do not try to return to your apartment."

"Do you think Barasco was telling the truth? My wife got a restraining order?"

"It's likely she did, yes. But I'll confirm that later."

I had to speak to Maria, talk some sense into her.

As if reading my mind, Freemont said, "Whatever you do, don't contact her. And you can't have any contact with your son either."

"I have to call him."

"Don't. If you want to stay out of jail, listen to me on this, man. Don't call him, don't text him, don't show up at his school. Stay away from your family. When the dust settles, we'll deal with all of that, but right now my primary concern is to keep you out of jail."

"But my son needs me."

"I get that," Freemont said. "I love my son, too. But if you're in jail, he won't have you at all, so I'm advising you to stick with the big picture. You hear what I'm saying?"

I understood why Maria was angry at me and felt betrayed, but she didn't have to bring Jonah into it. She knew I was a great father.

"I shouldn't be surprised," I said. "This is why I did it." I realized how that had sounded. "Not *it* like that—I mean it in why I went online in the first place. I mean why I went on that website and met Sophie."

"I understand," Freemont said.

Like before, I got an annoying vibe that he didn't believe me at all.

"Can I ask you for a favor?" I said. "I have no money and I need to get a MetroCard and something to eat. I'll pay you back, I promise."

He opened his wallet and said, "Will thirty help?"

"Yes," I said, "thank you."

He handed me the bills and asked, "So where you headed now?"

"I'll probably stay with a friend," I lied.

The truth was I had nowhere to go. I didn't have any extended family in the city. I had a lot of friends from A.A. in town, but they had families, and I didn't want to burden them.

"Cool, well let me know where you land." He handed me a business card. "I'll reach out to you in the morning and we can meet up, maybe at my office downtown, maybe around midday."

"I have to work tomorrow," I said. "I'm not sure of my schedule."

"Okay, well, reach out when you know, and we'll figure out a time."

We shook hands—my grip firmer than his.

"Thanks again," I said, "for everything."

"Good luck," he said.

He got a cab on Canal Street and headed away.

I went into the first restaurant I saw and ordered pork dumplings and shrimp lo mein to go. Standing on the sidewalk in front of the restaurant, I wolfed down the food, barely chewing. As the grease and sodium hit my gut, I remembered my vow to eat healthier and to get my body in shape for a wild affair with Sophie. All of that felt like a dream. Or a dream that had turned into a nightmare.

I finished the food and discarded the containers. Heading along the no-man's-land, between Chinatown and Little Italy and SoHo, panic hit. I had no place to go—I was, for all intents and purposes, homeless. My pulse was pounding; I couldn't get a full breath. I told myself I wasn't having a heart attack, it was just panic, but this didn't make me any calmer. I had to talk to Jonah—hear his voice one last time, tell him I loved him. I had my cell out, typed in: HOME. But, right as the call connected, I ended it.

I wasn't dying. Well, I tried to reassure myself anyway. I knelt in in the vestibule of a closed jewelry store, taking steady, even breaths until the panic attack subsided.

I agreed with Freemont that it would be a bad idea to go uptown tonight, but what else was I supposed to do? Sleep on the street? Ride the subway back and forth all night?

I craved a drink, and I thought, *Why not just do it?* I couldn't think of a single argument against it. After all, at this point, what did I have to lose? I remembered passing a dive bar on the previous block and headed back there.

The bar was small—three stools. A scraggly, depressed-looking guy sat in one of them, nursing a pint, staring at the small TV propped up in the corner, showing a hockey game. The young bartender, a thin guy with a long, dark hipster beard, came over to me and said, "What can I get ya?"

"Rum and Diet Coke."

My old favorite drink. I hadn't ordered one in years, but saying those words felt natural, like I'd never stopped.

As I watched the bartender prepare the drink, I felt like I could smell the rum. We alcoholics have a natural way of picking up on the scent of booze, but from about ten feet away? And I could already taste the first sip, the alcohol seemingly going from my tongue to my brain in an instant. Then that rush of relaxation and relief would hit. Ahhh. Drinking was such an escape that just *thinking* about drinking felt like an instant vacation from reality. Why had I quit anyway? To save my marriage? Yeah, like that had helped. Marriage—in quotes. Maybe if I'd kept drinking, I wouldn't have had as much conflict with Maria the past several years. I would've had an outlet for my anxiety and could've stayed pleasantly drunk.

The bartender put the drink down in front of me, then said, "Nine dollars. Start a tab?"

Jonah was the first one I'd apologized to when I went into A.A. Although he'd only been two years old at the time, I'd knelt by his crib and told him how sorry I was, and that I hoped he'd forgive me someday.

Now I was about to have another reason to apologize.

"Sir? Did you want a tab or not?"

I'd been staring at the drink, mesmerized.

"I'll pay it out," I said.

I put a ten down and left the drink on the bar, untouched.

I rushed out of the bar, like I was trying to get away from a grenade. I didn't feel like I was safe until I was about three or four blocks away.

On the podium at A.A. meetings, I've told people that sometimes in order to change your life, you have to bet on yourself. That's what I had to do now. I'd had a moment of weakness, but I'd been smart enough to see the devil in disguise. Now the ridiculousness of Barasco harassing me had to end, and Lawrence Ward had to be arrested. Why was it taking so long? Was Freemont right? Did Barasco have some evidence he was planning to use against me?

I wanted to see Jonah; that's all I cared about. I wanted to hug him, and laugh with him, and play our leaf-catching game, and teach him how to play guitar.

To hell with waiting for the cops to find the killer.

It was time to get my life back.

# CHAPTER FOURTEEN

A FEW YEARS ago, in an A.A. meeting at St. Monica's Church on the Upper East Side, I'd sponsored an ex-cop named Anthony Sorrentino. A narcotics addiction had gotten Anthony kicked off the force and his life spiraled. He started dealing, got busted, did six years at Sing Sing. In jail, he found God and got clean, but unlike a lot of addicts, he *stayed* clean when he got out. In A.A. we hit it off—well, at first. He asked me to be his sponsor and I helped him through a couple of crises, but he had a complicated personality. Our fallings-out always happened suddenly, for seemingly no reason. We'd be buddy-buddy one day, meeting for coffee and talking about life, and then the next time I saw him, he wouldn't talk to me or even make eye contact. When I probed to find out what was wrong, he'd either snap, cursing me out, or ignore me—depending on his mood. Then, after some time went by, he'd come up to me at a meeting and give me a hug, like I was his best friend in the world. We all have our demons, I guess, but Anthony's were worse than most.

I wasn't sponsoring Anthony anymore and hadn't seen him in several months. I had no idea how he felt about me lately—if he considered me a friend or foe, but I'd heard, through the A.A. grapevine, that he was working as a P.I. While it was unusual to ask an ex-sponsoree for help, I couldn't think of a better option.

I walked along Hester Street, where it was a little quieter, and called Anthony from my cell. I got a busy signal. I remembered that he had a landline with no call waiting. I tried a few more times, and finally got through.

"Hey, Anthony," I said. "It's Jack. Jack Harper."

Either by his experience as a cop or as a recovering addict, he must've recognized the desperation in my tone.

"I know who it is, you're on my caller ID. What's wrong, Jack?"

"I need your help," I said.

Must've caught him on a good day because he said, "So what're you waiting for? Get your fuckin' ass over here."

* * *

Anthony lived in Long Island City in Queens, just one subway stop out of Manhattan, about a half hour ride from Chinatown. I'd been to his place several times before, usually when he was in the midst of a crisis and needed my help. Now the roles had reversed. I didn't feel shame, knowing that, as a fellow addict, he'd understand how quickly fortunes could change.

Over the past several years, a lot of construction had taken place in Long Island City. I barely recognized some streets, and it seemed as if at least a few new buildings had gone up on every block. Years ago, when Maria was pregnant with Jonah and we still had a decent amount of money in savings, we'd considered buying an apartment here. Would things have been different if we'd moved out here? We could have found a cheap one-bedroom apartment, fixed it up, and, as the real estate market picked up, flipped it, maybe cleared a hundred grand. We could have used the hundred K as a down payment on a bigger place, a real two-bedroom. Or maybe we could have flipped a second apartment and *then* gotten the bigger place. Flipping apartments sometimes isn't easy, but with my real estate savvy we could've pulled it off. Maria had been against the move then—she didn't want to move out of Manhattan, and we wound up staying. Living in a small space for years had definitely had an adverse effect on our marriage. The financial pressure had weighed on us, too. In an alternate universe, Jack and Maria may have fought less, had less resentment toward each other, stayed closer, continued having sex. One decision, like moving to Queens, may have changed everything.

Anthony lived in one of the few older buildings in the neighborhood that hadn't been demolished, although it probably should have been. It was a narrow, semi-dilapidated five-story tenement, sandwiched between two new buildings under construction. Obviously, the owner of Anthony's building hadn't been willing to sell to the developers.

I rang Anthony's apartment and, without talking to me on the intercom, he buzzed me up. The building didn't look any better on the inside. As I headed up the stairs, I saw mouse droppings, and on a landing, a water bug scampered by.

On the fourth floor, Anthony was waiting in the hallway in front of his apartment. He was in gray sweatpants and a wifebeater. He seemed heavier than the last time I'd seen him; he must've put on at least fifteen or twenty pounds, mainly around the stomach.

"Hey." He gave me a big hug. Yep, I'd definitely caught him on a good day.

"Thanks for letting me come by," I said,

"Hey, anything for you, buddy. You know that."

Remembering all the times Anthony—in an opposite mood—had treated me like total dog shit, I said, "Yeah, of course I know that."

I followed him into the apartment. It was a very small, maybe four-hundred-square-foot one-bedroom with a separate kitchen and a counter/breakfast bar. Unlike other times I'd been here when the apartment was in disarray with dirty dishes piled on the table and counter, and laundry and newspapers strewn everywhere, this time it was clean and well organized. The simple square table had nothing on it except a branch of lucky bamboo in a narrow vase.

"I want to hear everything," Anthony said. "Coffee?"

He gestured toward the Keurig machine.

"Sure," I said.

"I don't have decaf, caffeinated cool?"

"Always," I said.

As he went in the kitchen to make the coffees, he said, "Have a seat, make yourself at home."

I remained standing.

"Thanks again for having me over," I said.

"You look like shit."

I wasn't offended. Anthony had a directness I appreciated.

"Feel like shit, too, man," I said.

He must've picked up on the shakiness in my tone. He said, "So, talk to me. What's going on, Jack?"

Struggling not to cry, I said, "I almost had a drink."

"Happens," he said. "But you didn't, that's the important thing. You talked yourself out of it."

"Barely," I said.

A tear reached my upper lip. Anthony didn't offer me a tissue or say, *I'm sorry*, or some bullshit cliché like that. I appreciated that. I didn't want sympathy or assurance that everything would be okay. I wanted help.

After taking maybe a minute to compose myself, I explained to him how I'd met Sophie online, leading up to how I'd discovered her body. I was open and honest about everything that had taken place—including all of my bad decision-making—knowing that, as a fellow addict, he would accept my behavior and wouldn't judge it.

When I told him about the aggressive questioning from Barasco, he cut me off.

"I knew Nick Barasco back in the day." Anthony sounded bitter. "I'm not surprised he's been dicking you around. He used to walk around like he thought he'd be police chief someday, but the guy's not even a good detective."

"Thank you," I said. "I'm glad I'm not the only one who feels that way about him. I was starting to feel like I was going crazy."

Anthony had served the coffee and was sitting across from me at the kitchen table.

"So what's going on now?" he asked.

In a matter-of-fact tone, I summarized the rest, including how Maria had locked me out of my apartment and how I'd had to spend a night in jail. I didn't feel any shame in telling Anthony about this, especially since he was an ex-con.

When I was through, as I'd expected, he seemed unfazed. He said, "Well, if you need to shower, or want to spend the night here, mi sofa, tu sofa."

"Thanks," I said. "I appreciate that, man."

"But first, I need you to look me in the eye," he said.

I looked at him.

"Did you do it?" he asked

"No," I said.

"Your eyes shifted when you said 'no.'"

I didn't realize they had.

Making sure I was staring right at him, not blinking at all, I said, "No, of course I didn't. Come on."

"I believe you," he said. "I know a thing or two about criminals and you're not a criminal."

"I wish Nick Barasco thought like you."

"Putting my police cap on, maybe he thinks you know something, or you're protecting somebody," Anthony said. "I'm just spitballing, of course, 'cause I don't know the details. But it sounds like he's using the pressure techniques you gotta use these days. You can't take a witness into a back room anymore and slap him around, or stick a broomstick up his ass anymore. So what can you do instead? Threaten the witness with evidence you might or might not have."

"There's no evidence because I didn't do anything," I said.

"You gave her CPR," he said. "That puts your DNA at the scene. Also you met her online, so that has shady connotations built into it, if you know what I mean."

"Her husband killed her," I said, "I'm positive."

"Well, you know they're checking the husband out thoroughly, 'cause that's what they always do when a married woman is killed. But you said he has an alibi, right?"

"That's what Barasco said."

"You think he's bullshitting?"

"Maybe. The thing I don't get—if he doesn't have an alibi, why wouldn't they just arrest him?"

"Good question," Anthony said. "Well, either it's true and he does have some kind of solid alibi, or they think the alibi has holes in it. Maybe Barasco thinks if he pressures you enough, you'll give something up, something they need to make their case more solid. My point is it's always a waste of time to try to get in the head of detectives in these situations because you never know what the real M.O. is. That's why lawyers always tell their clients to keep their mouths shut."

"I know I need a better lawyer," I said, "but I obviously can't afford one. That's why I thought that maybe—"

"Of course I'll help you," Anthony said. "You even need to ask?"

"Really?" I was surprised. The way things had been going for me lately, I'd expected him to tell me he was too busy or there was nothing he could do to help me.

"After everything you've done for me?" he said. "If it wasn't for you, I'd probably be back inside right now, or maybe even dead."

"I think you're exaggerating."

"Am I? I don't think so. You're one of the good guys, Jack."

Again, I felt fortunate that I'd caught Anthony on a "good day." He could have just as easily told me to go fuck myself.

"Thank you, man," I said. "I really appreciate this."

"No thanks necessary. I'm working on a couple other cases right now, but I know how to walk and chew gum. I'll check out the husband first. What did you say his name was?"

"Lawrence Ward. He lives in White Plains."

"I know White Plains," Anthony said. "My uncle had a landscaping biz up there. That was my first job in high school. You got an address?"

"No. I know he works at a pharmaceutical company in Stamford."

"That's more than enough info to go on," Anthony said.

"What can I do now?" I asked.

Anthony looked at me. "Want me to be honest?"

I nodded.

"Take a shower," he said. "You fuckin' stink."

* * *

When I came out to the living room, sans prison grime, towel around my waist, Anthony was on an iPad, Google Earthing Lawrence Ward's house.

"Soundview Avenue," he said. "Nice hood. Must have some serious coin."

He was sitting on a chair at the dining table, putting his sneakers on, as if getting ready to head out.

"They're definitely well off," I said. "I mean to own a townhouse in the city plus a big house in White Plains?"

"Means he could afford to hire somebody to knock off his wife if he wanted to," Anthony said.

"I've thought about that," I said. "It would explain how he has an alibi."

"The police are looking into that, I'm sure," he said. "Question is why didn't they get anything on him yet? My opinion? His alibi's bullshit."

"The detective said it's airtight."

"Yeah, the detective who's trying to nail you for it. I've been there, done that. Detectives are the biggest bullshit artists on earth, especially the ones under pressure to make a bust."

"So you think her husband killed her?"

"Going from my gut here, but yes—yes I do. The way he killed her, with the tie, sounds like it could've been a crime of passion."

"But she didn't die from strangulation," I said.

"Right, but why wrap the tie around her neck when she was dead if he didn't have to? There's something twisted about that—and I'm not talkin' about the tie. I mean something sexual. You're thinking, *Then why not use his hands?* Well, you said she'd brought the tie with her, right? So it might not have been his intention—it was just opportunity. He sees the tie, decides to strangle her. Maybe he thought he was being smart—didn't want her to fight back and get DNA in her fingernails, was looking to cover his tracks. On the other hand, if it was a pro job, maybe the killer was trying to make it look like a crime of passion. The husband knew she was online, cheating on him, so—"

"She didn't cheat," I said.

"But she was planning to," he said. "That's why she went there, right? And how do you know you were the only guy?"

"That's what the detective said."

"Well, on that count he might've been right. Maybe she had a string of affairs and the husband knew it so he hired a hit man, told the hit man to make it look like a crime of passion. The more I think about this, the more sense it makes."

From the closet near the front door, Anthony took out his leather jacket.

"Where you going?" I asked.

"I'm working on a case up in the Heights."

"This late?"

"Surveillance," he said. "Guy I'm tailing works at a bar, gets off late, so I'll be burning the midnight oil. But actually it's only about twenty minutes to White Plains from there, no traffic this time of night, so I might do a cruise-by of the house. More importantly I'm gonna get in touch with some of my old buddies in Homicide—they can fill me in on where the cops are at in the Sophie Ward investigation. If there are any witnesses, I want to talk to them, too . . . But you make yourself at home—there's some roast beef in the fridge and I got a fresh loaf of rye. You're probably exhausted. Bet you didn't sleep much in lockup."

"Yeah, I am zonked," I said. "But, uh, slight problem for tomorrow. I don't have any clean clothes."

"Right, clothes." He headed into the bedroom, saying, "I'm probably a few sizes ahead of you, but you can pick out any tee shirt you want from the bottom drawer of my dresser. For underwear and socks, I don't think you wanna wear mine unless you're up to date on all your shots. Why don't you wash yours out in the sink and use the blow-dryer? It's in the hall closet."

He returned from the bedroom and handed me a pair of faded jeans.

He said, "I left a set of keys for you on the dresser. The silver one's the front door, the gold one's to the apartment. You probably need some money, too, right?"

"I can't take money from you," I said.

"You've lent me before," he said.

"I have?"

"Don't you remember? It was when you first started sponsoring me. I didn't have any work and I was living on my friend Tommy's couch on Staten Island. You lent me five hundred bucks."

I remembered now. He'd paid me back a few weeks later.

"Right," I said, "I almost forgot."

"But I didn't," he said. "You were there for me then, and now it's my turn to be there. It's called loyalty. You're a good guy, Jack—one of the best people I know. Good people deserve loyalty."

He was taking money out of his wallet.

"Here's a hundred and forty-somethin' bucks," he said. "It's all I have on me, but it's okay, I'll hit an ATM later. I'll give you whatever you need, and you pay me back when you can."

"Gotta be honest," I said. "I don't know when that'll be."

"Whenever you can's good enough for me." He smirked. "What else am I gonna do with my money, buy H with it?"

I smiled then said, "Thanks man. I owe you big-time."

"The way I look at it," he said, "you already paid me."

When he left, I called home again and got the same message—the call couldn't be completed as dialed. I knew Maria was angry, and she had every right to be, but if the situation were reversed, I would've put my feelings aside and at least let her know that Jonah was okay. This wasn't about me and Maria—it was about Jonah. I knew our marriage was beyond repair, but I hoped she'd realize that hurting me in a vindictive divorce would only mean hurting Jonah, too.

Since Anthony had agreed to help me, I felt much better about everything—I wasn't alone anymore, I had a teammate. I'd been at low points in my life and recovered and I'd do it again. As I sometimes said at the podium at A.A.: "The great thing about being at the lowest point of your life is you know things can only get better."

A-fuckin'-men.

# CHAPTER FIFTEEN

WHEN I OPENED my eyes, I was disoriented. At first I thought I was on my couch in Manhattan and Jonah was asleep several feet away behind the flimsy wall. Then reality kicked in, and I remembered that I was in Anthony's place in Queens.

It was dark outside, but I was wide awake. I'd charged my phone overnight with Anthony's charger. I glanced at the display: 6:33 a.m.

On my way to pee, I glanced into Anthony's room, but he wasn't there and the bed was still made. The guy had dedication, no question about that. I was proud of him—he'd been through so much, struggling with his demons, but he'd survived. More than survived—he was working hard, building up a P.I. business. And, I had to admit, I was proud of the role I'd played in helping him to get back on track. The way my life had been going lately, it was nice to have something to feel good about.

I rinsed out my socks and underwear and blew them dry, then got dressed in my borrowed clothes. The jeans were big, but with my belt they fit all right. Most of the tee shirts were huge, so I checked in his dresser. I couldn't find one in the top three drawers, so I checked the bottom drawer. I spotted a couple of possibilities; as I pulled the shirts out, I saw the syringes.

There were four of them at the bottom of the drawer. As a fellow addict I should've been able to see through his bullshit, but I tried to stay positive. Maybe he wasn't using again; maybe there was some other possible explanation. Maybe it was drug paraphernalia from his past, or he could've taken the needles from someone he was sponsoring. Unfortunately, I couldn't muster up enough denial to believe any of this. While I felt, well, stupid for trusting him, I reminded myself that I hadn't had any better options. Even if he was using again, it didn't mean he couldn't help me. I had to hope for the best.

I found a plain black button-down that was about my size. I checked myself out in the bathroom mirror. I had a couple of days of scruff and the bags under my eyes were darker than usual, but I decided that, all things considered, I looked pretty good.

As I wolfed down a roast beef on rye with mustard sandwich, I went online on my phone and checked to see if there was any news about Sophie. Hopefully, the police had made an arrest, Maria would take me back, and this nightmare would end.

I couldn't find a story about an arrest in the case. Worse, the only new stories were about me.

I wasn't major news, but several local sites had reported about how I'd been arrested on Sunday and charged with resisting arrest. The stories mentioned that I had been questioned in connection with the death of Sophie Ward, and had discovered her body. One article, on the Spectrum News online site, included a quote from Detective Nick Barasco: "Jack Harper remains a person of interest in this case."

I tried to stay positive. "Person of interest" sounded a lot better than "murder suspect." And once Anthony dug up some dirt and Lawrence Ward was charged, I would be vindicated completely.

Okay, maybe I was a little too optimistic, but getting down wouldn't get me out of this any faster. Sometimes if you want good things to happen you have to act like good things are already happening. What do the life coaches call it? *Faking it to make it? Creating your own reality?*

A new reality—that's exactly what I needed.

I left Anthony's apartment, telling myself that I'd have my life back soon, that it was only a matter of time.

I tried my best to believe this.

* * *

I was determined to have a normal Tuesday. I'd go to the office, immerse myself in work, follow up some leads, maybe show a couple of apartments. It would be good to take a vacation from my problems for several hours.

I rode the subway into the city. I knew something was wrong when I entered my office and Brian and Claire didn't even glance at me. Normally at least one of them would say hello to me, but they both stared at their monitors like I didn't exist.

"Hey, what's going on?" I asked.

I hoped the icy reception wasn't for the reason I suspected, because they'd read the news stories about me.

Then I looked toward my desk and saw that everything was gone. All the papers and files, my PC—everything.

"What the hell?" I said.

Brian and Claire were still staring at their PCs.

"Come on, this is ridiculous," I said. "I know you're not working, so what's going on? Seriously, Brian, what's up? Come on, Claire, talk to me."

"Leave the premises immediately, Jack."

I turned and saw that Andrew Wolf had stepped out of his office. He was in black—black pants, black shoes, a black button-down. He was glaring at me like an executioner.

"What's happening?" I asked. "Why did you take away all my stuff?"

"Because you don't work here anymore."

His voice was even-toned, no affect. He'd made a decision, and I knew there was nothing I could say to change his mind.

But I tried anyway, saying, "I think you're making a big mistake. If you'd just let me—"

"You have to go—right now, Jack."

"Wait," I said, "if this has to do with what I think it has to do with, you have it all wrong."

"I'll bank transfer any outstanding commissions. Leave or I'm calling the police."

I couldn't get arrested again. Even if the cops showed up to just investigate another complaint about me, and Barasco found out, it wouldn't lead to anything positive.

"Okay, relax, I'm not causing a scene," I said. "I know why you're concerned, but just so you know, there's another side to this. The main thing is I'm innocent—I didn't do anything wrong."

"Your employment is terminated," Andrew said. "There isn't anything to discuss."

"I understand and I'm leaving," I said, "but can you just tell me what's going on? We've known each other a long time now. What's it been five, six years? I think I deserve some sort of explanation."

This seemed to resonate with him. Or he just wanted to say whatever he had to say to get rid of me.

"A detective came by here yesterday. He told me about the whole situation."

"He has it in for me," I said. "I don't know why, but he does."

"Jack—"

"Did he tell you that I didn't actually *do* anything? That I'm actually just a person of interest in the case? That I—"

"He told me your wife has a restraining order against you."

"That isn't true," I said. "See? He makes things up." I turned toward Brian and Claire, our audience. "Come on, tell him you believe me. I work with you guys every day, you know what kind of person I am. A friend of mine, just last night, told me what a great guy I am, how I helped him when he was down and no one else would. Doesn't that mean anything? If some self-absorbed cop comes in here, tells you a bunch of lies about me, you just believe it? Doesn't our history count for *anything*?"

I knew I was rambling, struggling to connect with them on anything.

Andrew had his phone to his ear. "I'm calling the police, Jack."

"Come on, you guys know I'm not a killer," I said to the room. "This is ridiculous."

"The phone's ringing," Andrew said.

Brian and Claire wouldn't look at me.

"Fine, whatever," I said, and stormed out to the street.

"Son of a bitch!" I yelled and kicked the first thing I saw—a bag of garbage.

I continued around the neighborhood, cursing at Andrew, saying, "Spineless asshole," and, "Rich fuck." Then I noticed people looking at me with fear and disgust, and trying to avoid me, the way I used to try to avoid the ranting lunatics in the neighborhood.

I sat in the public, outdoor seating at the Starbucks on 85th and 1st. As I calmed down, I realized that while the ranting was new, my behavior was familiar—blaming others for my problems. Andrew had fired me, but had Andrew made me go on Discreet Hookups? Even Rob McEvoy hadn't forced me to go on. I was the one who'd made the bad decisions; I was the one who'd fucked up. But it was always easier for me to get angry than to self-reflect. Call it my fatal flaw.

But at least I knew I had a problem, which meant I wasn't so far gone, right? I was doing the best I could to get my shit together and had to resist falling into the trap of becoming too hard on myself. Blaming myself could be just as destructive as blaming others. I had to give myself a pass.

Also, there was always the chance that my perception could be warped. Stress could do that to a person.

Maybe my whole life wasn't as fucked up as it seemed. Maybe it just felt that way. After all, I had Anthony working for me now.

I texted Anthony: *Hey, anything going on?*

He got right back to me: *How you doin? The jeans fit?*

The response didn't exactly inspire confidence. I was in trouble, depending on him, and he was asking about his jeans? I hoped he was taking this seriously and I hadn't misjudged him. I'd lost my family, my apartment, my money, and now my job, and I was counting on a recovering hard-core drug addict, an ex-con, to bail me out?

I responded: *Great any news???*

He replied right away: *In middle something big call u later.*

I wasn't sure what to make of this. Did "something big" mean a break in the case? At least he didn't sound like he was strung out on heroin. At this point I'd take any encouragement I could get.

I started walking again, realizing I was only a few blocks from Jonah's school. It was nine thirty—Maria must've dropped him off an hour ago. I could go to the school, just to see him and say hi, let him know I was okay.

Without weighing the pros and cons of this, I headed over there.

I knew Florence, the security guard, very well. I'd known her since Jonah had started going to the school, for kindergarten.

I entered the school and went up the short stairwell and approached her at her desk. She was a heavyset black woman, about fifty years old. While she was usually smiling, in a good mood, she had the tough-ass vibe of someone you didn't want to mess with.

"Hey, Florence, how are you?"

"Hangin' in there," she said. A copy of some tabloid magazine was open in front of her. "Woke up today, that's one good thing, right?"

"Now I feel a lot better about my own life," I said.

Even though what I'd said wasn't particularly funny, she laughed.

"I have to give my son his lunch, he forgot it," I said.

I patted my coat pocket, to imply his lunch was in there.

"A'right," she said. "Have a great day."

"You, too," I said.

After I signed in at the main office, I went right to Jonah's classroom on the second floor. I just wanted to tell him I loved him and give him a reassuring hug. I only planned to stay in the school for a few minutes, tops.

The hallway was empty except for a girl who passed by me, clutching a hall pass, probably on her way to the bathroom.

"Hey," I said.

She looked away, maybe remembering what her parents had told her about not talking to strangers.

That, or she'd gotten a bad vibe about me.

Through the windowed door, I peered into Jonah's classroom.

His teacher, Lauren—blond, pregnant, in her twenties—saw me. She seemed concerned, even a little panicked. I wasn't sure why. Was she just surprised? If so, why the panic?

I smiled, then shifted my eyes toward the students to indicate that I was here to see Jonah. She remained where she was, still with that odd deer-in-headlights look, as if trying to figure what to do.

I needed to talk to her, explain why I was here. As I entered the classroom, she rushed over, blocking me from opening the door fully and entering.

"You're not supposed to be here, Mr. Harper."

"I just need to talk to Jonah for a second."

"Please go away."

I saw Jonah—he was at his desk, waving to me. It was so great to see his face. It had only been about two days since I'd seen him last, but it felt like years.

I motioned with my arm for him to come over to me.

"Mr. Harper, you have to leave right now," Lauren said.

Jonah came over. After what I'd been through the past couple of days, it was amazing to see him.

"Hey, kiddo," I said, and hugged him and picked him up a little.

Lauren, sounding panicked, like I was a school shooter or something, said to another boy, "Go get Ms. Wong. Right now, out the back door."

The boy darted out of the classroom. I noticed the remaining kids looked scared.

"Whoa, what's going on?" I said. "Everything's gonna be okay," I said to the class. "I'm just here to talk to Jonah for a couple minutes, that's it."

"Mom said I can't talk to you," Jonah said.

The whole class, and Lauren, had overheard this. I felt embarrassed, even humiliated.

Bending down, I whispered into Jonah's ear, "Mom's just angry right now and that's okay. Sometimes people get angry, okay? But I just came here to tell you I love you and everything's going to be okay. Okay?"

Then I looked in Jonah's eyes and saw he was crying. He was shaking a little, too.

"Come on, stop it," I whispered. "It's me, Daddy. I love you."

"I love you, too," he managed to say before he began full on bawling.

It hit me that by coming to the school I hadn't made things any better. I'd made things much, much worse.

"Get away from the child."

I looked back over my shoulder and saw that Florence and the principal, Ms. Wong, had entered the classroom. This wasn't affable Florence of a few minutes earlier. This was angry, no bullshit, ready-to-beat-the-crap-out-of-me-if-she-had-to Florence.

Jonah was still crying. Fuck, why did every positive thing I tried to do dissolve into a total shit storm?

"Don't worry, it's okay," I said to Jonah.

"Away!" Florence grabbed my wrist with a clamp-like grip and pulled me backward so hard I stumbled.

Lauren went to Jonah and tried to calm him down.

"Okay, okay, I'm leaving, you can let go," I said to Florence.

"Damn right you're leaving," Florence said, pulling me into the hallway.

"It's okay," I said to Jonah, but I didn't think he heard me.

"I'm sorry," I said to Florence. "It was a misunderstanding. You can let go of me now. I'll leave right now."

She let go.

"Nobody told me you weren't allowed into the school."

"Nobody told me either," I said.

"I could put your ass in jail, you understand that?"

I didn't know if this was true or not, but I didn't want the school to notify Maria. If Maria exaggerated the situation, reported that I'd tried to kidnap Jonah from school, I'd definitely go back to jail, and might not get out so quickly next time.

"I'm sorry," I said. "I'm leaving and I won't come back, I promise. I'm sorry if I put you in an awkward position."

"Just get your ass outta here," she said.

Leaving the school, I felt energized. While coming to see Jonah had been risky, I was still glad I'd done it. When he first saw me, I could tell how happy he was. He'd only gotten upset because of Lauren's reaction, because he was confused.

Heading toward the Lexington Avenue subway, I was excited about the future. Soon things would return to normal, I'd get another chance, and this time I wouldn't make the mistake I'd made before—I wouldn't take the positive things in my life for granted. I'd gotten into a rut in my marriage and with work, but I wouldn't take those little moments for granted again. I'd get a new job—in real estate, or maybe something music related. I'd always wanted to teach music; maybe I'd teach, work with kids.

I checked my phone, hoping that Anthony had gotten back to me. I got his voice mail.

"Hey, Anthony, it's Jack at um . . . I guess around ten o'clock. Just checking back to see what your big news is. Hope big means good. Talk to you in a few."

In front of the 77th Street station, I waited for him to reply. Sometimes I didn't get service on the train and I didn't want to miss anything.

Twenty minutes went by and the only text I got was from a client—well, I guess ex-client—asking me if I had any new studios to show him.

I responded: *Thanks for the interest! I'm currently transitioning to a new agency. Good luck with your search!*

Then I texted Anthony: *getting on train TTYL*, then headed back to Queens.

* * *

Entering Anthony's apartment, I said, "Hello?"

No answer.

The lights were out; the apartment looked the same as when I'd left. A quick inspection seemed to confirm that he hadn't been home.

I checked my phone—still no voice mail or response to my text.

I was losing patience. What was up with the guy? He knew I was anxious, desperate, at a low point in my life, and he keeps me hanging like this?

I texted him again. Just *Hey.*

Still nothing. I could call him again, but what use would that do? Another voice mail wouldn't reduce his response time to the first one.

Then I noticed the red streaks on the floor. I flashed back to the townhouse, when I'd discovered Sophie's body, telling myself, *This is impossible. This can't be happening. Not again.*

Still in denial, I thought, *How did ketchup get on the floor?* Then the charade ended and full-blown panic hit.

"Fuck," I said. "Holy fuck. No, no, no."

I still didn't want to believe this was happening. There had to be some explanation to this—well, an explanation beyond the obvious one.

Fueled by this slim hope, I followed the trail of blood into the bathroom.

He was lying facedown in a glistening pool of dark-red blood. A butcher knife had been jammed into his lower back.

Instinctively, I wanted to yank the knife out of his back, to try to save my friend. But as I reached for the handle, I stopped myself.

*Was I out of my fucking mind?*

After what had happened at Lawrence and Sophie Ward's townhouse, did I really want to contaminate another crime scene? I backed away from the body out of the bathroom. But, big problem. I'd stepped in the blood and had tracked blood from the bathroom to the kitchen.

So much for not contaminating another crime scene. I could just tell the truth, tell Barasco I'd walked into an apartment and—for the second time in about a week—discovered a dead body. Yeah, that would go over great. I'd tell him that somebody was setting me up, and he'd come up with some vague motive why I'd want to kill Anthony—we'd had a fight about something—and I'd be charged for a double homicide. I'd taken the honesty route after I discovered Sophie's body, and where had that gotten me?

Using a wet paper towel, I wiped down the apartment the best I could, focusing on areas I knew I'd touched, like the doorknob and locks on the front door, but also areas I didn't think I'd touched, like the table and countertop in the kitchen. Although I didn't see any blood on the bottoms of my shoes, I wiped them down, too, and then I scrubbed the floor—from the front door to the bathroom. I put all of the paper towels into a plastic bag that I found under the sink. I wiped anything I touched, but I'd seen enough *CSI* to know that it was nearly impossible to clean up a crime scene entirely. Evidence of me—a strand of hair, fiber from my clothes—had to be somewhere. When the forensics teams found the evidence, I could claim that of course my DNA was in the apartment because I'd been staying here. If I'd left evidence on or near Anthony's body, or if forensics found the remnants of one of my bloody footsteps, this would be much harder to explain.

The buzzer from the intercom rang.

It wasn't particularly loud—probably the sound of a normal intercom buzzer—but it sounded practically deafening.

I tried not to panic. Kids and random delivery people always rang the buzzers to walk-up buildings—it was one of the big advantages of living in a doorman building. Besides, it was just the buzzer to the outside of the building, not like the doorbell was ringing.

The buzzer sounded again—longer this time, someone pushing down and maintaining pressure. After the buzzer sounded for a third time, there was a long period of silence.

Figuring the person had given up, I dampened a wad of paper towel, then bent down and wiped the floor of the kitchen. Some pink showed on the wad of paper towels, confirming my fear that there was still blood on the floor.

Squatting, panic hit when I heard footsteps on the stairs—someone coming up.

Still, it didn't mean the person was coming to this apartment. A delivery person, or a visitor to another tenant, could have pressed random buzzers just to get into the building.

Only the footsteps were getting louder. Then the person seemed to reach the landing right outside the door and then:

The doorbell rang.

Again, the noise jolted me, but I didn't make a sound. I stayed still, barely breathing, as only a couple of feet separated me from whoever was in the hallway.

The doorbell rang a few more times, then:

"Anthony? You home?"

It was a woman, with a heavy Brooklyn, or maybe Staten Island, accent—*Anthony* sounded like *Ant'nee.* Was she Anthony's girlfriend? He'd been married years ago, but he hadn't mentioned another woman in his life.

"Anthony, you there?"

She rang the bell again and then started banging on the door. If anyone else on the floor was home, they'd definitely overhear the racket she was causing.

"I see a light on under the door," she said. "I know you're there."

How did a light prove someone was home? People left lights on all the time.

"Come on," she said. "Open up or I'm gonna get in there somehow."

What did that mean? Did she have access to a key from a neighbor?

Figuring I was better off just letting her in, I said, "One sec." I put the wad of paper towel I was still holding into the plastic bag, then put the plastic bag under the kitchen sink. "Sorry, just, um, putting some clothes on."

I shut the bathroom door, then, finally, opened the front door.

The woman was dark-skinned, maybe Indian. She had shoulder-length black hair, and was in jeans, Nikes, and a blue hooded sweatshirt. She was stocky, had big shoulders.

"Who are you?" She looked and sounded surprised.

"I'm just, um, a friend," I said.

The hesitation must've sounded suspicious as hell, but I hoped she hadn't noticed.

*C'mon, Jack, focus.*

"Is Anthony home?" she asked.

"No, he isn't," I said, "can I help you with something?"

"You know when he's comin' back?"

"No. No, actually I don't."

"Who are you?" She sounded demanding, suspicious.

"A friend of his," I said.

"Name?"

Now this was getting officially weird.

"How about you tell me your name?" I asked.

She looked past me into the apartment. "You living here now?"

"I'm sorry, who are you?" I asked.

"He didn't tell me he was living with someone, so I hope for his sake you're not. This is a major violation."

"Look, I have no idea what you're talking about."

She glared at me for a couple of seconds, then reached into her pocket for something.

Paranoid, I thought, *Gun,* and may have even backed away a little.

Then she held up a badge and said, "Officer Singh. Can I come in, please?"

All of the positivity I'd had earlier had vanished. I didn't know how I'd ever believed my life was on the verge of getting better, but I guess this was typical. Without occasional surges of optimism, how would I repeat my mistakes?

# CHAPTER SIXTEEN

I WAS FUCKED.

Maybe an average person wouldn't notice any traces of blood or other evidence of a murder in an apartment, but a cop?

"Sure," I managed to say. "Come in."

I stood aside and let her pass.

For a crazed moment, I thought, *I should probably kill her.* While I had no intention of actually killing her, in the moment it seemed like the only possible way for me to avoid spending the rest of my life in jail.

I shut the door.

She glanced around, heightening my feeling of impending doom, then said, "Where's Anthony?"

"Anthony?" I asked. I'd heard her clearly; my thoughts were just scattered.

"Yeah, Anthony," she said.

Why was she here to see Anthony? Was it possible this had nothing to do with me?

"Um, he's not home right now," I said, fighting off the image that had appeared in my head of his body, bleeding out, on the bathroom floor.

"So who are you?" she asked.

"Jack. Jack Harper."

I was afraid she'd make the connection that I was the Jack Harper who was a person of interest in the Sophie Ward murder case. But I didn't want to lie either.

"He didn't mention any friends named Jack Harper," she said.

"I'm his sponsor," I said. "Well, ex-sponsor."

"How long you been staying here?"

She hadn't made the connection. Or if she had, she wasn't letting on.

"I'm not staying here," I said.

Now she was looking at the pillow and blanket that I'd folded and left out on the couch.

"I mean, I crashed here last night, yeah," I said. "But I'm not *staying* here. What's this all about anyway? Did Anthony do something wrong?"

"Yeah, he did somethin' wrong. He was supposed to meet me this morning at a diner in Sunnyside, but he didn't show."

"Oh," I said. "Well, I know he was working on a case last night."

"Makes no difference to me," she said. "He had a time scheduled, was supposed to report at nine a.m., and he didn't show. When was the last time you spoke to him?"

"This morning. Around nine-thirtyish."

"He mention anything 'bout meeting me?"

"Actually I didn't talk to him," I said. "We texted. It was short. He didn't say much."

"He say where he was?"

"No. No, he didn't."

"Son of a bitch," Singh said. "This is another possible violation. Guy likes to play with fire, don't he?"

"Sorry, but I'm still confused," I said. "*Violation?* What sort of violation are you talking about?"

"I'm Anthony's parole officer," she said.

Anthony had worn a tracking bracelet when I first met him, but I'd thought he was finished with parole.

"He's on parole?" I asked.

"For another seventeen months," Singh said. "He still has to make regular check-ins. I can take him in right now for this, so if you know something, know where he is, you better fess up."

"I don't know anything, I swear," I said. "I wish I did."

She glanced at her phone, then her gaze met mine again.

"So what's this about a case he's working on?"

I didn't see the point in telling her. Maybe just paranoia, but after my experiences with Nick Barasco, I didn't want to say anything incriminating.

"Not sure," I said, "but I know he expected to be out all night."

"Out where?"

"He mentioned a case he was working on in Washington Heights."

"A case." She sounded sarcastic. Then she asked, "Are there any drugs on the premises?"

"Drugs?"

"Heroin," she said. "Any heroin here?"

I didn't want to tell her about the needles I'd found in his dresser drawer, as it would lead to a search of the entire apartment—including the bathroom.

"No," I said. "I mean, I have no idea, but I don't think so."

"If I look you up, I won't find out you're his drug dealer, will I?"

"What? No. I'm not a drug dealer, I'm a real estate agent."

"Where do you work?"

"Well, I, um, don't work at the moment," I said. "I'm sort of in between jobs."

She looked at me like she thought I was full of shit.

"Why do you think there's heroin here?" I asked.

"I've been suspecting that Anthony started using again," she said.

"Really?" I tried to act surprised.

"Yeah, really," she said. "He hasn't missed an appointment yet, so maybe he's strung out somewhere. Maybe he's in the Heights—that's where he sometimes goes to score."

Feeling like an idiot for believing anything Anthony had told me, I said, "Well, I don't know where he is, but as soon as I hear from him, I'll tell him to get in touch with you."

"Yeah, you better do that," she said. After another long, suspicious glare, she added, "Have a nice day."

When she was gone, I was going to continue wiping down the place, then I thought, *What's the point?* When the body was discovered, Officer Singh would report that I'd been in the apartment, so covering my tracks didn't matter anymore. I just had to get the hell out of here.

Then my phone rang, only a number I didn't recognize displaying. Usually I let calls from unknown numbers go to voice mail, but I was so distracted that I picked up without really thinking it through.

"Hello?"

"Mr. Harper?"

"Who's this?"

"It's me, Marcus Freemont. Your attorney."

"Hey."

I prayed he had good news for me.

"There's been a development," he said.

*Development* didn't sound good.

"Okay," I said.

"Did you get a new criminal attorney yet?"

"What's going on?" An all too familiar feeling of dread was setting in.

"Detective Barasco wants you to come in again," he said.

"What the fuck? Why?"

"Calm down, it's not a disaster. I mean, not necessarily. He has new evidence apparently."

"That's insane. New evidence of what? I didn't do anything!"

"Where are you right now?"

I hesitated, deciding there was no way I was telling him where I was. So cops could swarm the place? There was no way I was going back to jail.

"I'm out," I said.

"Out where?"

"Walking?"

"I mean where're you *staying*?"

"What evidence? Tell me what the hell's going on."

"It would be better if we could meet, maybe at my office."

Yeah, right. Meet at his office so he could tell Barasco I was there? That wasn't an option either.

"Just tell me or I'm hanging up on you," I said.

"Okay, don't panic, but they found DNA. *Your* DNA on the victim."

"Of course they did," I said. "I gave her mouth-to-mouth. Is that all they've got?"

"Look, I only know what he told me five minutes ago," he said. "I don't know where the DNA was from, or what in particular he's referring to."

"It can only be from mouth-to-mouth!" I screamed.

"You've gotta relax, man," Freemont said.

"You call me and tell me the cops want to bring me in for something I didn't do and you want me *to relax*? I lost my job today, all right? I may've lost my fucking family. What the fuck have you lost?!"

I'd screamed so loud my throat hurt.

Remaining calm, he said, "Detective Barasco also said you tried to kidnap your kid from school today."

That son of a bitch school. The principal must've called Maria or maybe the police directly.

"I didn't try to kidnap him," I said. "I tried to give him a hug."

"I told you to stay away from him."

"It was just a hug."

I heard his deep breathing. I pictured him with his eyes closed, trying hard not to get flustered.

"Did you hire a criminal attorney or not?" he finally asked.

"I told you, I can't afford a lawyer. Look, I need time. Can you buy some time for me?"

"It doesn't work that way, Mr. Harper."

"What doesn't work what way?"

"If they have a warrant for your arrest, then you can't just—"

"Warrant? Who said anything about a warrant?"

"Nobody did."

"Then why did you just say it?"

"Because I assume that's his next step, that's all. He's probably getting a warrant right now, or trying to get one."

"Then stop him," I said. "That's your job—you're still my lawyer."

"There's nothing I can—" He cut himself off, then said, "Look, maybe a friend or family member can lend you money for a good criminal attorney."

"You know I don't have access to any money."

"Can you tell me where you're staying?"

"If you won't represent me, I'm not telling you shit."

"I didn't say I won't represent you, man. I'm just being honest, telling you what I'd tell my brother if he was in your situation."

"You'd tell your own brother to turn himself in, if you knew he was innocent?"

"Yes," he said. "Yes, I would."

"I think you're full of shit," I said. "That, or you don't believe I'm innocent."

I heard him deep breathe.

"I'll meet you, okay?" he said. "Come to the Manhattan South on 23rd. It looks much better in these instances if you come in on your own, if they don't have to pick you up. And who knows? Maybe they won't get a warrant, maybe it's all some sort of bluff. But we won't know that until we get down there and—"

I ended the call.

When he called back, I sent the call to voice mail. Then I went into settings and blocked his number.

There was no way I was going to an interrogation room with Nick Barasco again, subjecting myself to that barrage of bullshit.

I rushed out of the apartment, out of the building. I had one more option; then I'd be out of moves.

I would've rented a Zip Car or called an Uber, but without a credit card that wouldn't work. So I hailed a city cab.

"White Plains," I said. "As fast as you can get there."

# CHAPTER SEVENTEEN

"I DON'T GO to White Plains," the driver said.

Of course he did. What cabbie *wanted* to go to Westchester?

"You have to," I said.

"No, I only have go to the five boroughs," he said. "Get outta my cab."

"Look, this is an emergency," I said.

"I don't care," he said.

There was no way I was going out. Hard to find another taxi, and the next driver could have the same attitude.

"I'll give you a big tip."

"Sorry, I don't go to—"

"How much do you think the ride will cost?"

"Come on, buddy, just—"

"I'll pay you double the fare."

"It's sixty dollars at least."

"Here, how's one twenty?"

I showed him the bills. This would only leave me with twenty-seven dollars from the money Anthony had given me. I'd have enough to afford a train ticket back to the city. After that, I had no idea where I'd get money for food or—oh, yeah—where I'd sleep tonight, but I'd worry about that later.

"Okay," the driver said. "Get in."

I didn't really have a plan—well, a full plan—but I knew I had to do something to clear my name, make this whole thing go away. I'd go to Lawrence Ward's house, use my phone as a voice recorder, somehow get a confession, and then replay it for the police. I knew the whole idea was risky, maybe crazy, but, seriously, at this point what did I have to lose? After all, I'd already lost everything important to me. Was it a better idea to wait for Barasco to bring me in again and rely on my out-of-his-league Legal Aid lawyer to fight whatever charges he tried to bring up against me?

In White Plains, we passed houses—really estates—that had to go for five million or more. Then we reached Lawrence Ward's house, which wasn't the nicest in the neighborhood, but it was damn close. It was a contemporary, probably with four or five bedrooms on about an acre and a half. It looked even nicer than it had on Google Earth.

After I paid the driver—he clearly wasn't happy that I'd stiffed him on a tip—I headed along the stone walkway toward the brick stoop and the house's main entrance. A gray-haired guy raking leaves in front of the house next door glanced at me, then resumed raking.

Halfway along the walkway, I stopped and opened the voice memos app on my phone and pressed record. I had no idea what I would say to Lawrence or how I would get him to confess, but I wasn't going to leave here without *something* to use against him.

I continued up the stoop to the front door, rang the bell, and waited. I didn't hear anyone coming. It was very possible he wasn't home. I didn't know why this thought hadn't occurred to me sooner, but if he'd killed Anthony, he could've gone somewhere else afterward, maybe back to work.

As I rang the bell again, I flashed back to when I'd arrived at the townhouse in Manhattan, maybe a minute before I'd discovered

Sophie Ward's body. If I could've returned to that evening in Manhattan, had a do-over, I never would've gone into the townhouse. I would've gone home, to my wife and son, where I belonged.

Maybe coming here to confront Lawrence was an awful idea. My instincts were telling me to learn from my mistakes, to walk away. Better yet, run.

But when had I ever listened to my instincts? Besides, it was too late to leave now. I heard footsteps approaching. A second later, the door opened.

It was hard to tell in the picture I'd seen online, but I'd expected Lawrence Ward to be a foreboding, muscular guy. Instead, I was facing a wiry guy, about my height, with a neatly trimmed dark beard.

"Yes, can I help you?" he asked.

He didn't sound like I'd expected either. His voice was high-pitched, whiney.

"Lawrence Ward?" I asked.

Then he squinted and said, "Wait, I recognize you. You're *him*. You're Jack Harper."

I glanced at his clothes—he was wearing dark jeans and an untucked gray dress shirt—to see if there was any obvious evidence that he'd killed Anthony, like blood on his sleeves, but I didn't see anything. Of course, that didn't mean he hadn't showered and changed; he'd had enough time to.

"I know you killed your wife and my friend, or had them killed," I said.

"Son of a bitch," he said, and tried to close the door.

I shifted, blocking the door, then forced my way into the house. I still didn't have a real plan, but once you force your way into a stranger's house, there's no turning back.

The foyer was practically the size of my entire apartment, and beyond it was a dramatic winding staircase.

Backing away from me, into the living room area, Lawrence had his cell phone out, and was saying, "I'm calling the cops."

"Go ahead, call 'em," I said. "You can confess everything to them, too."

"No," he said, "I'm calling them so they can arrest you for breaking into my house, you crazy son of a bitch."

I knew this wouldn't sound *great* in my recording. I needed a confession, or something that incriminated him in the murders.

"So, make the call," I said. "I'll wait here, and we can tell the police together."

Of course, as a wanted murder suspect, I didn't want to chat with the police, but I also wanted to call Lawrence's bluff.

After mulling it for a couple of beats, all of a sudden he turned and rushed back toward the huge chef's kitchen. There were a rack of knives on the counter. He grabbed the largest one.

Wheeling back around toward me, he aimed the knife at me like a sword.

"Interesting choice," I said. "Since I just saw Anthony's body with a knife in his back."

"You have no idea what you're dealing with," he said.

Was that a confession? Sounded like it, but I needed more.

Before I could get him to elaborate, he lunged at me with the knife. If I didn't back away at the last moment, he would've stabbed me in the chest.

"Hey," I said, "what the fuh—"

Lawrence swiped at me again, skimming my arm.

I might've screamed, thinking, *How'd this happen?* A couple of weeks ago, I was a normal Upper East Side dad/real estate agent, hanging out with my son in playgrounds after school. Now I was fighting for my life with a crazed killer.

When he tried to attack me with the knife again, I grabbed his forearm above his hand gripping the handle. He was much stronger than he looked, and it was easy to imagine him killing Anthony and Sophie. I saw the cold, evil determination in his eyes, and I knew he wouldn't let me leave here alive. My only chance was to get the blade away and somehow subdue him.

He was relentless. I was squeezing his arm as hard as I could, trying to keep him away, but I couldn't hold him back. The tip of the blade was maybe two inches away from my neck. If I gave in, for just an instant, the blade would go into my neck.

I was thinking about Jonah. How I didn't want him to grow up without a father. How I wanted to be there for him.

Maybe these thoughts helped me garner a little more strength because I could tell that Ward's grip on the knife was starting to loosen, and then it fell, clanging onto the floor.

As Ward reached for the knife, I tackled him, and we fell onto the floor. I'd lost control, acting impulsively. He tried to push me off him, but I took control, managing to flip him on to his back. I punched him in the face and heard something crunch. I punched him again and again, using both fists. For a few moments, I felt like I was outside myself, watching Jack Harper beat the crap out of Lawrence Ward. It had been a long time since Jack Harper had hit someone, and Jack Harper had to admit that it felt exhilarating, freeing.

I had my hands around Ward's throat. I must've been squeezing for a while because his face went reddish purple, and he didn't seem to be breathing. I didn't stop squeezing though, telling myself that this asshole had cost me my marriage, my job, maybe custody of my son, and I told myself that if I just kept squeezing, if I didn't let up, I could make all of my pain go away.

Then, when I realized I was squeezing the neck of a dead man, I let go.

My rage had turned to panic.

*This isn't happening . . . Maybe he isn't dead.*

No, his eyes were open and still. Definitely dead.

"Fuck," I said. "Fuck, fuck, fuck, fuck, fuck."

Pacing like a caged animal, I tried to figure out what to do. Run? Hide the body? Call the cops? All the options seemed bad, especially the last one. How could I possibly explain what had happened to the police? Even if I convinced them that I'd come to White Plains to get a confession from Ward, would they believe that he'd tried to attack me with the knife before I'd strangled him? Probably not. And, worse, I hadn't gotten the confession from Ward. The only semi-incriminating statement he made was, *You have no idea what you're dealing with.* On my recording, it would sound like I'd broken in and attacked him.

I stopped pacing, trying to focus. The room felt like it was wobbling and my spiraling thoughts made less and less sense.

I decided I had to leave, but first I had to cover my tracks. There were napkins on the kitchen counter. I wetted a wad of them and then wiped the doorknob and the floor around Lawrence's body. I tried not to look at the body, holding my hand up in front of my face. Why was I getting a feeling of déjà vu? Cleaning up crime scenes was starting to feel like a bad habit.

Then I noticed blood on my arm from where Lawrence had cut me. It wasn't a deep wound, but the blood looked like it might have dripped. Great, so now I'd be leaving blood behind, as well as hair fibers and God knew what else.

I was searching for a drop of blood somewhere on the wooden floor when I heard the police siren. Was it a coincidence, a police car headed somewhere else in the neighborhood? Or had someone called the cops on *me*? The neighbor, I suddenly remembered. He'd probably seen me force my way into Ward's house.

I backed away, stumbling a little, but careful not to touch anything; like it mattered. I left the house and sprinted out to the sidewalk. The siren was getting louder. Not wanting to be too conspicuous, I walked as fast I could, with my head down slightly. At the corner, I turned right. I knew this was the general direction of downtown White Plains, but I had no real destination—I just wanted to get away.

At the next corner, I looked back over my shoulder and saw the speeding police car turn on to Lawrence Ward's block. Coming from the distance, I heard another siren. This officially was not a coincidence.

To hell with walking—I ran as fast as I could, maybe faster than I'd ever run in my life. I just wanted to get away, put as much distance as I could between myself and the house. I told myself that I was making up the nosy neighbor story, the police could've been going there for many reasons, but this didn't give me any reassurance. Even if no one had seen me in the house, the police would find plenty of damning physical evidence—including my blood. Even if the neighbor couldn't ID me, there was someone who definitely could—the cab driver. When the cabbie heard about a body discovered in White Plains, he'd remember that he'd dropped me off at the house. This was worse than Sophie's murder—there was much more evidence against me this time. I even had motive for wanting to kill Lawrence as I'd been telling Barasco for days that he had killed her. Barasco could easily create a story that I'd come to White Plains looking for revenge.

Gasping, I had to walk for a while. Up here I had no chance; if the local cops weren't looking for me already, they would be soon.

The city—I had to get back to the city. I'd feel safer in crowds.

Using Google Maps, I saw that the White Plains Metro North station was about a mile away. I ran about a block, then slowed to a walk as the ambulance I'd heard zipped past me. Then I continued, alternating walking, jogging, and running. It was the longest mile I'd ever traveled. Finally I saw the power lines of the train tracks up ahead, and then the concrete, industrial-looking train station.

In the ticket area, I checked the schedule—the next train would arrive in twelve minutes. It was better than having to wait an hour, but time wasn't on my side.

From a ticket machine, using cash, I bought a one-way ticket to Grand Central. Now I only had about twenty bucks left, but it really didn't matter. The police had probably discovered the body about ten, fifteen minutes ago. If somebody had tipped them off about me, or they suspected me just because I was already a person of interest, then there would be a—what did the police call it? APB—yeah, an APB on me. One of the first places they'd check would be the train station.

While there were only a few people in the waiting area, I felt uncomfortable. In the state I was in, with my agitation heightened, I was afraid someone would notice me.

So I went up to the platform, toward where the back of the train would arrive, and where no one was waiting.

Okay, only eight minutes now until the train arrived. I was feeling a little better about my chances of making it back to the city.

Until I saw the transit cop arrive on the platform.

He'd come up the same steps I'd come up. He was stocky with thick gray hair and a mustache. He stopped near the middle of the platform and then turned in my direction. He seemed to be looking right at me, and then he began walking along the platform in my direction.

I had nowhere to go. There were no exits at this end of the platform—I'd cornered myself. I could jump onto the tracks, but if the transit cop had really recognized me, how far could I get?

So I stayed where I was and stared at my phone intently, as if preabsorbed. My only chance was that he didn't know who I was and was walking toward me for some other reason.

I heard his footsteps approaching, then saw him in my peripheral vision.

"It's running behind."

His voice had startled the shit out of me, but I tried to react naturally, unfazed.

"Sorry?" I said.

"The train," he said. "Signal problems at Fordham. Everything's behind."

"Oh. That's too bad."

I continued staring at my phone, hoping he'd leave me alone.

"You live in the city?" he asked.

He didn't seem to have any idea who I was, but, my luck, I had to meet a chatty transit cop.

"Yeah," I said, hoping the one-word answers would give him the not-so-subtle message that I wanted to be left alone.

"Grew up in the Bronx," he said. "Two blocks from Yankee Stadium. Man, that neighborhood's changed. Back in the day, off season, the place was a ghost town. Now they got bars with fuckin' happy hours there."

I didn't say anything, hoping he'd leave, pretending to be busy tapping out an email.

"You Yankees or Mets?" he asked.

*Seriously?*

"Sorry, I just need to send something," I said.

"Whoa." He sounded offended. "You don't have to be rude about it. Just thought I'd tell you about the delays in case you wanted to know."

"How long's the delay?"

"Now you being friendly?" He sounded like a disappointed teacher. "Was a half hour before, but they got it cleared up. Should only be five or ten minutes."

"Thanks," I said.

He muttered something that included the word "nasty" and walked away.

I looked down the track, hoping to see the light of a train approaching, but there were no trains as far north as I could see. At least I'd gotten rid of the transit cop, but the exchange hadn't helped my situation. If he got an APB on me, he'd remember me and my rudeness.

While I was staring at my phone, I figured I might as well Google myself, to see if I was a murder suspect. Nothing new came up in the results, but that didn't give me much reassurance. It would take time before anything about Lawrence Ward's death made it into the news.

*Lawrence Ward's death.*

I'd been in such a frenzy to get away from the house, I hadn't fully processed what I'd done.

I'd killed him. Actually killed him.

I'd had no choice. If I didn't kill him, he would've killed me. But is that how it would look to a jury? I'd come to his house, and I had plenty of motive to kill him. Maybe I could make a case; maybe forensics would support my case. This seemed unlikely, though, what with a Legal Aid lawyer defending me. And what about Sophie's murder? I'd still be on the hook for that, especially since the guy who could prove that I hadn't killed Sophie was dead.

Then I had a thought that actually made me shudder. What if Lawrence Ward hadn't killed his wife or Anthony? What if evidence at Anthony's apartment implicated someone else? Then I'd just killed an innocent man.

One positive about panic—it helps time pass. A southbound train had appeared in the distance, and a couple of minutes later, it arrived at the station.

I boarded the nearly empty car and had three seats to myself. As the train pulled away, I stared out of the blotchy window, at the bleak industrial landscape, my thoughts swirling, thinking about everything that had happened since meeting Rob for lunch that day, to going on Discreet Hookups, to meeting Sophie, to becoming a murder suspect, to possibly becoming a murder suspect again.

"It's insanity," I said.

At least I was aware I was talking out loud, which meant I wasn't insane.

Or did it?

At many times in my life I'd felt insane. Those times were usually associated with drinking, but could I blame everything on alcohol? Everyone in recovery knows that alcohol is just the symptom.

I'd killed Lawrence Ward, so maybe I'd killed Anthony and Sophie, too, and had just blocked it out. Maybe discovering two bodies didn't seem like a coincidence, because it *wasn't* a coincidence. Maybe nobody was setting me up because I was the only killer.

I had to admit—it seemed as logical as any of my other theories. All this time I'd been telling myself that Barasco had some sort of vendetta against me, but maybe he'd been focusing on me for good reason. Hell, if I were the detective in charge of this case, I'd focus on me, too. I had been arrested before for assault, I had a history of violence, and I'd been at, not one or two, but *three* murder scenes, with motives for two. Maybe Sophie had threatened me, said she'd tell Maria that I'd met her on Discreet Hookups, so I'd snapped and killed her. See? It all made sense. That would explain why her blood had been on me, and why I'd been trying to convince Barasco that Lawrence Ward was the actual killer. Which led to my motive for killing Lawrence—so the police couldn't verify his alibi for the first murder. It hadn't been self-defense, as I'd been telling myself. I'd murdered him with the intention of blaming a "hit man."

I had to get a hold of myself. I was starting to lose it—as I had those other times.

I took a deep breath, tried to focus.

*Step two: Came to believe that a Power greater than ourselves can restore us to sanity.*

"Come on, God, if you really can restore people to sanity, restore me now."

Just because I'd had crazy episodes didn't mean I *was* crazy. I was sober now, I was a dad, I was a good person. I'd made some mistakes, but I'd gotten on a path, and none of that had changed when I'd met Sophie Ward.

But was this true, or was my belief that I wasn't crazy just another rationalization? After all, I'd always been a master of rationalizing my bad behavior, so if I *had* snapped and killed a couple of people, why would I admit it to myself? I'd even blacked out before, had long and short gaps in my memory, so why couldn't that have happened again? My past blackouts had been related to drinking, but had drinking been the real cause? Or maybe I had been drinking all along and had been in some kind of crazed state of denial all this time.

"Hey."

"What?" I nearly screamed.

The conductor, a heavyset guy, was waiting for my ticket.

"Oh, sorry," I muttered as I dug into my pocket.

"You okay, pal?"

"Yeah, fine. You just, uh, startled me."

I gave him my ticket and he placed another one into the holder atop the seat in front of me.

He gave me a long look, then went and took the ticket of somebody behind me.

I still felt crazy, but that didn't mean I *was* crazy. I was just caught in the maze, that's all, but—I reminded myself—I'd been caught in mazes before and had always found my way out.

I had to keep searching.

* * *

Though my ticket was to Grand Central, I got out at Harlem. I was antsy on the train, felt trapped, and I had no real destination anyway. I just needed air; needed to move.

Wandering along mobbed 125th Street, I felt much safer and more anonymous than I had in White Plains. No one even looked at me; I could've been invisible. City people were so caught up in their own dramas that no one cared about mine—that's what I told myself anyway.

I headed downtown on Lexington. After a few blocks, I checked the local news on my phone, to see if there was anything new about me.

There was—a few articles, but with the same content.

I read the headline: MAN FOUND DEAD IN WHITE PLAINS, SUSPECT AT LARGE.

There was only one paragraph, mentioning how I'd been a person of interest in the murder of Sophie Ward and now was wanted for murdering Lawrence Ward.

I was terrified—not for myself, because I knew the police would come after me—but for what Maria and Jonah would think when they found out. For Maria, it would just confirm what she'd already feared about me. I didn't know what she'd told Jonah, but Jonah had to know that I'd done something bad in order for the school to ban me from seeing him. When this news broke, though, Jonah would be certain to hear about it, and he'd grow up thinking his dad was a killer, and who knows? Maybe he'd be right.

Crossing the street, walking slowly, feeling dazed, I knew I didn't have much time. That transit cop in White Plains knew I had headed back to the city, and the conductor had seen me as well. Returning to Anthony's apartment was out because Officer Singh knew I'd been there.

Every option led to a dead end; I was out of moves.

Or was I?

There was one way out of the maze—the option that had always been there. It had been my way out of trouble since I had my first drink when I was fourteen years old. Alcohol had never been the source of my problems, but it had always been my easiest escape.

And, wouldn't you know it? There was a liquor store on the next corner. I went in, grabbed a bottle of Bushmills from the shelf, and paid for it, using almost all of my remaining money.

Knowing New York City was serious these days about enforcing the "open bottle law," I went around the corner and ducked into an alley. I opened the bottle and drank as much as I could until my throat burned and I needed to take a breath. Drinking felt natural, like I'd never quit, and maybe I hadn't. Maybe those times at A.A.—my tearful speeches at my annual anniversaries—had been total bullshit. Maybe quitting had just been another lie I'd told myself that I wanted to believe.

* * *

"Hey, asshole . . . Hey, asshole."

I opened my eyes, slow to realize that I was splayed in the vestibule of a building. A guy was pushing a door against the back of my head.

"Yeah, yeah, okay," I slurred.

I shifted enough for him to jimmy past me. He was Latino, maybe in his sixties.

"You better be outta here by the time I get back or I'm callin' the cops," he said. "Fuckin' bums, cloggin' up my halls."

The guy left. When he got outside he was still yelling at me, but I couldn't make out what he was saying.

I still had no idea where I was, or how I'd gotten here. I remembered being in the alley, taking the swig of whiskey, and then everything had gone black.

Failure and self-loathing struck me with a lethal combination—I drank again, I got *drunk*. All the time, energy, and commitment I'd put into resisting alcohol for years—six years and over five months, to be exact—had been wiped out with one bad decision.

I struggled and finally got to my feet. I was still drunk, or at least buzzed, the whiskey odor on my breath. I had my phone and wallet with me and the keys to my apartment. I had to get home to have dinner with Maria and Jonah, and then get Jonah ready for school.

Then I experienced the jolt, the sudden light-headedness you get when you receive devastating news, as I remembered that I didn't have a family anymore and was wanted for two murders. I cried—no, sobbed. I hadn't cried like this since my dog died when I was eleven years old. But this was worse—much, much worse. I'd lost my whole family and the reasons why seemed absurd, fake, like they weren't even my reasons. They had been the reasons of some other Jack Harper who'd inhabited my body for a while, but now the real Jack Harper was back, and I just wanted to have my typical, dull, semi-miserable life back. Maybe I'd been afraid to settle, felt I deserved more, but if I could go back, I wouldn't complain because I'd know that if you make dramatic changes, things can get better, but they can also get much, much worse.

But unfortunately this wasn't *It's a Wonderful Life*. I couldn't go back and make different choices. The mistakes I'd made were irrevocable and nothing was going to save me.

On the street, I thought I'd recognize something, but I didn't. Well, aside from recognizing that I was somewhere in Manhattan; then it clicked that I was in Spanish Harlem. Baby steps, right?

It was still light out, but it was getting dark. As I headed down the block, toward the nearest intersection, I glanced at my watch—5:38. It seemed like I'd only "missed" an hour or two, but it was still terrifying—not just that I'd blacked out from drinking, but that the experience seemed so familiar. Maybe I'd been drinking and blacking out all along and was just beginning to be honest with myself.

I saw the street signs as I approached the corner—117th and Madison. I wasn't far from the alley I'd gone in to drink. I'd bought the booze to escape, but as always, the escape didn't last long enough. I guess that was to be expected though; if the escape lasted permanently, there wouldn't be any alcoholics.

Sadly, even if I wanted one, I couldn't afford another escape; I couldn't even afford to get anything to eat. If I showed up in a homeless center, or for a free meal at a church, how long would it take somebody to recognize me?

I'd told a friend in college—after another friend had killed himself by jumping from the roof of the science building—that I would never want to kill myself, because I could always find one thing to live for. Well, that had been a lie, because as I tried to come up with a list of reasons to live, I couldn't come up with a single one. Jonah wasn't even a compelling reason to live; in fact, he was a reason to die. What son needs to grow up with the stigma of having a father who's serving a life sentence in prison? I couldn't possibly have any positive influence on his life; I'd be an albatross. But if I died tonight—ah, if I died!—he'd still have to grow up without a father, and with the stigma of what I'd done. But, eventually, I'd be forgotten, and Maria was an attractive woman, she'd meet someone else. There was still hope for Jonah to have a normal, happy life, but that hope didn't include me.

Before I ended my life, I needed to do one good thing for Jonah, something that would make him happier and that would cause him to think about me in a positive way. Actually, the idea had been percolating in the back of my mind for a couple of days—since my night in prison. It would be tough to pull off, but why not try?

As I walked, I called the California number. Rob McEvoy picked up before the first ring, then said, in his smooth, smarmy voice, "Hey, my brother."

I hadn't rehearsed, or even thought through, what I'd say to him—I was totally winging it.

"We have to talk," I said.

"Sorry I've been out of touch," he said. "Didn't mean to flake, but life's been crazy."

*His* life's been crazy?

"You think I give a shit?" I said.

"Whoa." He sounded shocked. "What did I say?"

"Yeah," I said, "like you don't remember?"

"Remember what? Are you okay, man?"

"No, actually not okay. I'm actually pretty much as far away from okay as you can possibly get."

"If this is about the apartment, I said I was sorry," he said. "Life got in the way. It's not that I'm not interested. I totally am. It's just that—"

"I don't give a fuck about the apartment," I said, "and I don't give a fuck about you, you lying, cheating son of a bitch."

He'd never been a friend, and now that we weren't in a band together, and he wasn't even a potential client anymore, I didn't have to be on eggshells; I could let loose, not kiss ass and pretend I liked him.

"Look, man, I don't know what's going on, if you think you're being funny or whatever, but I have to—"

"You're gonna do whatever I tell you to do," I said.

"What the fuck?"

On the phone, in the background, I heard cars honking.

"Where the hell are you?" I asked.

"Manhattan actually," he said.

He was in the *city*?

"Where in Manhattan?" I asked.

"Midtown," he said. "I meant to give you a buzz to let you know I'd be in town again but, like I said, things have been crazy. When I got back to L.A. things got sort of, well, out of hand. So I've been dealing with that, then this big deal that I'm about to close and . . . Anyway, I'm heading into a meeting now. Can I call you back?"

I could tell he just wanted to get rid of me. Yeah, right.

"No, not later," I said. "Meet me right now."

"Look, man, I just told you I'm—"

"You think I give a fuck about your meeting? Is your life more important to you than your meeting?"

"Look, I'm hanging up on you—"

"Hang up, I'll destroy your life the way you destroyed mine."

That was good—I was proud of myself for coming up with that on the fly.

"Jack, what's going on, man? Why the fuck're you acting this way?"

"Meet me now."

"I'm walking into drinks at Soho House with a top recording artist and his manager. I can't just—"

"Meet me or you'll never see your wife and kids again. Your choice."

I sounded like the villain in a Bond movie, but there was nothing jokey about my tone. I was on a roll.

"Jack, dude. What the fuck?"

There was fear in Rob's tone. He was catching on that I wasn't bullshitting.

Keeping the intensity going, I said, "You heard me, you fucking prick."

"Look, I don't know what's going on, but maybe you should just chill for a while. Are you home? Can your wife help you?"

"I don't have a wife anymore," I said. "And if I call your wife and tell her everything I know about you and Discreet Hookups, my bet is you won't have a wife either."

Long pause—all I heard were cars honking. My threats were clearly resonating.

"Come on, what's going on, Jack?" he finally asked. "Is this a joke? You fucking with me?"

"If I end this call, your life's over, Rob."

"Jack, what the—"

"One—"

"Jack, why would—"

"Two."

"Okay. Okay, I'll meet you, I'll meet you. Just calm down, all right?"

"I'll text you instructions," I said, and ended the call.

Finally, I felt like a winner.

# CHAPTER EIGHTEEN

I TEXTED ROB to meet me at the Starbucks at 96th and Lexington. When he arrived, I was waiting near the door. I immediately noticed that this wasn't affable Rob from a couple of weeks ago. This was pissed-off, terrified-as-shit Rob.

It was a beautiful thing to see.

He looked around, like he didn't spot me right away, even though I was only about ten feet away, leaning against the counter by the window, staring right at him. Then his gaze settled on mine and he seemed surprised, taken aback, by my appearance no doubt. I probably looked, appropriately, like I'd been through hell.

Meanwhile, he looked like his usual slick, smarmy self. He was in expensive jeans, looked like Diesel, an untucked black button-down, a designer sport jacket, and recently shined shoes. He looked so groomed-looking, so clean, so arrogant. Everything about him disgusted me.

He came over to me. A couple of people were close by—a long-haired guy tapping away on his laptop and a woman chatting on her phone.

"Please." He sounded short of breath. "Tell me this is all a joke, man. You're pissed off I flaked on the apartment. That's what this is about, right?"

"Gimme twenty dollars," I said.

"What?"

"You heard me. Twenty. Right now."

The guy on the laptop looked over. Rob, seeming maybe relieved because he thought he was going to get off by giving me twenty bucks—yeah, right—opened his wallet and handed me a twenty.

I got in line and when it was my turn, I bought a turkey sandwich, two muffins, and two packages of mixed nuts. I didn't care what I was buying; I was starving and needed food.

When I returned to Rob, I'd already stuffed about half a muffin in my mouth and I couldn't chew fast enough. I didn't care that I had crumbs all over my chin.

"What's going on with you, Jack? Are you okay? Maybe you should, like, talk to somebody."

"A shrink!" I screamed. "You think I need a shrink?"

People around, including laptop dude, were looking over at me.

Paranoid that somebody in here would recognize me and call the cops before I had a chance to do what I needed to do, I said, "Let's go. Across the street to the playground."

"Why?" Rob asked.

"Let's go."

I'd taken Jonah to this playground many times over the years. He loved the artificial "Rivers of the World" stream. We used to find twigs and then race each other—whosever twig made it to the end of the stream first was the winner.

The playground was empty now, and dark—the only light from lampposts on 96th and Lexington. I sat on a bench, the same bench I used to sit and watch Jonah play when he was a few years old—not letting him out of my sight. Those happy memories of being a stay-at-home dad contrasted sharply with where I was now and seemed to be almost mocking me.

"Now you gonna tell me what the fuck is going on?" Rob said. "I don't know why I'm sitting here, feeding you muffins in a playground, when I'm supposed to be in a meeting, hashing out a multimillion-dollar licensing deal."

"Good to know you'll have some money coming in," I said. "You're gonna need it."

"What's that suppo—" Rob winced, catching a whiff of my breath.

"Are you *drunk*?" he asked.

"Was," I said.

"I thought you quit drinking."

After I swallowed another bite of muffin, I said, "We're here to talk about you, not me."

"What about me? What do you want, Jack?"

"Two hundred thousand dollars."

He gave me a look like he hoped I was joking.

"I'm serious, what do you—"

"Oh, I'm very serious, too. Two hundred thousand is the commission I would've gotten if you bought that apartment. And you should feel lucky, getting off easy after what you did."

Actually two hundred thousand was way more than what I would've gotten for my commission, but Rob didn't have to know that.

"Did?" Rob said. "What did I do except not make an offer on an apartment?"

"You told me about Discreet Hookups," I said.

He paused, absorbing this, trying to make sense of what I was saying.

Then he said, "So?"

"So that site led to me ruining my life, and now I'm going to ruin yours. Well, unless you pay me."

"Whoa, slow down," he said. "So that's what this is really about? You went on that site?"

"Yes," I said.

"Why?" he asked.

I thought of the reasons—unhappy in my marriage, insecure in general, midlife crisis, craving for excitement—but nothing seemed to explain it in full.

So I said, "If you didn't tell me about the site, I never would've gone on it. I'd still be living in my apartment, with my son who I love more than anything, and oh yeah—my marriage wouldn't be over and I'd have access to my bank account."

"Is this some kind of joke?" he asked. "Did one of the guys from the old band put you up to this?"

He looked around, as if maybe hoping to see Tommy, our old drummer, jump out from behind a tree.

"About the money," I said. "I'll text you my wire transfer info and you can transfer the money into my account as soon as I leave here."

"You're out of your mind," he said.

"You're right, I probably am," I said, remembering my recent blackout. "But what does that have to do with anything?"

"Why would I give you a fuckin' cent?" he said.

"So your wife doesn't find out about what a cheating scumbag she's been married to all these years?"

"You wouldn't tell my wife anything."

"I wouldn't?"

He could tell I was serious.

"Look, man," he said, "I don't know what happened to you on that site, and if you think I'm responsible, I'm sorry for whatever I did, or said, or whatever, okay? But, please, cut me some slack, bro. My life's complicated as fuck right now, man. The shit hit the fan when I got back to L.A. after my last New York trip, okay? A woman I'd fooled around with a few times, a waitress from Swinger's, came by the house and—well, you can imagine how that scene went down. You were right, bro—I was playing with fire the whole time. I don't know how I was deluded, so oblivious. Anyway, I went to my healer and talked it through and I decided to cash out while I was still ahead. Figure I've had my fun, sowed my middle-aged oats, and now I can focus on my family again. The wife and I, we had a long talk. It was really amazing—we opened up to each other in a way we hadn't in years. It was like we'd been chatting for years, but we were finally having a *talk*. Anyway, we're going into counseling, gonna try to work shit out. We have our first session set up for when I return to the coast. So, as you can imagine, the last thing I need in my life right now is any more drama."

He was obviously pandering, trying to get my sympathy. He'd always been a big drama queen, going back to our days in the band. Whenever he was unhappy about a song selection or there was some other conflict, he'd go on about whatever his drama *du jour* was, in an attempt to manipulate the situation.

But that wasn't going to work this time.

"So you're staying in your marriage," I said, trying to stay calm.

"That's the plan," he said. "I mean I never had any intention of leaving, as you know. My wife, God bless her, gets it. She knows how hard monogamy is, so she's willing to hear me out. But I'm still jonesing for that apartment. My wife and I'll use it—it'll be good for us to, you know, rekindle. Maybe we'll give it to one of the kids someday. My girl wants to go to NYU—maybe she'll stay in the city. What I'm trying to say is, you'll get your commish, all right? If not on this apartment, then another one. And I, for one, am willing to forget today ever happened."

The idea that Rob was staying in his marriage, that he wouldn't lose anything, made me even more determined to fuck him over.

"I know her number," I said.

"Who's number?" He seemed confused.

"Your wife—Julianne," I said. "It's public, on Facebook. I already have it programmed into my phone."

I showed him my phone with his wife's number, which I'd entered while waiting for him at Starbucks.

"Why're you doing this?" he asked.

"Revenge," I said.

"Revenge? I didn't even do anything to you." He paused, squinting. "Wait, what happened to you on Discreet Hookups?"

"You'll hear about it in the news," I said.

"The *news*?"

"About the two hundred thou," I said. "Wire transfer's probably the best way. When I leave, I'll give you fifteen minutes to get it done. I know there'll be a lag before the money appears in my account, but you can CC me the wire details. If I don't get those details in fifteen minutes, your wife gets a phone call, and you can forget about rekindling. You think she's understanding? Well, let's see how understanding she is when she hears about all the trolling you've done on D-Ho. You'll be lucky if your kids ever even want to talk to you again. If there's a God—and I believe there is—you'll wind up on the street, sleeping in vestibules."

"Two things," Rob said. "One, I don't know what the fuck you're talking about. Two, there's no way I'm wiring you that money."

"Then say goodbye to your family," I said.

As I stood, he grabbed me by the wrist.

"I don't have two hundred thousand dollars lying around," he said.

"If you were ready to plunk down two million dollars on an apartment you were planning to use as a fuck pad, you can afford to give me ten percent. My *deserved* ten percent."

I saw the terror in his eyes.

Still gripping me, he said, "I get it now. I was confused for a while, maybe 'cause this all caught me off-guard, but now it's so obvious. This is all because of jealousy, isn't it? You're jealous, not because I had more talent—you had tons of talent, too—but because you couldn't let go of the dream like I did. I moved on, but you stayed in fantasy land, thinking you were gonna be a rock star someday. I meet guys like you all the time—fuckin' dreamers, afraid to take risks. You can't deal with the fact that I made it and you didn't, so this is the only solution your sick mind can come up with—to try to take it away from me."

"I had a good career," I said. "I was making money."

"Yeah, as a studio musician, with all the other failed wannabes. It must suck to be you—feeling like the industry fucked you over, feeling like successful guys like me got what you deserve. Is that why you were cheating on your wife? Because you felt empty inside? Because you had nothing going on, except trying to sell a fucking apartment? I bet you blame her, too, but you should be blaming yourself."

I yanked my arm free, then said, "I'll be checking my email."

As I unlinked the kiddie gate and exited the playground, I heard him scream behind me, "You're a fuckin' loser, Jack! A loser!"

"Not tonight I'm not," I said to myself.

I didn't feel bad for Rob, but I knew he was right. I was scapegoating him for my problems, the way I'd scapegoated people my whole life. My parents, Maria, promoters and managers who didn't give me a "fair shot." He didn't force me to go on to Discreet Hookups; hell, he hadn't even really encouraged me. I'd made that decision on my own. If I were counseling myself, I'd tell myself that I had to take responsibility for my actions.

"Fuck that," I said out loud as I headed down to the subway station at 96th and Lexington.

Just because Rob hadn't directly ruined my life didn't mean he was a good guy. He knew I was vulnerable, in a bad marriage, and he'd planted ideas in my head. He was like a lot of addicts I knew—trying to get people to sink as low as they felt inside. He was an empty man and he wanted me to feel empty, too. He deserved to lose everything, he deserved to suffer. This wasn't about revenge; this was about justice.

I checked to make sure there were no cops or MTA employees watching, then I jumped the turnstile.

On the platform, I waited for the train to arrive. I saw the light in the tunnel, felt a little wind, so it wouldn't be long.

I didn't know if Rob would actually go through with the wire transfer. He'd seemed sufficiently terrified when I'd left him, but it depended on how much his marriage actually meant to him. Either way, I felt like I'd done a good thing. If he wired the money, Maria and Jonah could use it to help have a happy, stress-free life. If he didn't do the transfer, well, at least I'd die knowing that, in the end, at least I'd tried to do something positive for my family.

The roar of the approaching train grew louder, the headlights blaring like the eyes of a vicious monster.

I was looking forward to death. It would be a relief from the shit show my life had turned into, that was for sure. I just wanted the pain to end. I wanted peace, darkness.

As I bent my knees, about to take my dive into eternity, I already felt the train's beautiful impact, the relief of my spiraling thoughts shutting down, when somebody tackled me, pinning me down to the concrete platform as the train whizzed by.

"Don't worry, I got ya, I got ya," the big guy said.

I heard a woman say, "Oh my God, I'll call nine-one-one."

Other people were just screaming.

I tried to get up, but the guy wouldn't let me budge, and then I was struck by what seemed like the worst realization possible.

I was alive.

# CHAPTER NINETEEN

THEY MUST'VE INJECTED me with something because I'd stopped screaming and was just staring at the roof of the ambulance, trying to prepare for whatever came next.

As they carried me out of the ambulance toward a building, I glanced at the signage:

BELLEVUE

Figured. Where else would they take a guy who'd tried to jump in front of a train?

They took me to a small hospital room that had a bed, a table and chair, another chair in the corner, some equipment for examinations, and not much else. They didn't leave me alone. An aide, maybe some sort of guard, remained in my room at all times, obviously to make sure I didn't try to kill myself again.

Nurses and doctors examined me, like a normal physical, and then a psychiatrist, an attractive gray-haired woman named Dr. Lindsay, asked me questions, mainly about my general psychological state like:

"Do you ever feel helpless?"

"No."

"Do you ever feel alone and isolated?"

"No."

"Do you ever feel like you're not in control of the decisions you make?"

"Never."

I knew that she and the other doctors were just doing their jobs, but the last thing I wanted was for them to determine I was insane. If that happened, they might commit me, and I'd wind up on suicide watch indefinitely.

Why didn't I jump a second sooner? If I had, I would've been wiped out. I hadn't seen any newspapers or news online, but the guy who'd saved me was probably considered a hero. He thought he'd done a great thing, saved a good person.

If he only knew.

Although I felt calmer, thanks to whatever drugs they'd given me, I was still planning to jump in front of a train, or slit my wrists, or OD the first chance I got.

Or, if I wound up in jail, I'd kill myself there.

No one had mentioned anything to me about the police investigation, but they knew my name and had to know I was a murder suspect. Maybe they didn't want to alarm me, or maybe Barasco had instructed them to not mention anything about the murders.

Then Dr. Lindsay asked the question that she'd been building toward:

"Why did you try to kill yourself, Mr. Harper?"

"I didn't," I said.

She'd been entering all off my responses into an iPad. She added this one as well, then said, "Witnesses say you were about to jump in front of an oncoming train."

"Well, they're wrong," I said.

"But several people have reported seeing you about to—"

"I have no desire to kill myself, I swear. I love my life."

She entered this, then said, "Thank you for your cooperation, Mr. Harper. I'll let you rest now."

As she headed out, I asked, "How long do I have to stay here?"

At the door, she turned back and said, "I'm not in charge of that decision."

I sensed she was lying.

"You can't keep me for more than twenty-four hours, right?" I asked. "Isn't that the law?"

"Rest, Mr. Harper," she said as she left the room.

The aide remained in the room. His name was Cuvis. Hoping he'd be my ally in here, or at least give me information, I tried to strike up a rapport with him. But he wouldn't talk to me, unless it was about bodily functions. I asked him if I could have my phone back—my personal belongings had been taken away—and he told me I'd have to discuss that with the doctors. I noticed that there were no sharp objects around me—no pens and no knives, not even a plastic one was served with my dinner. I considered trying to jab the plastic fork into my throat but a) I didn't think it would kill me, and b) Cuvis was staring at me while I ate.

He even came into the bathroom with me.

"You're really gonna watch me shit, too?" I asked.

"Yes, I am." No bullshit tone; this was clearly his career, his wheelhouse—suicide watches.

I tried to go, but with an audience, I was too tensed up.

Back in the room, I said, "I guess it's true what they say—you know, about a watched pot never boiling."

Jeez, I couldn't even get the guy to smile.

* * *

The stagnant air with the combination faint odor of disinfectant and feces was sickening. The dinner last night reminded me of a cross between mediocre airplane food and the TV dinners my mother used to "prepare" for me when I was a kid. I wouldn't have minded going back to prison—if it meant getting out of Bellevue.

More nurses and doctors visited. I asked them when I would be allowed to leave, but they all avoided the question. Then a doctor told me I could discuss my situation with Dr. Lindsay.

When Dr. Lindsay returned, I said, "So what's going on? Are you going to release me today or what?"

"A detective from the NYPD wants to speak with you," she said.

"Nick Barasco?" I asked.

"Yes," she said. "Are you aware of why he wants to talk to you?"

"I don't have amnesia," I said. "I'm just surprised he didn't come sooner."

"He's wanted to talk to you since you were admitted here," she said.

Her gaze hardened as she studied my reaction.

"Oh, I get it," I said. "You wanted to make sure I'm sane. Well, I'm totally sane, okay, so you can send him in at any time."

"I highly suggest you consult with your lawyer first," she said. "The detective mentioned a lawyer who's represented you before." Dr. Lindsay looked at her iPad. "Marcus Freemont."

"He's not my lawyer," I said.

"Well, you should have someone—"

"I want to represent myself."

"I'm not sure it's a matter of *representing*, it's a matter of consulting. I really think you ought to talk to someone before you—"

"So what've you determined about me so far?" I asked. "You think I'm crazy? That's the bottom line, the elephant in the room, so let's just get it out in the open. What's your diagnosis, Doctor? Come on, let's hear it."

"You're experiencing extreme agitation," she said.

"That doesn't sound like medical lingo. You sure you're a doctor?"

She remained stone-faced.

"See?" I said. "You're the one who won't answer my questions, hiding behind your psychobabble, and you think *I'm* crazy?"

I felt abnormally hyper and unguarded, maybe some side effect of whatever drugs they'd been pumping me up with.

I wasn't looking at Cuvis, but I knew he was watching me, making sure I didn't lash out at the psychiatrist.

"I think you've been experiencing a lot of stress," she said, "and that's manifesting as—"

"You didn't answer my question," I said. "Am I crazy or not?"

"My job is to evaluate you, Mr. Harper, and—"

"I know what your fucking job is."

Cuvis came over, ready to escort Dr. Lindsay out of the room, but she held up her hand to him—the stop sign.

"To answer a question you asked me earlier," she said to me, "you'll be released when I determine you're fit to be released, and when the police feel it's safe to release you. There's no set time table, but remaining cooperative with the process is probably a good idea."

Great, now she sounded like Nurse Ratched from *One Flew Over the Cuckoo's Nest*.

"Fine, I'll do what you *suggest*," I said, leaning on suggest for a little passive-aggressiveness. "You want me to call Freemont, I'll call Freemont. Does that mean I can get my cell back?"

"*We'll* contact him," she said.

As she left the room, Cuvis didn't stop watching me.

* * *

I knew what their M.O. was. They'd keep me here until they gathered enough evidence to deem me crazy and commit me, maybe for life. Why did that guy have to grab me on the subway platform?

New York is full of assholes; my luck, I had to cross paths with the one nice guy.

Dr. Lindsay returned to my room and asked me many of the same questions she'd asked me during her first visit. This was obviously more of their grand plan to drive me insane. I tried to stay patient, but how long can anyone stay patient answering the same damn questions over and over again. Eventually I raised my voice—didn't shout, just raised it—and she tapped something into her iPad.

Their plan was so effective that even I began to wonder if I was crazy, and the belief that I wasn't crazy, and they were just trying to make me think I was crazy, was a manifestation of my craziness.

See how twisted they were making me?

* * *

I was at the desk, picking at another delicious TV dinner, when Freemont arrived. He looked at me, I thought, in a disappointed way, like a parent who'd been called to school because his kid has been sent to the principal's office.

"We meet again," he said.

"Hey," I said. "I'd invite you to join me, but I don't think you'd be into the recycled turkey."

Ignoring my attempt at an ice-breaking joke, he glanced at Cuvis, who was sitting stone-faced in the corner—hey, maybe it was my delivery—then said, "Can you wait outside?"

"Yeah, but I'll have to keep the door open," Cuvis said.

Freemont sat in the chair that Cuvis had vacated. "This would've been a lot easier if you turned yourself in like I suggested."

"I want to confess," I said.

"Confess, huh?"

"That's right," I said. "I killed Sophie Ward, then I killed Anthony Sorrentino and Lawrence Ward. I'm a cold-blooded murderer. You know how they say the killers are the ones you least expect? The nice guy who goes to work every day? The husband, the father? Well, that's me. I'm a nice guy on the outside, evil on the inside. But I didn't try to kill myself. I don't want to go for an insanity plea because I'm not insane."

The best-case scenario for me would be a quick conviction and a death sentence. Unlikely in New York, but it was worth a shot. Otherwise, I'd kill myself in my jail cell the first opportunity I got. Well, that was my plan anyway.

"I agree with you," he said.

"Agree with what?"

"That you're not insane. I had a talk with Dr. Lindsay. She says you have no signs of mental illness, you're just playing games with yourself—her words not mine. You feel guilty about things so you want to take responsibility, but I'm here to tell you, you can let go of all that now. I think you're gonna walk."

"I don't understand," I said. "What're you talking about?"

"I mean, the police got their man and he's dead. The cops know Lawrence killed Anthony Sorrentino. By the way, man, if you're gonna hire a P.I., you should really tell your lawyer about it."

"I didn't hire him, he's a friend from A.A."

"There's no way *that* could go wrong," Freemont said sarcastically.

"Wait," I said, "so how do they know Lawrence—"

"Killed him? Witness saw him leave the building. DNA on the body, DNA on Ward's body."

"What about Lawrence Ward's murder?" I said. "They can't think he killed himself?"

"No, they know you killed him."

"Then how'm I gonna walk?"

"You'll have to explain exactly what went down at the house and why you went there in the first place, but the police know that was self-defense."

"They do? How?"

"Well, it helps that there's video of the entire incident. Ward had a security system at his place. You'll have to explain why you strangled him, though. On the video, it looks like you could've let up, but you didn't. You'll have to explain how you panicked, your adrenaline kicked in, something like that. That shouldn't be hard to explain since it was his weapon. You'd just been attacked and all so it makes sense you'd want to defend yourself. Given the police now know that Lawrence Ward killed Anthony Sorrentino, I don't anticipate a problem. In other words, the cops don't seem too upset that Ward's off the board. It's not like you killed some innocent guy. You killed a killer."

I was trying to absorb all of this, figure out what it meant.

"What about Sophie Ward's murder?" I asked. "Before Anthony and Ward were killed, you wanted me to come down. They were ready to arrest me."

"I never said they were going to *arrest* you," Freemont said. "You know, you should really clarify these things before you block my number. You were a person of interest, yes, but I think they know they don't have enough to build a case against you. Besides, now that Ward killed Anthony, it seems more likely that he killed his wife, too. There may be a hole in his alibi—the police are looking into it. Anyway, Anthony was probably getting too close to the truth, so Ward took him out. That's the theory the cops are working with now anyway. As long as no new information comes up that involves you in any way, I think you'll be in the clear."

"Sorry for blocking you," I said. "So I'm not going to be charged with anything?"

"Assuming the questioning goes the way I hope it's going to go—no, you won't be charged. So you can stop all the game playing, all right? Just be honest with the doctors, yourself, and, most importantly, with me. After you get whatever treatment you need, yeah, you're gonna get out of here. I don't get it, why aren't you smiling? You should be happy."

"Happy." I let that linger, then added, "I'm in fucking Bellevue. I've lost everything. If I get out of here I won't have money to take a subway, I'll have nowhere to stay. I'll be homeless, begging on the streets. And you're talking about happy?"

I knew I was being a little melodramatic, but still—it wasn't far from the truth.

"I know it's rough," Freemont said, "but people bounce back. You're a smart guy, resourceful. You said you're in A.A., right? I'm sure you can find a friend's couch to crash on till you get your life in shape again."

"Yeah, that worked out great for me the last time."

Freemont half-smiled at my morbid humor, then said, "Tell you what. I have a guest room in my house in Brooklyn, Kensington. If you can't find someplace to stay, you can stay with us till you can."

"You don't have to do that."

"I know I don't."

I was moved, but didn't want to break down in front of him.

"Look, Jack," he said, "you worry about rebuilding one step at a time. First, we get you out of here, clear your name, and then you worry about your other issues. But you should feel good about this—this is a good development. Things'll get better for you, I promise."

I didn't see how getting out of Bellevue as a free man would necessarily make my life any better, but I did see a positive in the situation.

When I got out, I'd definitely have another chance to kill myself.

* * *

Later, Cuvis told me I had another visitor. I figured it was Barasco to charge me with at least one murder.

"Send him in," I said.

"Her," Cuvis said.

I figured it was Dr. Lindsay, returning for more evaluation of my mental state.

Instead, Maria entered.

I didn't expect to ever see her again, outside of divorce court. She remained near the door with a neutral expression that I read as cold. Had she come here to tell me I was an asshole, that I'd ruined her life, that she was going to divorce me and take Jonah away to another state or country?

Bracing myself, I said, "I know you probably hate me right now, but thank you for coming. It means a lot to me."

She looked like she was trying to see through me. I'd seen this look before—her death stare. It was usually right before she lashed in to me with a tirade, and this would be her worst ever. She'd locked me out of our apartment and gotten a restraining order when she thought I'd killed one person; what would she do now?

Well, at least we were in a hospital, with guards, so there was a limit to how angry she could possibly get.

"I guess you've heard about what happened," I added. "It's been a crazy few days."

"How are you?" she asked.

She didn't sound angry, but maybe this was just the dawn before the storm.

Going for a preemptive strike, I said, "Look, I'm sorry. I know how angry you must be right now, and I don't blame you. I'd be angry at me, too, if I were you. I just hope we both can put Jonah first right now, not put him through any more than we already have. How is he by the way?"

She continued to stare at me ambiguously for a while, then said, "He's fine. He misses you."

She was still being civil. I didn't know why she was being civil, if it was part of a ploy, but I wanted to enjoy it while it lasted.

"I miss him, too. Where is he now?"

"In school—the sitter's picking him up."

"How's he doing?"

"He likes his teacher a lot. His reading's getting better."

"That's good, I knew he'd catch up. He's a smart kid. He gets it from you."

She didn't seem upset, but I was still expecting her to lash out at me.

"Look, I know you hate me," I said. "If you're here to tell me off one last time, can you just make it quick? I've been through a lot lately."

"What do you mean?"

"I know you came here to yell at me," I said, "tell me what a piece of shit I am. So let's just get it over with."

"I'm not angry at you, Jack."

I let this sink in, then said, "You're not?"

"No," she said. "Actually I'm happy to see you."

"You are?" I didn't believe her.

"Yes," she said. "You don't owe me any apologies either."

"But after everything I—"

"No, it was my fault," she said. "I overreacted. Actually, I was afraid if I told you I was coming, you wouldn't want to see me."

"I wouldn't want to see you?"

"I locked you out of your home," she said. "I stopped your credit cards, had you arrested."

"I mean, besides that?" I smiled, trying to make it into a joke, though I didn't think there was anything really funny about any of it.

"I was hurt," she said. "The detective was telling me about that website you were on, how you might've been cheating on me, but like I said . . . I jumped to conclusions and that was wrong. Not just for you, for Jonah. I wasn't thinking. I'm sorry."

It occurred to me that since I'd known Maria she hadn't apologized to me. I didn't think "sorry" was in her vocabulary.

"I wasn't cheating," I said. "I was just flirting. I mean, I'm not making any excuses for my behavior, I know what I did was wrong. But it's not like it was a habit. It was a onetime thing, I got sucked in, I made a mistake. I don't know if you heard, but I'll probably be getting out of here with no charges filed. I want to go into therapy, into counseling, do whatever it takes to figure myself out."

"I know you're getting out," she said, "and I want to help you."

"What?" I'd heard her; I just wanted to hear it again.

"I want to help you." She took a few steps toward me and stopped. "I mean, I won't say I'm totally past this, because I'm not, but you're still my son's father, and I want to give you the benefit of the doubt. I talked to my cousin Michael, and he put me in touch with a great criminal lawyer. It's ridiculous that you're using that Legal Aid guy."

"He's done a good job for me so far."

"Then you have to quit when you're ahead. You're going to use Michael's contact and you'll get everything taken care of. If they don't charge you with anything and try to keep you here, we'll fight it. Michael says they can't keep you here involuntarily. Have you talked to the police yet since you've been here?"

"Since I was admitted here?" I said. "No."

"That's good," she said. "You don't want to say anything without a great lawyer representing you."

"Why are you doing all of this for me?" I asked.

She seemed confused. "What do you mean?"

"Being so nice," I said. "I mean, I did a horrible thing to you and Jonah. I caused all of this."

"No," she said. "You didn't." She came over and held my hand. "I know we've had problems over the years, but I didn't want any of this to happen to you, and you definitely don't deserve it. I just panicked when Detective Barasco told me you were on that website. I assumed the worst, but what woman wouldn't? But I know you, Jack. I know you're not a bad person, and I know you're a great father. We'll need more openness in our marriage and more honesty going forward, that's for sure. I know I've been opposed to counseling, but that's probably a good idea, too." Her eyes looked glassy. "I want you back, Jack. *We* want you back."

While everything she'd told me sounded genuine, somehow I still didn't trust it. I thought I'd lost her forever.

She moved closer. I thought she might kiss me, but instead she pulled back and said, "We'll talk more . . . later."

I watched her leave.

* * *

A couple of hours later, a woman, about fifty years old, with short curly brown hair, in a conservative, uncomfortable-looking navy wool dress, entered and said, "Mr. Harper?"

"Yes," I said, "who're—"

"Rachel Goldman. I'm a criminal attorney. Michael Brant suggested I meet with you."

"Oh, right," I said. "Thanks for coming down, but I don't think this is necessary. I have a lawyer."

"It's a big mistake to use a Legal Aid attorney for a case like this," Rachel said. "One slipup and you'll wind up in jail, maybe for the rest of your life."

Realizing she could be right, that I should probably quit while I was ahead with Freemont, I said, "Well, I'm willing to hear what you have to say."

She pulled up a chair and asked me to explain everything that had happened since I'd met Sophie Ward online. At times, she interrupted me to clarify something, then had me continue. Although she was humorless and didn't have as much personality as Freemont, she did seem much more experienced.

When I started telling her about what had happened at the house in White Plains, she interrupted with, "Did Lawrence Ward tell you anything about his wife's murder?"

"You mean did he confess?" I asked.

She nodded.

"No," I said. "I mean, not really. He said, 'You don't know what you're dealing with.' Is that a confession?"

"Is that all he said?" she asked.

"Yes," I said.

"Are you sure?"

"Actually I have the whole thing recorded."

"You do?" She seemed surprised.

"Yeah," I said. "I was hoping to get a confession, but I didn't."

"That's great," she said. "I'll have to listen to the recording. In the meantime, it would be a good idea to not mention anything specific about what you discussed, so there are no contradictions."

"Got it," I said.

"If you'd like to work with me, you'll need to inform your current attorney that you no longer require his services."

Using Rachel's phone, I called Freemont and explained the situation. He didn't exactly sound crushed.

"Makes sense, man," he said. "If I were you I'd do the same thing. Good luck with everything, I mean that."

A few minutes later, Barasco arrived.

"Hey, Rachel," he said.

"Nick," Rachel said.

"You two know each other?" I asked.

"We've crossed paths," Barasco said. "So, out of curiosity, how are you affording her services?"

"My client won't answer that question," Rachel said.

"Protecting his boundaries already." Barasco said to me, "Looks like you're already getting your money's worth."

Barasco questioned me about my whereabouts on the day that Anthony and Lawrence were killed. He sounded straightforward, not antagonistic like in previous questionings. I explained that I took a cab to White Plains and what had happened between Ward and me.

"You knew there was a warrant for your arrest when you went to White Plains," Barasco said. "Is that correct?"

"No, I didn't know," I said, "and I wasn't planning to run away. I just wanted to clear my name, see my son again."

"And what transpired at the house?"

Rachel interrupted with, "Mr. Harper has a recording of the incident that I haven't reviewed yet."

"A recording?" Barasco looked at me.

"I was hoping to get a confession from him," I said.

"I'd like to hear that recording, too," Barasco said, "but as you know we have security footage of the incident. We know he came after you with a knife and you killed him trying to defend yourself."

"That's true," I said

"So why didn't you stick around for the cops to get there?"

I glanced at Rachel who nodded, indicating it was okay for me to answer.

"I panicked," I said. "After what had happened in New York, I thought I'd get blamed for the murder, just because I was there."

"Understandable," he said. "What happened next?"

I described how I'd taken a train back to the city, but left out that I got drunk. But I knew I'd be talking a lot about that at my next A.A. meeting.

I also didn't tell him about meeting Rob McEvoy. He didn't bring it up, so he didn't seem to know, or care, about it.

"What about the subway?" he asked. "Were you planning to jump in front of that train?"

I was sick of the stress of not telling the truth.

"Yes," I said.

"How come?"

"Because I'd lost everything," I said. "I didn't think I had any reason to live."

"Do you feel that way now?"

Thinking about how, if this all went well, I'd be able to see Jonah again very soon, I said, "No. No I don't. I want to live. I don't feel suicidal at all anymore."

He had several more questions about what I'd seen at the house in White Plains, and I gave him honest answers. It was so much easier to be honest than to come up with lies.

"We still need to hear the audio of what had transpired in the house in White Plains," he said, "and you're still not off the hook for Sophie Ward's murder."

"Is there any additional evidence connecting my client to Sophie Ward's murder?" Rachel asked.

"Not at the moment, no," Barasco admitted.

"You'll let us know if that situation changes," Rachel said.

I liked this woman.

Barasco left.

I emailed Rachel the audio file, then she left, too.

About a half hour later, Rachel returned, holding a Ziploc. "Good news, you're being discharged. Here are your possessions."

I realized that the Ziploc contained my wallet, phone, keys, and loose change.

"I listened to the recording and played it for Barasco. He seems satisfied. He still can't prove that Lawrence Ward murdered his wife, but he had no plans to charge you for that murder either."

Rachel and I walked along the corridor together, toward the elevators. Leaving Bellevue, after I'd been prepared to be institutionalized for maybe the rest of my life, felt surreal.

I spotted Dr. Lindsay leaving an office. She sort of smiled and raised her hand, a little wave goodbye, like I was a classmate on the last day of school.

*Have a great summer, Jack. See you in the fall!*

"This isn't school," I said.

"What's that?" Rachel asked.

I didn't realize I'd spoken out loud.

"Nothing," I said.

We got on an elevator.

When the doors opened in the lobby, I saw Maria.

Although she was smiling and seemed sincere, it was hard to fully trust her. Was this just a game for her? Was she trying to get payback? Was she just trying to hoover me back into the marriage, just to dump me in some humiliating way? Well, I'd find out soon enough.

I went over to her and didn't say anything.

We left Bellevue together.

# CHAPTER TWENTY

In the cab, we exchanged some small talk, mostly about Jonah. Otherwise, we were silent.

When we approached our apartment building, Maria asked, "Do you have your cash card?"

I was about to remind her that the card didn't work.

"I reactivated it," she said.

I paid, then we headed into the building.

I could tell that Robert was uncomfortable seeing me, after how he'd treated me the last time, but I was in too good a mood to hold a grudge.

"Robert," I said. "How've you been?"

"Fine." He sounded relieved. "How about you?"

"Feels great to be home," I said.

Before we'd left Bellevue, Maria had told me that Jonah was home with Carly, the sixteen-year-old babysitter we sometimes used who lived in the building with her parents. My pulse was pounding in anticipation of seeing him.

At the door, I dug into my pocket for my keys.

"Those still won't work," Maria said. "But I'll get you a new set right away."

When Maria began to turn the key in the lock, I heard Jonah say, "Is it Daddy? Is it really Daddy?"

It reminded me of the times he was three or four years old and, if he hadn't seen me all day, he'd run to me and jump into my arms and I'd pick him up and hug him.

The door opened and he shouted, "Daddy, Daddy!" and he ran toward me.

I lifted him up—it wasn't as easy as when he was a toddler, but I barely noticed. I lifted him up so high his head almost reached the ceiling as he laughed with pure joy.

I noticed that Maria had turned away and seemed to be wiping tears from her eyes.

"He's been so excited all night," Carly said.

"You've been excited, huh?" I said, looking up at Jonah, at his round, still baby-like face.

"Yes," he said. "I missed you so much, Daddy."

Tears gushing, I said, "Well, I missed you, too, kiddo. So, so much."

* * *

Carly returned to her apartment, and I hung out with Jonah in his room, talking about sports and what he'd been learning in school, until it was time for him to get ready for bed. Then I kissed him goodnight and I went to our bedroom where Maria was lying down, reading on her Kindle.

Although my clothes had been washed in the hospital, I was eager to put on my actual clothes.

I opened the dresser drawer where my tee shirts usually were, but saw my jeans there instead.

"Oh, I put your stuff back into your drawers today," Maria said. "I'm not sure if it's all where it's supposed to go."

"Back?" I asked.

"Yeah, I'd moved your stuff into suitcases and boxes." She sounded ashamed. "I'm sorry, Jack. I was just so hurt. I mean when I found out you were actually there, at the townhouse, that you lied to me, I—"

"It's okay," I said. "It's all over now. I'm back home, where I belong. I'm gonna shower."

There's nothing like your home shower, especially after you've been showering at Bellevue for a couple of days.

Later, I entered the bedroom with a towel around my waist. Maria, in panties and a baggy tee shirt, was lying in bed on her back, staring at the ceiling.

"What's wrong?" I asked.

She didn't answer, so I didn't push it. When she was ready to talk, she'd talk.

I let the towel fall to the floor. When I got into bed, Maria still hadn't budged.

Then she said, "Can you really forgive me?"

"You didn't do anything wrong," I said.

"I treated you awfully," she said. "I was just so hurt, felt so betrayed, but I know it's no excuse for doing what I did to you—locking you out of the apartment, lying to the police. I know I'm being melodramatic now, but when Barasco told me what you'd done, it felt like the worst pain possible. My behavior, though, is inexcusable, and I need to take some responsibility. Does this make any sense?"

"It makes total sense." She looked like she wanted to kiss me. Instead, she said, "I forgot to ask you one thing."

"What?" I said.

"The other day, two hundred thousand dollars arrived in our bank account," she said. "Do you have any idea how it got there?"

# CHAPTER TWENTY-ONE

"Two hundred thousand dollars?" I said, though I'd heard her.

"Yes," Maria said. "From a Citibank account."

I'd planned to check my bank account when I got my cell phone back, but I'd been so excited to see Maria and be home with my family again that I'd forgotten. I hadn't even checked my texts and emails.

"Wow, it's really there," I said. "Rob really did it."

"Oh, so then you know about it," she said.

"Yeah," I said, "but I can explain why—"

"I didn't want to bring it up right away," she said. "I mean, I thought I'd let you mention it first. At first, I thought it might've been for the apartment you'd mentioned, maybe commission? But that didn't make sense, because why would he direct deposit commission money into our personal account?"

Now that I was back, and she'd forgiven me, I wanted things to be different. I wanted to be honest, no matter what the consequences. Maybe she'd be horrified by what I'd done, judge me for it, but I'd been lying to her, and to myself, for way too long and what had it gotten me except pain and torment?

"I blackmailed him," I said.

I braced myself for the fallout, whatever it entailed. I figured she'd lose it—scream, curse, cause a scene. Well, that's what would've happened a couple of weeks ago if I'd told Maria news that upset her. Jonah would wake up terrified, and Maria, or a neighbor, would call the police. Then Maria would throw me out again, block me from my bank accounts, start a custody battle.

What I didn't expect was for her to remain as calm as a psychotherapist and ask, "Why, Jack?"

Maybe she was just restraining herself, trying to play the role of "the understanding wife." But I explained, the best I could, why I'd done it. How I was distraught, thought I'd lost everything, and how it didn't seem fair for Rob to get off unscathed. As I spoke, I realized how petty and vindictive, even crazy, I must have sounded. I'd blackmailed, actually *blackmailed*, an old friend, for two hundred thousand dollars because he'd told me about a website? Who *does* that?

At the same time, it felt good to be honest with her, like a huge burden had been lifted.

"Look," I went on, "I know it was a stupid thing to do. I wasn't thinking straight at the time; I was in a bad way. I'd even started drinking again. Yeah, I went off the wagon, I was really starting to lose it, and, in the moment, it seemed like a good idea. I wanted to do something for you and Jonah—just one good thing. I'd done so many bad things lately, made so many mistakes, that, I don't know, I thought this would make up for it. But now I realize how stupid that was, how I was just scapegoating Rob, making the same mistake I've made so many times before. I didn't have to listen to him, I *chose* to listen to him. But, don't worry, I'll work on this now and become a better man, I promise. This whole experience has scared the shit out of me—I've hit my real rock bottom. I'm going back to A.A., and I'll apologize to Rob and wire that money back to him, and I'll—"

"No," Maria said.

She sounded very serious.

"No, what?" I asked.

"No, you're not returning that money to him."

She still didn't sound like she was joking, but I said, "You're joking, right?"

"I just want to move on," she said. "The money's already in our bank account, and Rob wouldn't have given it to you if he didn't want to give it to you. He probably felt bad, realized what he'd put you through, and thought giving you the money was the least he could do."

"Maybe that's true," I said, "but I still have to call him and—"

"No, it's our money. We need it."

Definitely not joking.

"Come on," I said, "you really can't expect me to keep that money."

"*Our* money," Maria said. "It's in *our* bank account."

"But weren't you listening to what I was saying?" I said. "It's actually Rob's money."

"No, it's our money now. He wired it to *us*, to our joint account."

"But he only did it because I threatened him, because—"

"Because he knows he did something wrong," Maria said. "Don't you get it? Rob's not a good guy. You've known that for years. I remember the stories you used to tell me about him. He's always been an asshole, a player. He lies, cheats—"

"I know," I said, "but that doesn't mean—"

"Yes," she said, "it does. Don't you get it? You were right—it is *all* his fault. He knew what he was doing—he was encouraging you, trying to hurt you. He's like a scummy drug dealer, an enabler. He knows it, too. That's why he gave you that money, because he felt guilty—"

"No, he did it because—"

"Because he wanted to do it, Jack, because he wanted to redeem himself. People don't do anything they don't want to do. Trust me,

I'm right. By keeping the money you're *helping* him. If that money really meant anything to him, if it was really going to destroy him, do you think he really would've wired it? That money's probably like his lunch budget for the next few years. But we *need* the money, it could make a difference for us. It could be a down payment on an apartment, pay for Jonah's college. How many problems for us were caused by money? All the arguments we've had about your career, how our apartment's too small, how we're not putting enough away for retirement. All of those fights wore us down, put a wedge between us, made us drift farther and farther apart. But now we have a chance—to start again, without all of that stress. I feel like we're getting along better already, and I know you feel the same way. He was looking to do something good, Jack, just like you were, so you both got what you wanted."

Although I knew what Maria was saying didn't make much sense, somehow it *all* made sense.

"I have an idea," I said. "How about we put the money aside for a couple of weeks, or a couple of months, and then decide what to do."

She continued glaring at me, until she managed to smile.

"That does sound like a reasonable compromise," she said. "Good idea—let's just keep the money in the bank and agree we won't touch it . . . for a while."

I knew we hadn't resolved the issue, but at least we'd tabled it.

She was looking at me like she wanted me to kiss her, so I did. We hadn't kissed, *really* kissed in a long time. Feeling as awkward as a teenager, I leaned in.

Her lips didn't feel familiar at all; they felt like a stranger's lips. I was distracted, flashing back to discovering Sophie's body, Anthony's body, killing Lawrence, almost jumping in front of the train.

"Are you okay?" Maria asked.

I realized I was drenched in sweat.

"Yeah," I said, "fine."

Maria lay on her back, and I climbed on top. I tried to take control, rejecting my thoughts and memories and trying to focus on Maria. Her body felt unfamiliar, more toned, and then I flashed back to when Maria had visited me at Bellevue—her cold glare. I wanted to refocus on us, in the present, but my mind kept drifting to the past.

I wasn't close to getting a hard-on.

"It's okay, we don't have to do it tonight," Maria said. "It's nice just lying next to you."

I turned away onto my side, and Maria hugged me from behind, spooning me.

I was still sweating.

* * *

In the morning, while Maria showered and got ready for work, I checked my texts. I'd gotten a lot of messages from A.A. friends and acquaintances and old sponsors checking up on me, making sure I was okay, and, yes, I'd gotten a couple of texts from Rob.

The first had been sent a day after I'd almost jumped in front of the train:

> *Hey bro just heard about you on the news feel awful, had no idea how desperate you were man. I feel so bad for telling you about that site. It wasn't my intention to fuck things up for you, hope you know that bro and if I knew how bad you were doing I never would've let you leave that playground*

In another text he continued:

> *Anyway bro feel bad about how things went down I know you were counting on that commish so I'm wiring the 200 K into*

*your account lets just both move on forget this ever happened sound cool??*
*I know you are a good guy and you don't want to do anything to hurt me or my kids*
*Robby*

I read the messages a few times. Unlike the messages from my A.A. friends, Rob's concern didn't seem genuine. He'd wired that money out of fear that I'd ruin his marriage, not because he cared that I'd almost killed myself. The guy obviously had zero empathy.

Maybe Maria had been right; maybe we *did* deserve that money.

I made Jonah breakfast—French toast, his favorite. I made some for myself, too, and, as we sat at the table eating, he told me about the fantasy football team he'd started. When Maria came by, she kissed me, and it was obvious how happy Jonah was—not just because his dad was back home, but because his parents were happy. He'd never seen his parents like this. Over the years, I'd thought I'd been hiding the tension in my marriage from him, but he'd been picking up on it, and it had affected him, as it had affected all of us.

When Maria was leaving for work, I kissed her goodbye and gave her a tight hug.

"I wanna hug, too," Jonah said.

Our family hug would've made a great Christmas card photo: Jonah, grinning widely between his mom and dad, looking like the happiest kid in the world.

Later, Jonah and I walked to school together. Although it wasn't quite my normal routine, because I had no job to go to, it was still great to be back to being a dad again, back where I belonged.

At school, going by the awkward looks I got from other parents and some kids, it seemed obvious that if they hadn't seen me or read about me in the news, they'd heard the rumors. A couple of moms,

Stacy and Geri, from the PTA, were discussing preparations for the school's upcoming annual Halloween "Boo Bash." I was about to offer to volunteer, as I had in previous years, but when Stacy and Geri saw me they had panicked expressions and headed into the school to avoid me.

"Hey, come on, don't be ridiculous!" I called after them.

Florence, the security guard, came over.

"What's goin' on out here?" she asked.

"Nothing," I said and rushed away.

Without any job to go to, I had a free day until Jonah's pickup time at two forty. I was eager to start job hunting, try to land another real estate gig, but after everything I'd been through lately, I decided I was entitled to some me-time.

I went to Le Pain Quotidien on 1st and 83rd and had a coffee and croissant and browsed someone's abandoned *New York Times*. I didn't feel like returning to my apartment, so I headed to Central Park. I walked partway around the reservoir. It was chilly and started drizzling—a perfect museum day.

It had been a long time, maybe a year, since I'd been to the Metropolitan Museum of Art, or to any museum. Years ago, Maria and I used to go frequently, and as I climbed the steps, I flashed back to the times we had carried Jonah up the steps in his stroller—her holding the handles, me lifting from the bottom. I hadn't seen any plays or movies in movie theaters or live bands recently either. Living in New York City and not taking advantage of the cultural activities was a shame; I'd taken too much for granted lately.

I texted with Maria: *@ The Met.*

Several seconds later, she replied: *Nice Thinking about you too :) I'll cook dinner!*

When was the last time Maria had cooked? Three, four years ago?

I responded: *Sounds great!*

I went to my favorite part of the museum—the Impressionist wing. After checking out my favorite Renoirs, Gauguins, Seurats, Degas, I went over to the Van Goghs.

I checked out some of my faves—*Pair of Shoes*, *Self-Portrait with Straw Hat*, *Mother Roulin with Her Baby*.

Then I went over to the still life: *Vase with Irises*, and read the description:

*In May 1890, just before he checked himself out of the asylum of Saint-Remy, Van Gogh painted four exuberant bouquets of spring flowers, the only still lifes of any ambition he had undertaken during his yearlong stay: two of irises, two of roses, in contrasting color schemes and formats. In the Irises he sought a "harmonious and soft" effect by placing the "violet" flowers against a "pink background," which have since faded owing to his use of fugitive red pigments.*

I'd always liked the painting, but now it had additional meaning for me. I know, I know, grandiose, but I, too, had just come out of an asylum, so I could identify with Van Gogh's restrained mania in the painting, and of course his use of fugitive reds reminded me of Sophie.

Distracted by my own troubles and reconnecting with my family, I hadn't thought about her much the past few days, but now I felt as gutted as I had when I'd discovered her body in the bedroom of the townhouse. The poor woman, and her family—they were the biggest victims in all of this. Sophie hadn't talked much about her family, but her loved ones were probably still suffering, wanting closure.

"Are you okay, sir?"

The security guy, who had a foreign accent, had come over to me. I realized I must've looked as awful as I felt.

I sat on a bench, staring at the painting, as more memories of Sophie swarmed me. Our devious, late-night chat sessions, how she'd awakened the dormant, adventurous side to my personality, how close we had gotten so quickly, and her explanation for why she'd chosen the name Fugitive Red, because "love fades." She'd been so unhappy, trapped in a bad marriage, desperate to make a connection. And we *had* made a connection. Maybe an online relationship wasn't a real relationship, but our emotions had been real. I was glad that I'd at least allowed her to feel some joy and hope in her life before she'd died.

"Powerful, isn't it?"

I didn't realize that a slight, elderly woman had sat down next to me. I also didn't realize that I was crying.

"Yes," I said. "You know that pink background was once red."

"What?"

I couldn't tell if she couldn't hear me or couldn't understand me.

"The background," I said a bit louder. "But the big question is did Van Gogh know that the red would fade? Is that why he chose the red? To make a statement about love fading over time after he was released from the asylum?"

The woman seemed perplexed. I felt ridiculous.

"Never mind," I said. "Have an amazing day."

* * *

Maria made one of her old specialties—chicken piccata, rice with pine nuts, and sautéed spinach. For dessert, she'd picked up Jonah's favorite: chocolate mousse.

After dinner, I washed the dishes and Jonah dried, then the three of us watched TV—the original *Star Wars* because Jonah had never seen it. Seeing Jonah so excited made me feel like I was seeing it for the first time as well. I could tell that Maria felt the same way.

Later, when Jonah was in bed and I was saying goodnight to him, he asked, "When can we see the sequels?"

"Soon," I said.

"How soon?"

"Very soon."

"This weekend?"

"Maybe."

"I can't wait. Are you gonna stay married to Mommy?"

I was caught off-guard, but I had no reason to hesitate.

"Yes," I said. "Yes, I am."

I kissed him goodnight on the cheek, then joined Maria in the bedroom.

Sex was awkward. I was still distracted and sweating a lot, and Maria didn't seem that into it either.

"That was incredible," Maria said afterward, snuggling against me.

I knew she had to be exaggerating at least a little.

"Yes," I said. "I know."

* * *

The next day, Saturday, we decided to have a family day. We took the Q-train to Coney Island, went on some rides, including the Cyclone, and then walked along the Boardwalk to Brighton Beach. We had stuffed cabbage and pierogies at a casual Russian restaurant and then returned home and watched *The Empire Strikes Back*.

Later, after Maria and I had more awkward sex, she said, "I have an idea, let's go on a date night. We haven't done that in ages."

Maria sounded like she genuinely wanted to get closer to me and improve our marriage.

"Sounds like a plan," I said.

On Sunday, we arranged for Carly to babysit and went to dinner at a restaurant where we used to go frequently, Elio's on 2nd

Avenue. We sat outside and Maria had a glass of wine with dinner and I had water. I had five days of sobriety and wasn't planning to go off the wagon again.

Afterward, Maria suggested going to Carl Schurz Park. We walked through the park to the promenade and sat on a bench looking out at the East River.

Holding my hand, Maria said, "This feels so nice."

My gut was screaming at me not to trust any of this. Rationally, I knew that I'd been with her long enough to know that the idea of us getting back to the "good times" in our relationship was just a fantasy.

But when had I ever been rational?

"Yes," I said. "It does."

* * *

On Monday morning Maria went to work, and I took Jonah to school. Jonah seemed anxious and wasn't his usual chatty self. At drop-off, I didn't feel like hanging around to chat with the parents. Instead, I went to a coffee bar on 85th, and sat in the garden, sipping coffee, searching for a job online.

The two hundred grand in our bank account still didn't feel like it was ours, but, admittedly, knowing that the money was there was a huge stress relief and eased my desperation. If Rob hadn't deposited that money, I would've been desperate for work right now, felt pressured by Maria, and been forced to accept the first opportunity that came along. Now I felt free to be pickier.

Andrew Wolf had emailed me the other day, apologizing for his "rush to judgment" against me, and offering my old job back "if I wanted it." I didn't even bother to respond—not because I held a grudge, but because after years of struggling and neediness, I finally had an opportunity to do what I wanted to do, and I planned to seize it.

Maybe this was my opportunity to get out of real estate and get back to doing something I really loved. I found a listing that intrigued me—an indie record company in Brooklyn was looking to fill a position in their PR department. While I didn't have PR experience per se, I'd done some band promotion in my twenties and my sales experience sort of tied in. I found a few more music-related positions that sounded cool, and then I worked on my resume. I didn't want to rush this, though. My plan was to spend the next week or so working on my resume and researching job opportunities, and then I'd set up interviews.

Later, I was going to grab some lunch in the neighborhood, when I thought, *Why not surprise Maria?* Years ago, way before Jonah was born, Maria and I used to meet for lunch on workdays all the time, but we hadn't done it in ages.

I walked to midtown, to Maria's office on 51st and Lexington. I'd been to the office a few times over the years, usually on days when I had an appointment in the afternoon and needed to drop off Jonah with Maria at work when we couldn't get childcare.

Brad at the front desk recognized me.

"She's expecting me," I said.

"Go right in," he said.

I walked through the row of cubicles, heading toward the windowed office where Maria worked. I knew she'd be surprised to see me and I was looking forward to her reaction. I figured she'd be happy, maybe run up to me and give me a big hug.

As I approached her office, I stopped when I saw she was standing, talking with someone—a man. I figured she was having a meeting, or about to end one, and I was going to come back later or just text her from the street.

Then I recognized the guy—it was Maria's friend Steve from Westchester. *Why was Steve here?*

I watched as they continued to talk. They both had intense expressions, like they were talking about something serious. I'd always been aware of the sexual tension between Maria and Steve, and they *were* exes. Was it possible they were having an affair or had been having an affair for years? Maria had always insisted that they were "just friends," but maybe I'd missed the obvious signs. I knew they spoke on the phone frequently, and texted and emailed. Some might even say this qualified as having an emotional affair, so why couldn't it have escalated to something physical? I recalled the possibly hypocritical advice Steve had given me about how I should never cheat on Maria. In retrospect, it all made sense—why would he want me to cheat on and potentially hurt the woman he was in love with?

Of course, I knew I was jumping to a lot of conclusions, but my mind was spinning.

I felt weird watching them and was about to turn and leave when Maria saw me.

Did I see a flash of panic in her expression? Seemed like it. Then she smiled and motioned for me to join them.

"Hey, what a surprise," Maria said, and then she kissed me.

"Hey," I said to Steve.

"What're you doing here?" Steve asked.

"I was about to ask you that same question," I said.

Maria cut in with, "Steve just stopped by to visit me. He was running some errands in the city today."

"Looks like we had the same idea, then," I said, glancing at Steve.

Steve didn't say anything, but he looked like he was reining in emotion.

"Why don't we all sit down?" Maria suggested,

"It's okay," Steve said, "I should get going. I have to take the kids to swimming practice later. I'll talk to you soon, sweetie."

He kissed Maria on the cheek, then left the office without making eye contact with me.

"Sweetie?" I said to Maria.

"Oh, stop it." She saw I was serious. "Come on, you don't really think something's going on with me and Steve, do you?"

"Is there?" I asked.

"No, of course not. He was telling me about his marriage, that's all. He and Kathy are thinking about getting divorced and he wanted a woman's perspective. Why are you looking at me like that?"

"I'm not looking at you any way," I said.

"I can't believe you don't believe me. Me and Steve? Seriously?"

"I never said I don't believe you," I said.

"Well, you're implying it."

"How am I implying it?"

We stared at each other for a few seconds, not blinking.

"So why did you come here anyway?" she said.

"Just to surprise you," I said. "Thought you'd like to grab lunch with me."

She smiled. "Actually, I'd like that a lot."

We went around the corner and bought salads and ate on metal chairs in a public space nearby.

After some casual conversation, Maria said, "Okay, about Steve. He's just upset that we're still together, that's all. When he heard about you in the news he felt protective of me and when I told him I wanted to work on my marriage, he was against the idea. So he came to talk to me."

"It's none of his business," I said.

"I agree with you," Maria said. "Actually, I was telling him that exact thing when you walked in. That's why he acted that way when he saw you."

Maria seemed sincere. I didn't have any reason to think she wasn't telling the truth.

"Sorry if I overreacted," I said.

"Don't be." She held my hand. "I understand why you thought what you thought."

"No, I definitely made an assumption and it's frustrating . . . I mean, I thought we were beyond all this."

"Beyond what?" she asked.

"The dysfunction," I said. "Things were so bad with us for a long time, I think we can both acknowledge that. But I thought we'd gotten past the past. I thought things would be normal now."

"They are normal," she said. "They are."

She let go of my hand and we continued eating our salads.

* * *

"I'm worried about Jonah," I whispered.

I had just tucked him in and joined Maria on the couch.

"Don't be," Maria said. "He's a happy kid."

"It's true, he *seems* happy, but I'm worried he's holding stuff in. He does that sometimes."

"He's been through a lot the past couple of weeks," Maria said. "He was so excited to see you when you came home, he's probably just rebounding from that now."

"I think we should consider getting him some therapy," I said.

"I don't think that's necessary," Maria said, sort of harshly. Then she said, "But if you're in favor, I'm in favor, too. I know you're more of a therapy fan than I am. By the way, I'm still open to going to marriage counseling if you want to. Actually, I think it would be a good idea."

"I'll try to check into it tomorrow," I said.

Maria grabbed the remote. "Let's watch something funny," she said.

She turned on the TV, found *Anchorman*. It was toward the end of the movie and we watched the rest of it—Maria laughing occasionally, and me, distracted, remaining stone-faced.

When the movie ended, Maria peeked into Jonah's room, then said, "Sound asleep," and turned off his light.

"We should wake him up so he can brush his teeth," I said.

"One missed brushing won't kill him," Maria said.

I didn't remember her getting into bed. I must've already been asleep.

# CHAPTER TWENTY-TWO

WHEN MY PHONE alarm went off in the morning, I dreaded getting out of bed as I remembered that today was Anthony's funeral.

Shawn, an acquaintance from A.A., had sent me a Facebook invite about it. Normally I would've wanted to be there to remember a good friend and support his family—I'd been his sponsor, after all—but I felt incredibly awkward. I'd been in denial about his death, hadn't even thought about it as much as I should have. As far as I knew, the details of Anthony's death were still unknown, but I couldn't help feeling responsible. While I knew, rationally, that I hadn't caused his death, that it could've happened on any case he was working on, or when he was a cop, this didn't make me feel any better about it.

But, to hell with it, I was tired of being the guy who shirks responsibility and avoids situations just because they're unpleasant. I'd been *that* guy for long enough.

I manned up and put on my darkest suit.

The funeral was on Long Island, in Smithtown; Shawn rented a Zip Car and drove me out there. Shawn was a young guy, about thirty, whom Anthony had sponsored. Shawn didn't know, or didn't seem to know, that Anthony had been technically working for me when he was killed, so I didn't fill him in on this information.

Anthony hadn't been religious, but his family was Catholic. Shawn and I viewed the body—I was impressed how the embalming had managed to make a murder victim appear peaceful—paid our respects to his family and friends. There were a few familiar faces from A.A.—Maggie and two guys whose names I didn't know—but most of the attendees were total strangers. I did get a strong "cop vibe" from several people; not surprising given Anthony's background at the NYPD. One cop-looking guy—stocky but not fat with thick gray hair and a gray mustache—seemed to be looking at me, as if he recognized me from somewhere. I told myself I was just being paranoid, or maybe we'd been at an A.A. meeting one time and I had forgotten meeting him.

Then I saw the gray-haired guy go over to Anthony's sister and say something to her. I'd met his sister for the first time several minutes earlier when I'd told her how sorry I was for her loss.

Shawn and I weren't planning to go to the cemetery.

"Wanna get going?" I asked him.

"Sure," he said, "how 'bout ten minutes?"

I was chatting with Shawn and Maggie, sharing our favorite Anthony stories, when I heard:

"Jack Harper?"

Anthony's sister had come over to me. Her eyes were reddish from crying, but she looked more angry than upset.

"Yes," I said.

"I didn't make the connection before when you came over," she said. "Who invited you here?"

She was talking loud. Shawn and Maggie were overhearing us, and so were several other people nearby.

I didn't think I'd ever felt more embarrassed and awkward.

"I read about it on Facebook," I said. "I just wanted to be here to support—"

"If I wanted you here, I would've invited you myself!"

Her tone had gone from raised to full-blown screaming. Now more people, maybe the whole funeral home, were our audience.

"Sorry," I said, "I didn't mean—"

"If it wasn't for you, Anthony would still be alive."

"That isn't true—"

"How's it not true?"

I hesitated, then said, "Because I—"

"He was my fucking brother, you asshole! Now he's gone! He's fucking gone!"

The gray-haired guy came over and pulled her away, then a few other people got between us.

I couldn't leave the funeral home fast enough, and Shawn wanted to get away, too.

When we got back in the Zip Car, I was distracted by my thoughts and didn't say anything. The scene at the funeral home—getting yelled at, with everyone watching—still felt surreal, like theater. I guess I was a little in shock.

Shawn, driving, didn't say anything either until we were passing LaGuardia Airport, almost back in the city.

"Why didn't you tell me Anthony was working for you?" He sounded like he was releasing pent-up anger, like he'd been trying to figure out how to bring this up with me since we'd left Smithtown.

"He wasn't actually working for me," I said.

"So you didn't hire him?"

For some reason, I felt guilty.

"He was doing me a favor," I said.

"Then why didn't you tell me, man?"

"I don't know," I said. "I guess I didn't think it was important."

"You didn't think it was important I know how my friend died?"

"I didn't mean it like that," I said. "Come on, give me a break, man."

Shawn maintained a serious glare for the rest of the trip.

When he dropped me off near my apartment in Manhattan, things were still awkward. When I got out of the car, he drove away without saying goodbye.

At home, I couldn't shake my guilty feeling, like I'd done something wrong. Maybe it was because I'd been lying when I'd told Shawn that I'd told the police everything I knew. Actually, I hadn't.

I still had about an hour before I had to pick up Jonah from school, so I sat on a bench in the garden of a church and did some searching on my phone. On our Verizon bill, I checked the numbers of calls and texts for the past couple of weeks, but nothing seemed unusual. Then I checked the recent history on our credit cards and Chase bank account. Nothing unusual there either.

At school pickup, a couple of Jonah's friends and their moms were headed to 16 Handles for frozen yogurt. I asked Jonah if he wanted to go with them, but, still acting sullen and not himself, he said he just wanted to go home.

"It's okay, you don't have to go if you don't feel like it," I said, wanting him to know that I respected his emotions.

At home, I hung out with Jonah, watching TV.

From her office, Maria texted: *stopping @ whole foods after work we need eggs?*

I checked the fridge, saw we had an almost full carton of eggs.

Sent: *No we're good.*

She replied, *Okay, leaving in few. Be home half hour!*

Back on the couch next to Jonah, he asked, "When can we see *Return of the Jedi*?"

"Soon," I said.

It was great to see Jonah excited about something, getting his mojo back. Kids—they were so resilient.

A couple of minutes later, I remembered that there was one credit card account I hadn't checked—a Discover Card that we rarely used.

I didn't carry the card with me in my wallet. We had a filing cabinet in the hallway closet where we kept our important papers, documents, and correspondence. In the "credit card" file I found my card, which had expired about three years ago. I didn't think I'd gotten a replacement card so maybe I'd deactivated the card and didn't remember it. I was going to forget the whole thing, then I decided I'd call Discover to see if a new card had been sent to me.

I waited on hold for a while, and then the representative, a man with an Indian accent, picked up. I explained the situation and gave him my card number and name.

"I'm sorry, sir," he said, "but you're no longer on this account."

"What do you mean?" I asked.

"The only name on the account is Maria Harper."

"That's my wife, but there has to be a mistake," I said. "That account was in both our names."

He asked me to hold. Then he returned and said, "Your name was removed from the account, sir. Maria Harper is the primary account holder and she removed you."

This seemed off, but did it mean anything?

"Is there anything else I can help you with, sir?"

"No," I said, "thank you so much."

I figured I'd ask Maria about the account later, or sometime soon. Then I had another idea. Just because my name had been taken off the account didn't mean I couldn't log on.

On my phone, I went to Discover.com online and tried logging on with my old password. Sure enough, the account information appeared.

I was surprised to see that the card had been used actively. Since Maria paid the bills, I could also see how this had been easy for her to hide. I was shocked to see hotel bills, restaurant bills, and bills from stores like Victoria's Secret and The Pink Pussycat, a sex shop in the West Village.

What the fuck? Had I accessed the wrong account? Was there some mistake?

I checked recent transactions—there were seven transactions listed, all within the past few weeks.

Six of the charges were for "Business Services," and the other was for $159.96 at Bloomingdale's.

*Business Services? What the hell?*

One of the "Business Services" charges was for $69. Four of the others were for $20. The others were for $10.

Wait, *$69*? The date of the charge, and the other charges, were from a few weeks ago, around the time I'd joined Discreet Hookups. Could it just be a coincidence?

I was too surprised, and had too much adrenaline pumping, to contemplate all of the implications. I went online and checked the transactions for the Visa card that I'd used for my Discreet Hookups membership, and sure enough there was a "Business Services" charge of $69, and additional charges from when I'd purchased credits.

Okay, so Maria had been on Discreet Hookups; but what did *this* mean? Did she go on to check up on me, to spy anonymously? But why had she kept that a secret, especially after I'd become a murder suspect?

The other charge at Bloomingdale's didn't seem significant.

Or was it?

I checked the Discover transactions again and saw that the transaction had occurred fourteen days ago.

The day Sophie Ward was murdered.

# CHAPTER TWENTY-THREE

MAYBE I WAS in deep denial, but I still didn't want to jump to conclusions. I kept thinking, *Maybe there's some explanation for all of this, something I don't understand.* After all, less than a minute ago, I'd been convinced that I was paranoid about everything, and my opinions tended to change rapidly, especially lately.

I called Bloomingdale's. It took a while before I could speak with the proper person, but she gave me all of the information I needed.

Next, I logged on to Discreet Hookups. All of my chats with "Fugitive_Red" were still there. In a Word file, I created a timeline of all of my chats.

"Hey."

Maria was standing in the doorway to the bedroom. I immediately clicked away the file, returning to the home screen. I didn't think she had seen.

"Hey, how are you?" I asked, trying to sound natural.

"What're you doing?" she asked.

"Oh, nothing," I said. "Just, um, checking out some possible work leads."

"Great," she said. "How was the funeral?"

Odd question. How was any funeral?

"Sad. Bleak."

"Well, I'm sure you're glad you went. I bought a chicken and some sides. Are you hungry?"

"No," I said. "I mean yes. Sounds great."

During dinner, the focus was mainly on Jonah, which was fine with me. I had a lot on my mind and I felt way more comfortable talking to Jonah than Maria. I realized halfway through the meal that I wasn't making enough eye contact with Maria. This was bad because I didn't want her to think that anything was wrong, so I made a conscious effort to look at her.

"Is something wrong?" she asked.

"No, why?"

"You keep staring at me."

"Oh, sorry," I said. "I didn't realize."

As I helped clear the table, I announced, "I think I'm going to hit an A.A. meeting."

"Great." Maria gave me a sexy look, biting on her lower lip a little. "I'll help Jonah with his homework, then maybe we can rendezvous in bed later."

She kissed me. Although my instinct was to pull back, I didn't.

I wasn't planning to go to A.A., though.

Instead, I cabbed it downtown to East 32nd Street, to Lawrence and Sophie's townhouse. There was a For Sale sign in front from, you guessed it, Wolf Realty. I had to smile, though I wasn't in a humorous mood. I walked up and down the block several times, taking pictures here and there with my iPhone. Then I returned to the townhouse and took some pics.

Back home, I went on Verizon's website and tried to log on to Maria's account. I thought it would take a while, or perhaps it would be impossible, to guess her password, but it turned out to be one I knew she used frequently. The log of her phone calls seemed to confirm that I was right about everything.

I still didn't want to believe it, though. I needed to be one hundred percent, and there was only one way I could get to one hundred percent:

A confession.

* * *

When Maria joined me in bed later, I didn't want to have sex with her. I didn't want to get her paranoid or suspicious either.

Lying side by side we kissed for a while, then she climbed on top, kissing me some more. I couldn't get excited; fight or flight kicking in?

"I'm just tired," I said. "I was up early and it was a long day."

After a long period of silence, she said, "You think I'm sexy, don't you?"

"Of course I think you're sexy," I said.

"I'm sorry," she said, "I know in these situations the worst thing you can do is take it personally, so I won't."

We fell asleep the way we'd slept during most of our marriage—facing opposite directions.

* * *

Although I couldn't sleep for most of the night, I woke energized, fixated on what I had to do.

I dropped Jonah at school, then I spent the day preparing for my talk with Maria. I needed to get Jonah out of the apartment, so I called Carly, our sitter, to see if I could drop him at her parents' apartment for a couple of hours. Carly was busy, had a test to study for, but when I told her I'd pay her an extra hundred, her schedule suddenly freed.

"Definitely," she said. "I can watch him the whole night if you want me to."

I told her that two hours should be fine.

Later, after school, Jonah was on his bed, playing a video game.

"Come on, get your shoes on," I said, "you're going to Carly's."

Surprised, maybe worried, he asked, "How come?"

"Because Mommy and Daddy want to spend some time alone together, that's why."

"But I don't wanna go."

"You have no choice."

There was no way I was going to put Jonah in front of another round of drama, especially when I had no idea how my talk with Maria would go.

After I dropped him with Carly on the sixteenth floor, I returned to our apartment and waited for Maria to come home. I activated the record feature on my cell phone, and placed my phone on the dining table.

When she arrived, holding a few heavy-looking paper shopping bags from Whole Foods, she said, "Hey, can you give me some help? These are heavy."

I took the bags from her and brought them into the kitchen.

"I probably bought too much stuff, but I want to start cooking more," she said. Then she looked beyond me, into the living room, and asked, "Is Jonah in his room?"

"No, I brought him to Carly's."

"Carly's?" She seemed confused. "Why?"

"I just thought it would be nice to have some time alone," I said. "You know, just to talk."

Maria seemed skeptical, like she didn't buy this explanation and assumed I had to have some kind of hidden agenda.

"A talk, huh?" she said. "What do you want to talk about?"

Did she suspect that I suspected her? Was she going to confront me when the whole point of this was for me to have a chance to confront her?

"Nothing in particular," I said.

"About what?" she said, as she put the milk and yogurts away in the fridge.

"We should probably sit down," I said.

"You're making this sound so serious," she said. "Should I be concerned?"

"Maybe," I said.

I waited on the couch until she put the frozen food away. Then she joined me.

"Hey, just realized, Jonah's out of the house." She put a hand on my thigh. "Maybe we should talk in bed. We haven't had the apartment to ourselves since you came home from Bellevue."

I pushed her hand away.

"What's going on with you?" she asked.

"A lot, actually," I said.

"Are you okay?"

"The evening Sophie Ward was killed," I said. "Where were you?"

I hadn't meant to blurt out this question, but I couldn't unsay it.

"I don't understand," Maria said, seeming surprised, not shocked. "Why are you asking me this?"

"We just never discussed this, that's all," I said. "I'm just wondering where you were."

"For what purp—?" She cut herself off, then said, "Wait, you don't think I had something to do with it, do you?"

I didn't answer.

"This is a joke, right?" she said. "A bad joke. You don't actually mean this?"

"I spoke to Carly when I dropped Jonah off tonight," I said. "She said on the night Sophie was murdered you had asked her to watch Jonah for a couple of hours."

"I had some chores to do around the neighborhood," Maria said. "I can't believe you actually—"

"You were fucking Lawrence Ward, weren't you?" I said.

Looking panicked, she said, "That's ridiculous."

"I saw the phone records from Verizon," I said. "It took me a long time to figure out your password, but I knew it would be some version of you mother's maiden name."

"I don't know why you're doing this," she said, "trying to make up a story when everything's been going so well."

"I have evidence," I said. "There are hundreds of calls to him."

"Lawrence Ward was a client of our company. We were discussing business."

"You really expect me to believe that he was your client, and it was just a coincidence that his wife wound up dead?"

"Well, it had nothing to do with me," she said.

For an instant, I thought, *Was it possible? Had I gotten it all wrong?*

It was incredible how she could always get me to doubt reality and my own instincts.

"You have to stop digging," she said. "Let's just go on with our lives."

She tried to grab my hand again.

I stood and said, "Stop with the bullshit already. I know everything. This is why you took me back, isn't it? Forgiveness, my ass. You just wanted to make sure Lawrence didn't tell me anything about you before he died. That's why you wanted *your* lawyer with me while I was answering Barasco's questions. What if Lawrence did tell me something? What would you have done?"

"You know what I think you should do?" Maria said. "I think you should call your psychiatrist at Bellevue and describe these symptoms. You're acting extremely paranoid and unstable right now, Jack."

"I also noticed some credit card charges," I said, "on our Discover Card—well, it used to be our card anyway. I know you were on Discreet Hookups, just like I was. At first I thought you were just checking up on me, but there was another charge on the same card for one hundred and fifty nine dollars and ninety-six cents. The transaction occurred at three thirty-eight p.m. on the day Sophie Ward was killed."

Maria's eyes showed she was processing this. Then she said, "I have no idea where you're going with this."

"What did you buy at Bloomingdale's that day?" I asked.

"Um, a blouse, I think," she said.

"You think?"

"I mean, yes, I bought a blouse. And I'm not sure why I used that card. Maybe I used it by accident. Why? What difference does it make?"

"I think the amount is odd," I said. "Ninety-six cents."

"What's odd about ninety-six cents?"

"If you'd bought one item, like a blouse, the price would've ended in ninety-nine. The six indicates you bought four items. There's no sales tax in New York State on a single item of clothing under one hundred and ten dollars."

"I think you're being absolutely ridiculous now, Jack. Maybe you need medication."

Now I was the one looking at her intensely.

"I mean, who the hell cares what I bought?" she said. "What does that have to do with—"

"One fifty nine ninety-six is about the price of four ties, if the ties were thirty-nine ninety-nine each. There's no tax on clothes at that price in New York State."

"I'm calling Bellevue," she said. "Right now."

I grabbed her phone from her.

"Hey, give that back," she said.

"You went to the townhouse that day before I got there. It's possible to zigzag up the block and avoid any camera on the street, and that's what you did. I don't know exactly what happened at the house, but I imagine you confronted Sophie, killed her by smashing the vase over her head, and then wound a tie around her neck. You put the other ties in Sophie's bag to make it look like she'd brought them, then you left the way you came. It was probably just a few minutes before I arrived. Of course you knew exactly what time I'd arrive, because you're Fugitive Red."

I watched her reaction. Her smirk convinced me I was right about everything.

"It started the night I went out for a walk and left my laptop open," I continued, on a roll. "You assumed I was cheating and even though you're a cheater yourself, you felt like I'd betrayed you—I know how your mind works. That's when you, or maybe you and Lawrence, came up with your plan. It was the perfect way to get rid of his wife so you two could be together. As a bonus you could set me up for the murder. All you had to do was become Fugitive Red. I admit, you did a good job of sucking me in. I had no idea I was chatting with my wife those nights, but in retrospect it all makes sense. You were never in the same room with me when I was online, and who else would know how to become the perfect mirror for me? It was just like when I met you for the first time, when you were suddenly into rock music and you were my biggest fan. You'd preconditioned me for more abuse. But I don't blame you as much as I blame myself. I'm the one who fell for it. I actually thought I was connecting with Sophie, but I once thought I was connecting with you, too. I guess that's the whole point, right? I was the perfect sucker for your plan because you already knew exactly how to manipulate me.

"During all those chat sessions, I really thought I'd found my dream girl, kind of like when I first met you. The name Fugitive Red should've been a dead giveaway. If I wasn't so caught up in the excitement of connecting with someone, of getting some relief from our shitty marriage, I might've picked up on these things. You knew I'd read that article on fugitive reds in the *Times* magazine. You wanted me to think, *Wow, and we both love Van Gogh, it's like we're soul mates*. Love fades—that was a nice touch there. You know my weak spots so well, Maria. The joke was definitely on me. All that time I was cheating on my wife, I was really cheating *with* my wife. You knew exactly how to sext with me, because you talked about all the things you were never into doing. Who better to become my fantasy woman than the woman who knows me better than anybody?"

Maria had stood up during my monologue. She was facing me, staring at me with her wide, empty eyes. I'd seen this look at times over the years, usually when I criticized her for something and she felt hurt. It was like a mask came off—her charm vanished, and she was suddenly showing me her true self. For years, I'd refused to believe that this was the real her, though. I wanted her to be the woman I'd fallen in love with—I wanted to believe she was the mask.

Unfortunately the mask had been a fantasy, no more real than Fugitive Red.

Maria laughed, shaking her head, then said, "You deserved it."

Although I'd seen Maria's mask come off before, the coldness still startled me.

"How did I deserve it?" I asked.

"You think it's been easy being married to you?" She laughed again, though her eyes remained expressionless. Then she said,

"Where would you be without me? How many years did I have to support you because of your stupid music career that was going nowhere? If it weren't for me, you'd still be wasting your time as a washed-up musician. On top of that you checked out with your drinking—and you think *I* have problems? You were so self-centered you didn't even notice me for years. And how about when you got drunk and had that fight with that club manager? I had to carry you through that, too."

"You think you're the big victim, huh?" I said.

"You're damn right I'm the victim," she said. "That's why I had no choice but to get involved with Lawrence Ward and all those other men."

My stomach tightened. "Other men?"

"You think Lawrence was the first? How naïve are you? I've had dozens of men over the years. I was even fucking two other guys when we got married. How does that make you feel?"

"Sorry for you," I said.

"Bullshit," she said. "I can see how hurt you are right now. I love it—it makes me feel so justified. It's funny how you were so focused on Steve. He's another idiot who believes I'm in love with him."

I'd seen Maria's mask slip off before, but I'd never seen this much darkness. I stared at her, then said, "I've always known you were a narcissist, but I had no idea I was married to a full-blown psycho."

Her eyes looked dead again.

"I never said I was nice." She let that linger for several seconds, with a proud smirk, then added, "Okay, it's true about me and Lawrence—we had a thing going for years, and you were totally clueless. Lawrence hated his wife and I hated you—I guess in that way alone we were perfect for each other. We knew we had to find some way to be together. Me getting rid of you wasn't the problem since you obviously would've welcomed a divorce. Sophie was the problem. They didn't have a prenup and he would've lost at least half of his money and everything he owned to her. He'd thought about killing her, but he didn't know how he could get away with it.

"Then, that night, I saw your laptop open to that adultery site—talk about passive-aggressive! Typical Jack Harper—you're unhappy and you act out. If not with alcohol, with *something*. But I knew I'd stumbled on to the perfect way to solve all of our problems. I texted Lawrence and we came up with a plan. He could get rid of his wife and keep all his money, and I'd get rid of you. It was brilliant. All I had to do was become Fugitive Red."

"So you admit it," I said. "You killed Sophie Ward."

"I just did what I had to do."

I hoped my phone was recording all of this.

"Besides, it was all your fault," she said. "You had the balls to post a picture that I'd taken of you on a website for cheaters. Seriously, what kind of man does that? A sick man, that's who. And how about when I asked you if you still loved your wife and you said no? That hurt—it reminded me of how you had checked out of the marriage and deserted me."

"So you did all of this, killed a woman and set me up for it, for what purpose?" I asked. "Just to get back at me for something I didn't even do to you?"

"Fucking up your life was just a bonus," Maria said. "We knew the police would find your chat logs with Fugitive Red, and it would only help that you sounded gleeful about cheating on me. We almost had to bail on the whole plan, though. It was when you wanted to talk on the phone before meeting. I could've tried to disguise my voice, or gotten someone at my office to pretend to be Sophie Ward, but both options seemed too risky. Luckily I was able to talk you out of the idea."

"There's still one thing I don't get," I said. "The way Sophie was dressed. She was in a negligee at the townhouse, when I found her there. If it was really you the whole time, why would the real Sophie have been dressed like that? Why would she have been at the townhouse at all?"

"She thought she was meeting her husband at the townhouse. That was part of our plan—Lawrence had convinced her that he wanted to reconcile, and he told her to wait for him—Lawrence could be incredibly charming when he wanted to be. Guess we had that in common, too."

"What about Anthony?" I asked.

"Oh, that was totally your fault."

"*My* fault?"

"Who else? If you hadn't gotten that guy involved, he wouldn't be dead. Lawrence had to get rid of him before he went to the police."

"He wasn't a *guy*," I said. "He was a *great* guy. He was my friend."

"He was an addict who'd been in prison."

"So according to you that makes killing him okay?"

"Look who's talking—you killed Lawrence. Now *he* was a great guy."

"Yeah, a great guy who'd plotted to kill his wife."

"I don't hear you taking any responsibility for anything," Maria said. "But taking responsibility's not exactly your strong suit, is it?"

"Anthony had a family." My voice was wavering. "A family who loved him."

Before I could react, she grabbed my phone.

"Hey," I said.

"You think I'm an idiot?" she said. "You think I didn't know you were recording all this? I knew something was up, as soon as you arranged for Jonah to go to the sitter's. Maybe you think I'm that oblivious wife you ignored for years, then tried to cheat on me, so callously. You thought you were so clever, didn't you, sneaking around behind my back, but face it, Jack, you've always been at least two steps behind me."

I lunged for the phone again, but she moved back and I squeezed air.

She glanced at the phone. "Yep, just as I'd expected."

She was near the open living room window. I knew what she was about to do, but before I could react, it was too late.

"No!" I screamed as she tossed my phone out.

From twelve stories up, the phone would almost certainly smash when it hit the ground. With her gleeful smile, it was clear that the least of Maria's concerns was that the phone might hit someone on the head and injure, or even kill, them.

"Looks like now it's my word against yours," Maria said, "and who do you think the police would believe? A responsible, working mom, or an unemployed ex–mental patient?'

Her expression changed from twisted to seductive as she moved closer to me.

"Don't worry, I'm not mad at you, Jack. I know how much pressure you've been under lately and I certainly know about your history of bad decision-making. I know how bad you must feel for causing all of this tumult. But I'm willing to forgive and forget if you will."

She kissed me, sliding her tongue into my mouth.

Then she pulled back and said, "Everything is so good with us now. We had a rough spot, but we got through it. Come on, think about all the positives. We have Jonah, we have each other, and we have money. Money was always such a big issue for us. We can make a down payment on an apartment, take a trip to wherever we want.

How about Paris or Venice? That's what we need—a fun, relaxing getaway. How about over Christmas? We can leave Jonah with a friend, go away for a week. Have romantic walks during the day and fuck all night. I know you want that, Jack."

She squatted in front of me and unbuckled my belt. When she unsnapped my jeans, I kneed her in the face. She toppled over onto her back.

"Stay the fuck away from me," I said.

Although blood was dripping from her nose, she didn't seem stunned. If anything, she seemed pleased.

Maria, back on her knees, smiling now even though blood was dripping over her mouth, said, "You really think beating me up is going to help your situation?"

"I didn't beat you up."

"It sure as hell looks like you did. I'll tell them that you snapped, called me all kinds of horrible names, and they'll send you right back to Bellevue. And they might not let you out this time."

I hated that she was right.

"I'll tell them what you did," I said. "I have evidence."

"What evidence? A credit card bill? A phone bill? You think that'll actually *prove* anything?"

"I'll get more," I said. "The cops'll find more when I tell them where to look."

"They won't believe you." Maria was back on her feet now, blood dripping off her chin. "Face it, you're not a reliable person, Jack. You *never* have been. You're a violent alcoholic with an arrest record. You tried to kidnap your son from school."

"You're just twisting it again," I said. "You're the insane one, not me."

"Everybody thinks that I'm a loving, devoted wife, a victim."

"You're a fucking monster."

She came toward me. "You killed somebody, too, Jack."

"That was self-defense."

"Killing is killing," she said. "Face it, you're a violent man, Jack. You proved it tonight when you punched your poor, battered wife in the nose. With your police record and mental history, how will that look?" She was so close our noses were almost touching. "You liked listening to my confession. I could tell—it turned you on. Just like our chats turned you on, when you thought I was Fugitive Red. You have a dark, twisted, sadistic side, Jack. You try to hide it, but face it—you're just like me."

"I'm nothing like you," I said. "Thank fucking God."

I turned away from her and went toward the kitchen.

Big mistake.

I didn't feel any pain.

Just the impact on my head before everything went dark.

# CHAPTER TWENTY-FOUR

THE PAIN HIT when I opened my eyes. My head hurt like hell. I felt dizzy and nauseous and had no idea where I was.

Then I recognized the stove and refrigerator and realized I was lying on the kitchen floor. A burly uniformed cop was kneeling in front of me, asking questions I couldn't understand.

I tried to speak, but couldn't find the words.

"You're okay," the cop said, "but you have to stay still."

"Muh . . . muh," I said.

"What's that?" he asked.

"Muh . . . muh . . . Maria," I said.

"Who's Maria?"

"My . . . w . . . wife. We're is she?"

"We'll find your wife, okay?"

I tried to get up, but he held me down.

"Whoa, pal, you can't move till EMS comes here and checks you out. But you're conscious and talking—those are good signs."

I saw that Hector, the building's super, was in the vestibule; he'd probably let the cop into the apartment.

"Have you seen my wife?" I asked Hector.

"The doorman saw her leaving," he said. "She had blood on her so he called the cops."

"You have to find her," I said to the officer. "She's dangerous."

"Did your wife do this to you?"

"Yes," I said, "and she also killed a woman, Sophie Ward."

"The murder downtown," he said.

"Right," I said. "She did it. I have evidence and . . . You have to call Detective Nick Barasco and let him know what's going on."

"We'll get to the bottom of it, don't worry."

Then I had a thought that terrified me.

"My son," I said. "I have to get my son."

I tried to get up again, but he still wouldn't let me.

"Where's your son?" the cop asked. "Is your son in the apartment?"

"No . . . babysitter," I managed to say. "Upstairs."

I told him Carly's apartment number.

"We'll make sure he's okay," the cop said.

"Was my wife alone when she left?" I asked.

"I don't know," Hector said.

"You have to check now," I said to the cop. "Please."

"My partner's in the lobby, and she'll be up here any second with EMS. When she gets here I'll have her check on your son, okay?"

"Lemme call the babysitter at least."

"You have to stay still right now," the cop said. "Moving can be dangerous until you get checked out."

"Can *you* call her?" I asked.

The EMS workers arrived with the other police officer.

"Can you go check on his son?" the male cop said to her.

He told her the apartment number and she left. My pulse was pounding as I was imagining the worst—Maria had taken him somewhere. Or worse—maybe she'd killed him. Who knew what that woman was capable of?

A few minutes later she returned and said, "Your son's fine."

"Thank God," I said. "But he can't be alone. My wife can come and try to take him away."

"Okay, let's just try to stay calm right now," the cop said.

"I'm telling you, she's dangerous. You have to find her. Call Nick Barasco."

"Right now, you're just gonna have to stay still and do what I tell you to do," the cop said. "Is that understood?"

Although I didn't have any life-threatening issues, I was told that I'd probably suffered a concussion and had to go to the hospital for observation. I was able to leave the apartment by foot, walking alongside the cops and an EMS worker.

In the lobby, some reporters and other news crew had arrived, and some residents of the building had assembled as well. A few reporters shouted questions, but I ignored them. It was humiliating and I tried to look straight ahead, not make eye contact with anyone. Most of my neighbors had already heard about me in the news, knew I had been in Bellevue—they probably thought I was crazy after all.

At Mount Sinai Hospital, after a doctor examined me, a nurse arrived.

"Can I call my son?" I asked her.

"Of course you can," she said.

She let me borrow her cell, and I called Carly's. Her father answered. I asked him if it was okay if Jonah stayed there tonight.

"Of course," he said. "So what exactly happened? I heard the police had to go to your place."

I didn't want to alarm him and make him think he was in an unsafe situation.

"It's all going to be fine," I said. "But, do me a favor. If Maria calls, or shows up, don't let her into the apartment or near Jonah. Call the police right away."

"Okay," he said, "but why?"

"She just may be a little, well, unstable right now. Nothing to worry about at all, it's just a precaution. I really appreciate you watching Jonah. Can I speak to him?"

"Sure thing."

I waited a few seconds.

"Hi, Daddy," Jonah said.

"My favorite sound in the world," I said. "How are you?"

"When are you picking me up?"

"As soon as I can, but probably not till tomorrow."

"Can Mommy pick me up?"

"No, she can't either."

Detective Barasco entered.

"Hey, I have to go now," I said, "but I'll talk to you tomorrow. I love you."

"I love you, too, Daddy."

I ended the call.

"Why I am I getting déjà vu?" Barasco asked.

"Maria, my wife, killed Sophie Ward," I said. "She was also involved in Anthony's murder."

"How do you know this?" he asked.

I explained that I had phone records showing frequent contact with Lawrence Ward and that she was Fugitive Red.

"If you examine her iPad you can probably find cookies or whatever."

"I'll need to see whatever you have right away," he said.

"I have it backed up on the cloud," I said. "Just get me a laptop and I'll send you everything. But you have to find Maria right away and keep her away from my son. She tried to kill me."

"Why did she try to kill you?"

"If you don't mind, I don't want to talk to you about any more of this until my lawyer gets here."

"Look at you," Barasco said, "knowing all your rights."

Barasco said he'd come back later.

I called Marcus Freemont and said, "Guess who?"

"Oh no," he said. "What happened to your other lawyer?"

"Let's just say there's a lot I need to catch you up on," I said.

When Freemont arrived at the hospital, it was past midnight.

"You trying to visit every hospital in town before you die?" he asked.

"Ha, good to see you, too," I said. "Sorry I replaced you the other day, but I was pressured by my wife and—"

"No worries," he said, "I've had worse disappointments. So what the hell happened?"

I explained everything that had gone down at our apartment.

"The cops can find the pieces of my cell phone on the street," I said. "Maybe there's a way to recover the data."

"Doubtful," he said, "but I'll look into it. Hopefully we can get by without her confession, we'll see."

Barasco joined us.

"My client's ready to talk," Freemont said.

"Finally," Barasco said. "By the way, we're looking for your wife. Do you have any idea where she went? Does she have any relatives?"

"She has a cousin, Michael Brant. He's a lawyer. She has a friend Steve in Westchester, maybe he knows something."

"Text me all the contact info and we'll check it out," Barasco said. "So what do you have to tell me?"

I told Barasco what I'd told Freemont.

"Sounds like you did some good work there," Barasco said. "Of course, I'm gonna take credit for it."

I didn't think he was joking.

"Actually we already have unknown DNA from the Sophie Ward crime scene."

"That could be Maria's," I said.

"Could be," he said. "We'll have to run some more tests to confirm it, though. Send me the name of your wife's doctor and dentist, too, if you can."

* * *

The doctors made me stay overnight for observation. In the morning, as per hospital protocol, they transported me via wheelchair to the hospital's exit on Madison Avenue, and then I rushed out and hailed a cab.

I had no plan for what I'd say to Jonah. How could I possibly explain to him what his mother had done? How could he possibly understand, when I didn't understand it myself?

When I saw him, sitting on the floor with Carly, coloring in coloring books, I didn't even try to explain anything to him; how could I?

I just hugged him and told him how much I loved him. That was the best I could do.

* * *

Later, Freemont called me with some news—the DNA from the townhouse was linked to Maria. In addition, on Maria's iPad, they found cookies of her chat sessions as "Fugitive_Red" on Discreet Hookups. The police found a few witnesses who had seen Maria and Lawrence together at various Manhattan hotels, and supporting video provided additional evidence of their affair.

The bad news was the police hadn't found Maria.

"The cops are all over it now," Freemont said. "She's a top priority. They're looking all over New York State and in surrounding states."

"Yeah, but by now she could be out of the country," I said.

"Maybe," he said. "Have you noticed any withdrawals from your bank account?"

Shit, why hadn't I thought about that sooner? I'd been so worried about Jonah I hadn't been able to focus on anything else.

"Hold one sec," I said.

On my phone, I logged on to our joint bank account. Sure enough, the 200,000 dollars was gone.

"Fuck me," I said.

"What happened?" Freemont asked.

"Let's just say I don't think money is an issue for her right now," I said.

* * *

I was hoping that the police would find Maria and arrest her. But days, then weeks went by and the police had no leads. It was like she had vanished.

I tried to get back into a routine, rebuild my life and Jonah's life, but it was hard to move on. I knew Maria wouldn't stay away forever. At some point she'd return and try to get revenge, or try to see Jonah. I felt like I was constantly looking over my shoulder, waiting for Maria to appear at any moment. My thoughts became increasingly paranoid.

Some people with PTSD flash back to a particular event, but I had flashbacks to discovering Sophie and Anthony's bodies, killing Lawrence, my attempted suicide, and fighting with Maria. There were days I felt like I belonged back at Bellevue, but I fought through it. I knew I had a huge responsibility now to Jonah. I was the only support system he had and I couldn't let him down.

Jonah also showed signs of PTSD. He was anxious and depressed, and one day I had to pick him up from school after he had a panic attack.

We saw a family therapist together and psychiatrists individually. I was taking Paxil for my symptoms. Jonah wasn't on any meds because of his age, but his psychiatrist didn't rule out meds in the future if he didn't show improvement.

Jonah and I didn't talk specifically about what had happened. I didn't pressure him to, getting the vibe that he felt more comfortable talking to his therapist about it.

So I was surprised when, one day after school pickup, he said to me, "Did Mommy kill people?"

I didn't want to avoid the question. I'd talked to my own therapist about this very issue. Avoidance wasn't behavior I wanted to model.

"One person," I said.

"How come?"

I took a few moments, to organize my thoughts, then said, "I know this is hard for you to understand. But your mom had a lot of problems. It doesn't mean you'll ever have problems."

We walked for a while in silence. Leaves were falling from the trees, but neither of us tried to snag them.

"I miss Mommy so much," Jonah said.

"I know you do," I said.

We continued on.

* * *

*Step 10: Continued to take personal inventory, and when we were wrong, promptly admitted it.*

I sent a short email to Rob McEvoy, apologizing for what I'd done and for any pain I'd caused him. Then I blocked his number and blocked him on Facebook, so if he tried to contact me, I wouldn't feel pressured to respond. Rob had been a negative influence, and I had to get negative people out of my life.

I thanked Raymond Ferrara, the man who'd prevented me from jumping onto the subway tracks, for saving my life and apologized for not thanking him sooner.

I wanted to take full responsibility for everything I'd done and not blame others for my mistakes. But, going forward, I also wanted to focus on positive relationships and rid my life of negative influences.

I worked hard on my resume and went to job interviews. Finally, I landed a job in the PR department at a recording studio downtown. It wasn't a creative position, but it would help get me back into an artistic mind-set. I played guitar every evening at home. Music had always been my passion, but it was also a great form of therapy, and I realized how much I'd missed it over the years. I'd even written a few new songs—for myself. I wasn't planning to play them in public any time soon, but it felt amazing to just playing again, to have music back in my life. I was teaching Jonah how to play guitar as well. He loved it, had a natural ear. Thank God for music. I know this might sound corny, but music was helping us heal.

I attended A.A. meetings two or three days a week. I had a new sobriety date, and I was hoping it was the last one I'd need. I certainly had enough new material to give inspirational speeches for the rest of my life.

I spent just about all of my free time with Jonah. Especially now that he only had one parent to raise him, I wanted to be there for him as much as I possibly could. Except for going to A.A. meetings, I didn't use a babysitter. I was home with Jonah—cooking his meals, helping him with his homework. Evenings were much more peaceful than they used to be when Maria was living with us. There was no tension, no fighting. Best of all, I got to spend more time with my son.

Several months passed by. I checked in with Barasco every couple of weeks or so, hoping to hear news that Maria had been arrested, or at least the police had some new solid leads.

"We won't give up looking for her, I promise," Barasco said.

Over the summer, Jonah and I took a trip to California. We went to San Francisco, camped in Big Sur, and then drove down the coast to L.A. and Disneyland.

There was one weird incident at Disneyland. We were in line at Haunted Mansion when I thought I saw Maria in the crowd, about fifty yards away. It was hard to tell for sure, but the hair was the same—maybe a little longer—and that red dress looked like hers.

"What's wrong, Daddy?" Jonah asked.

I felt light-headed and dizzy. Someone passed in front of me, momentarily blocking my vision, and the woman in the dress was gone. I glanced in every direction, but it was like she'd disappeared.

I decided that my mind had been playing tricks—it wasn't her; I'd just confused her with someone else. I didn't give it much more thought and we enjoyed the rest of our vacation.

Back in Manhattan, it was a new school year, and for the first time in a long time, things felt normal. Jonah had made new friends in school and joined a soccer league. I took him to the soccer games, cheering him on.

On the night of the Halloween Boo Bash at the gym in Jonah's school, I hung out with the other parents. Rebecca, a recently divorced mom around my age, came over to chat. She'd been friendly with me before, always saying hi and smiling. Tonight was different. I could tell she was getting flirty, by the way she was making eye contact with me and how she touched my arm a couple of times.

"Hey, we should get coffee sometime," she said.

Just to get away, I pretended I was getting a call on my cell.

"Sorry, have to take this," I said, and went outside.

I didn't want to be rude, but I didn't want to lead her on either. I guess I should've been interested—she was pretty and smart and fun to talk to. It had been about a year since Maria had disappeared, and I felt more together emotionally, but I just didn't have any desire to date, or to get into a relationship. For the first time in a long time, I was liking my life again, and I didn't feel the need to make any big changes.

Later, back at our apartment, I helped Jonah with his usual nightly routine—homework, then washing up and getting ready for bed. Before sleep, he showed me some silly YouTube videos a friend at school had shared with him.

"G'night, kiddo," I said, then turned off the light and shut the door to his room.

"'Night, Daddy."

Now it was time for *my* nightly routine.

In my bedroom, I locked the door and got naked. Then I logged onto Discreet Hookups with my user name, FUGITIVE.RED, and my password, SOPHIE.

Yes, I needed an outlet, and this felt safer than trying to have an actual relationship.

I scrolled through the dozens of women I'd sexted with over the past several months, trying to decide who I was in the mood for tonight. SoSexxxy69 was online. She claimed she had a husband who traveled a lot and ignored her. Maybe it was all a lie, but I guess that was part of the thrill.

> SoSexxxy69: *Hey, how're you tonight, baby?*

I felt like I'd taken a first sip of alcohol after a long, hard day.

> FUGITIVE.RED: *Ready to party!*
> SoSexxxy69: *Awesome! Let's do it!*

We chatted for a while, exchanging our raunchiest fantasies.

Then it hit me. It made so much sense; I didn't know how I hadn't realized it soon.

FUGITIVE.RED: *It's you, isn't it?*

Long pause. Maybe I'd been wrong, just getting paranoid as usual.

SoSexxxy69: *Who?*
FUGITIVE.RED: *You know who.*
SoSexxxy69: *I don't know what you're talking about*
FUGITIVE.RED: *I know it's you okay? You can be honest with me I won't turn you in, I promise! I just want to know you're alive and safe*

I realized I could've been wrong about all of this. SoSexxxy69 could have been a lonely, married woman.

After a few minutes passed, I tried to send, *Are you there?* but my message didn't go through.

Instead I got: SoSexxxy69 *DOESN'T EXIST.*

She must have deleted the account.

"Damn it," I said.

It had been her—I was sure of it. I could tell by how she'd made me feel. Only she could've brought out that kind of intensity.

I pictured her on a tropical island, lounging by the ocean, sipping a cocktail, laughing her ass off, proud of herself for duping me again.

I guess I should've been angry; instead, I laughed with her.

It felt great to have my wife back.

# ACKNOWLEDGMENTS

THANK YOU TO my agent dream team, Joel Gotler and Murray Weiss, for their many close reads and spot-on editorial input. My longtime overseas publishers, No Exit Press and Diogenes Verlag, have supported me throughout my entire career and were early champions of *Fugitive Red*. And thank you to the whole crew at Oceanview Publishing for bringing *Fugitive Red* to life in the U.S. and Canada.

CPSIA information can be obtained
at www.ICGtesting.com
Printed in the USA
BVHW070013161118
533154BV00003B/11/P

9 781608 093281